"That's enough, Shasta," Alexander said firmly as he approached. "Leave the nice lady alone," he warned, lifting his daughter off the stool and setting her on her feet.

"It's all right, I have one at home just like her," the woman said, chuckling.

"She's far too inquisitive for her own good and some-times . . ." Alexander stopped short upon lookng at the woman for the first time. Today seemed to be the day for one awestricken moment after another. He knew he shouldn't, but couldn't help but stare.

Her flawless mahogany complexion gave off an almost ethereal glow, while her piercing gray eyes startled him as she sat watching his stunned reaction to her. He immediately got the sense she was used to it. The sharp lines of her face, perfectly chiseled cheekbones, and strong chin seemed familiar to him somehow.

She stood, stepping away from the counter. Alexander momentarily admired her hair, which fell in large, unruly black ringlets as it rested just short of her breasts. The ebony color and softness reminded him of a raven's soft wings. His gaze continued down a slender neck, past full breasts, to a small waist, amply round hips, and legs so long he had trouble swallowing.

Time *Will* Tell

Francine Matthews

BET Publications, LLC
http://www.bet.com
http://www.arabesquebooks.com

ARABESQUE BOOKS are published by

BET Publications, LLC
c/o BET BOOKS
One BET Plaza
1900 W Place NE
Washington, DC 20018-1211

All Kensington Titles, Imprints, and Distributed Lines are available at special quantity discounts for bulk purchases for sales promotions, premiums, fund-raising, and educational or institutional use. Special book excerpts or customized printings can also be created to fit specific needs. For details, write or phone the office of the Kensington special sales manager: Kensington Publishing Corp., 850 Third Avenue, New York, NY 10022, attn: Special Sales Department, Phone: 1-800-221-2647.

BET Books is a trademark of Black Entertainment Television, Inc. ARABESQUE, the ARABESQUE logo, and the BET BOOKS logo are trademarks and registered trademarks.

First Printing: October 2005

10 9 8 7 6 5 4 3 2 1

Printed in the United States of America

I dedicate this book to the giver of all gifts . . . God . . . and to the woman who gave me my first romance novel . . . Lucy Lawson, a.k.a. Big Grandma!

Chapter One

Jacqueline Carr sat patiently watching her father as he stood in front of the large picture window in his study. At sixty-three, he was still a handsome, well-muscled man with a full head of salt-and-pepper hair. Jacqueline supposed it was men like him who gave support to the theory that African-American men didn't get old; they simply became more distinguished with age.

Solomon brought a pipe to his lips, as was his habit when contemplating matters of great importance.

"You shouldn't do that," Jacqueline said gently.

Solomon turned, facing his daughter. She was truly a lovely sight to behold, he thought proudly. A man couldn't have asked for a more beautiful and trustworthy offspring. With the exception of the four years his daughter had gone away to college, she had spent her entire life on the 1850 Ranch. He often worried that she spent far too much time buried elbow deep in one task or another.

"Don't worry," he stated with a smile, "it isn't lit."

"Father," Jacqueline said firmly.

"Isn't it enough that your mother won't let me light the blasted thing in the house or anywhere else on the property? I suffered a mild heart attack, not a bout with cancer, for pity's sake."

Jacqueline said nothing but set her chin, giving her father a stern glare.

"Women," Solomon grunted, putting the unlit pipe back on its holder atop the old cherry-wood desk.

"It's our job to keep you healthy, whether you like it or not," Jacqueline reminded him. "So, what did you want to see me about?" she asked, changing the subject.

"I'm waiting on your mother, who is, as always, late," her father answered with a frown as he checked his watch.

"I am never late," sixty-one-year-old Leila said as she entered the room in her usual regal manner. Jacqueline couldn't help but smile. Leila was as refined as Solomon was rugged. If Solomon ran the ranch with an iron fist, then it was only fair that Leila did so with a sharp eye and a graceful disposition.

"That watch of yours hasn't worked since sixty-nine and you know it, Sol." She kissed her husband's cheek gently and did the same to Jacqueline before taking a seat.

Jacqueline noted the hot blush that enveloped her father's handsome face. Clearing his throat, he too sat down. Jacqueline was almost certain if he hadn't, his knees would have buckled from the effect his wife still had on him after forty-three years of marriage.

"I've a million things to do before we pack, dear,"

Leila began, exhaling tiredly, "so let us hurry things along, shall we?"

"Pack? Are you going somewhere?" Jacqueline asked with both worry and surprise.

Leila shot her husband a disapproving frown, which resembled the one Jacqueline had given him only moments before. "You didn't tell her?" she asked.

Solomon cleared his throat before speaking. "I was about to, but I thought the girl would be a bit distressed and in need of her mother to—"

"Tell me what?" Jacqueline interjected suspiciously.

"Don't blame your procrastination on me, Solomon Jacob Carr," Leila protested.

"Well, you were in fact late and . . ."

"You really must stop using me as an excuse to stall for time, dear," Leila said disapprovingly.

"He didn't tell me what?" Jacqueline asked again, sitting forward in her chair.

"I use no one . . . or at least not you . . . to get what I want. I simply thought the girl might be a bit shocked and would need you to calm her. You know how she gets when—"

At that, Jacqueline stood abruptly. "Hello! 'The girl' is standing right here. Now, will someone please tell me what the devil is going on?" she demanded.

Both Solomon and Leila sat staring as if baffled by their daughter's unexpected outburst.

Leila was the first to recover. "Well, tell her then."

"I will, in my own good time," Solomon retorted stubbornly.

"You're becoming an ornery old cuss in your old age, Solomon," Leila huffed.

"*Old!*" Solomon objected, standing, ready to do battle for his ego.

"Yes," Leila started, completely unfazed by his posturing, "and not only that, but—"

"Mother!" Jacqueline said, loud enough to distract Leila from the verbal battle Jacqueline knew she was enjoying. "I insist that you tell me what's going on!"

Leila raised an eyebrow at her daughter. "I see," she said, eyeing Jacqueline carefully. "You're twenty-seven and a mother to boot, which of course gives you the right to give your poor old mother orders, is that it?" she asked, giving Jacqueline a wounded look.

"There's no need to be disrespectful, Jacqueline. Your mother and I raised you better than that," Solomon interjected, coming to stand beside his wife and placing a gentle hand on her shoulder. "How would you like it if little Jasmine filled her tongue with such a challenging tone and spewed it at you?"

Jacqueline felt a twinge of guilt. "I'm . . . I'm sorry, Mother," she said sincerely. "I didn't mean to be disrespectful. I merely wanted the two of you to stop talking to one another as if I were not in the room and—"

Jacqueline stopped abruptly, recognizing her parents' stall tactics. "Now I know there's something going on!" she said, snapping out of the trap. "No more stalling. Someone just tell me what's going on!"

Solomon opened his mouth to speak but was interrupted before getting the chance. All eyes turned to the door as a cheery seven-year-old girl barged into the room, shooting past both Leila and Solomon to hug her mother around the waist.

"Did you hear, Mama?" the spirited brown-skinned girl asked, looking up at her mother with excitement gleaming in her eyes. "Did you hear about Nana and

Pop-Pop's trip? Can you believe they're gonna travel the entire world for a whole year and we get to take care of the ranch all by ourselves? Least that's what Ollie told me," she added thoughtfully, hoping eight-year-old Oliver hadn't been playing another one of his tricks on her.

Both Solomon and Leila moaned, shaking their heads at one another.

Jacqueline stood blinking at her parents in disbelief.

"Mama, say something!" Jasmine insisted. "Ain't it gonna be fun?" the girl asked, looking hopefully up at her mother.

After several seconds, Jacqueline looked down at her daughter. Forcing a smile on her face, she pushed long, thick waves of sun-bleached sandy-brown hair from her daughter's adorable face. She spoke slowly, making certain not to give away the panicked beating of her heart.

"Yes, pumpkin, that does sound as though it would be fun," Jacqueline agreed, correcting her daughter's grammar. "Even so," she said, placing her index finger beneath her daughter's chin, causing her to make direct eye contact, "you didn't knock before entering, nor did you excuse yourself before interrupting our conversation."

Jasmine looked guiltily at her mother. Releasing her hold on Jacqueline, she approached the edge of Leila's chair. "I'm sorry for being rude, Nana and Pop-Pop," she said grimly.

"That's quite all right, my little—"

"Now go play outside until we're done in here," Jacqueline said, cutting off Leila's coddling.

Jasmine walked to the door sadly, disappointed in

herself for upsetting her mother. She gave Jacqueline a quick glance before closing the door and was relieved to see the sly wink Jacqueline shot in her direction.

"Now," Jacqueline said irritably, "will someone please tell me how Father expects to take a trip around the world when he can't even make it to the other side of the ranch on horseback without getting winded? Did you both somehow forget that he suffered a heart attack less than six months ago?" she asked, crossing her arms in front of her.

"I don't think she'll settle for anything less than the direct approach," Solomon said under his breath.

"Apparently not," Leila agreed as they both shot Jacqueline guilty looks that much resembled their granddaughter's.

Solomon grew serious as he returned to his desk. "Sit down, Jacqueline," he said in resignation. "We'll explain everything."

Jacqueline obeyed.

"Doc Brown seems to think I need to get away for a spell. While the air out here is fresh enough, he believes a change of scenery would do me good. Truth is, I can't say that I disagree, and besides . . ." Solomon sighed, reaching for his pipe. "Your mother's been badgering me about taking a trip for years. She'd like to see Africa and Scotland, believe it or not," he said, putting the unlit pipe in his mouth.

"But you just had a heart attack," Jacqueline reminded him again. "You should be resting, not running around catching planes, booking hotels, and—"

"It was only a mild heart attack," Solomon said, cutting her off. "I consider it a warning, nothing more."

"A warning?" Jacqueline said, incredulously. "Dad,

no heart attack is a warning. If it were, the warning would be to take it easy, not do something as foolish as boarding one plane after another visiting foreign countries where you don't know anyone and are thousands of miles away from your physician!"

Solomon smiled sadly. "I prefer to think of it as a different kind of warning."

"What other kind of warning is there?" Jacqueline asked, puzzled.

Solomon sat back in his chair chewing the end of his still unlit pipe. "The kind that reminds you that you're getting old and that perhaps it's time you enjoyed your life," he answered, staring out of the picture window as he spoke in a reflective tone.

"I've worked the land all my life, and your mother's been right alongside me. We've invested blood, sweat, and tears into this place, just like my parents and their parents before them.

"I rise before the sun wakes in the morning, and go to bed long after it has retired for the day. Yet there's always something left undone—something that gets put off until the following day. Truth is," Solomon said, turning in his chair to face Jacqueline, "I'd like to know what it feels like to be as free as those wild horses you love so much.

"Then of course, there's your mother. A man couldn't get much luckier than to have a woman at his side who is as loyal as she is beautiful. She's given me the greatest pleasures in life, and I'll be damned if I'll leave this earth without taking the time to do something that would make her as happy as she's made me these many years," he concluded.

Jacqueline stared at her father not knowing how or if she should respond.

"I know this all sounds sudden, but your mother and I have been thinking about this for some time and then, well, I had difficulties and—"

"Difficulties? Dad, you had a heart attack!" Jacqueline stated with frustration, realizing she was beginning to sound like a broken record.

"We'll be fine, Jacqueline dear," Leila said reassuringly. "Your father received a clean bill of health from Doc Brown just yesterday. You must understand that a heart attack isn't necessarily a death sentence in this day and age. We understand your worry, but you must understand that your father needs this."

"But . . . a whole year?" Jacqueline worried. "You can't just up and leave for an entire year. Who's supposed to look after things here while you're gone?"

"You, of course," Leila said softly. The expression on her daughter's face was one that Leila would remember for the rest of her life. The poor girl didn't know whether to laugh outright at the thought, or cry with joy at the prospect of doing what she'd dreamed about since she was a child. Leila noticed the slightest hint of fear in her daughter's eyes as well.

"You've been training for this moment since you were old enough to walk, talk, and count, my dear. Your father and I have the utmost confidence in your capabilities. Now it is time for you to prove it to yourself."

"But . . . but—"

"But nothing," Solomon interrupted. "You've been champing at the bit for more responsibility around here since you returned from college years ago. It was wrong of me not to have done this when both you and Bryce—" Solomon stopped abruptly.

He rose to take a familiar stance at the picture window with his hands folded behind his back.

Jacqueline didn't have to wonder what he was going to say. She knew Solomon had loved her husband more like a son than an in-law. Bryce's death had been nearly as hard for him to accept as it had been for Jacqueline.

"Maybe if Bryce were here, I could have run the ranch with his help, but now . . . maybe it's not such a good idea," Jacqueline said thoughtfully.

Solomon turned, walking to stand directly in front of Jacqueline's chair. "You are my daughter. A Carr, by God! You're built from tougher stuff than most, girl," he insisted. "You've the blood of great African and Indian warriors running through your veins and don't you ever forget that.

"Your great-great-grandfather fought in the Civil War. Your great-great-uncle Simeon was a runaway slave who went on to found one of the wealthiest black communities in Oklahoma in the 1800s and," he said, bending forward until he was nose to nose with his daughter, "it was your great-great-grandfather Shadrack Augustus Carr who helped stake a claim for this very land during the 1889 land run.

"But," Solomon sighed tiredly, "you know the history of the 1850, so there's no sense in me rehashing it all now. Just don't you forget what I've told you all your life, child. You come from strong and good stock.

"Now, I liked Bryce. Your husband was a good man and truthfully," Solomon said, straightening, "I do miss the boy. But your husband is gone. Nothing we can do about that now. Nothing but maybe prove to you that you can stand on your own two feet, teaching your daughter how to grow into a strong woman in the process."

"But, Dad, I—"

Solomon shook his head. "Your mother and I have poured our lives into this place. Now we're tired," he confessed. "And we want to be the first generation to enjoy the fruits of our labor. We don't want to die in order to let our offspring have a chance to run the place."

Jacqueline walked in a small circle around her chair. Coming to stand before it again, she stared closely at her parents. "You realize this couldn't have come at a worse time, with the preparations for the annual rodeo going on, don't you?" she asked.

Solomon offered no response.

"Well." Jacqueline sighed. "I suppose if you'll organize the paperwork and tell me what—"

"No time," Solomon said, walking quickly back to his desk. "Flight leaves in . . ." He checked his watch, then looked at Leila. "What time is it?"

Leila's eyes shot to the window where she tilted her head slightly to get a better view of the sun. "It's six-thirty," she answered, before sitting back down again. "The flight leaves at midnight."

Solomon smiled playfully. "That's the Indian blood in her. See why my watch doesn't need to work?"

Jacqueline sat still as a tomb. "You . . . you mean, you're leaving . . . today?" she stuttered.

"That's right, my dear, as of twelve a.m., the 1850 is all yours. For the one year we're gone anyway."

"Actually," Leila interjected, reaching to take her daughter's hand in both of her own, "we signed all the paperwork a week ago. Technically this has been your ranch for nearly seven days already." She gave her daughter a moment to digest the information before continuing.

"Jacqueline, darling, we have every confidence in you. You just need to have a little in yourself. Bryce knew everything there was to know about cattle ranching and horse breaking, but you were always the one with the brains and more than enough grit to go around. Bryce knew it. Your father and I know it, and now it's time for you to know it too. Not here," Leila said, pointing to her head. "But you've got to know it in here." This time she pointed to her heart.

"Besides, it's not like we're leaving you alone. You've an entire ranch full of hardworking men and women who love you and want nothing more than your success. And let's not forget Cookie. She's been like a grandmother to you since the day you were born. She knows how to do more than just cook, and the kitchen is not the extent of her expertise." Leila smiled playfully. "If you have any problems she'll know what to do. Trust me, she always does."

"Enough of that soft stuff, Mrs. Carr," Solomon grumbled. "The girl's got grit and generations of strong blood behind her. She'll do fine. Now come," he said, walking over to extend an elbow to his wife. "We've got packing to do."

Leila gave Jacqueline an approving wink before allowing her husband, who she knew was trying to leave before he too got emotional, to lead her out.

At the sound of the door closing behind her, Jacqueline rose slowly to stand as her father had stood before the picture window. She let her eyes absorb the scenery outside.

Lush green rolling hills stood watch like soldiers

in the distance as the wind led soft pastel clouds of red, orange, purple, and yellow on a graceful dance in the early evening sky. Her full lips turned up at the corners as she made out a herd of wild horses frolicking about from one hill to another. She spotted a black stallion standing as if watching her from the highest hilltop.

Every evening since her husband's death seven and a half years ago, the horse breached the tallest hill as if calling to her, reminding her that her husband's spirit still remained nearby.

Jacqueline sighed. She missed the days when she had someone to share her innermost thoughts and feelings with. She missed Bryce's smile and the feel of his strong arms around her. Her smile broadened with the realization that she even missed the way he smelled after putting in a hard day's work. The scent of the outdoors, mixed with his own natural aroma, caused an old familiar heat to run through her.

She missed making love with him beneath a starry sky after they had secretly snuck off to the lake unnoticed. She missed being loved by a man even though she knew Bryce's love for her was outmatched by his love for the 1850.

She pushed back hot tears, wishing he had lived to see Jasmine born. "You would have been so proud of her, Bryce," she whispered. "You would have been proud of us both."

Jacqueline let her eyes roam closer to home where the corral to the left of the main house was full of horses that were not to be broken, but branded, then freed. They ran about in circles letting out snorts and whinnies as if calling to their friends on the hilltops.

The bunkhouse for the ranch hands, which sat to the right of the house, needed work. Yet the men never complained. Most of them, like Jacqueline, had been born and raised on the ranch and wouldn't have left it for any amount of money. There were plenty of other ranches in Oklahoma, but for anyone who had ever lived and worked on the 1850, it was and always would be home.

Jacqueline's heart fluttered nervously as she wondered if the men would be as loyal to her as they had been to her father. She put the question out of her mind as she looked beyond the stables to the trail leading down to the pond.

She smiled again, realizing it was more of a lake than a pond. Her great-great-grandfather had wanted the children of the ranch hands to have a place of their own. With the help of his sons, they started digging near the pond in hopes of expanding it.

Her grandfather planted trees along the edges for privacy as well. Then Jacqueline's father came along, repeating the custom with his only child, a daughter, until now, after nearly one hundred years, the pond had become a beautiful lake.

Her father was right, Jacqueline did love the 1850 and wanted with all her heart and strength to prove she could run it. Jacqueline had spent countless hours over the years sitting beneath her favorite tree down by the lake, writing down plans about how she would increase profits and expand the ranch.

Now here she was, standing in her father's study after having been handed her dream. She stood taller, prouder, and suddenly completely fearless as she made up her mind to make the next year an absolute success. She would not fail. She would show not only her parents, but also her ancestors, that even though she was the first woman born to the Carr family line in five generations, she was as strong and as smart as the men who came before her.

"Mama!" seven-year-old Jasmine squeaked, barging into the study. "Nana and Pop-Pop are leaving tonight!" She came to an abrupt stop after nearly tripping over the tip of the oriental throw rug.

Jacqueline smiled at her clumsy daughter, wondering if the girl would ever grow into her long limbs. "Yes, I know," she said, smoothing the frayed edges of her daughter's hair.

"Nana promised to send me beautiful dolls with pretty dresses from all the places she visits!" Jasmine said, fidgeting.

"Can I . . . *May* I go help Nana pack?"

"After supper you may help," Jacqueline answered, watching her daughter.

"After dinner? Oh, please, Mama, I did my chores and Nana said," she complained.

"After dinner, Jasmine," Jacqueline reiterated firmly. "For now I have something special for you to do."

Jasmine pouted. "Is it another chore?" the child asked suspiciously.

"Only if you think of it as such."

"What is it you want me to do?"

"Actually, it's something we can do together."

Jasmine ran a hand along the edge of her grandfather's desk, then stopped to look up at her mother. "What?" she asked again.

"You know how Pop-Pop and I go down to the pond every night to dig so we can make it bigger?"

"Uh-huh . . . I mean, yes, ma'am," Jasmine said cautiously. She sat at her grandfather's large desk.

The leather chair was huge and the desk nearly gigantic compared to the slender girl.

"Well, since Pop-Pop and Nana are going away for a year, I'll need someone to help me dig. Not just any someone but someone very strong, and to be honest, it would be nice to dig with a girl instead of a sweaty guy."

Jasmine laughed at her mother's turned-up nose and at the prospect that her grandfather could ever smell like anything but the fresh outdoors.

Being out at the lake after dark, doing something with her mother, who always seemed to find a way to make things fun; digging in the dirt without getting into trouble for doing so; and showing the men that girls could do a better job and not get all smelly, was enough to convince Jasmine that her mother just might be on to something.

"I'll do it!" Jasmine said. "I'll go get the shovels!" she called over her shoulder before Jacqueline could say a word.

"Watch out, world. The Carr women are about to step up to the plate!" Jacqueline said with a laugh as she too left the room and closed the door behind her.

Chapter Two

"What do you mean it fell through?" Alexander Hawkins roared. "I had that thing locked and in my pocket just six months ago! How could the deal have fallen through?"

Beverly watched Alexander pace the length of the office floor. He had every right to be upset. He had been working on one of the sweetest real estate deals to come along in ages. Now it looked as though all the hours of hard work and negotiations were nothing more than a waste of time.

"Sit down, Alexander, you're making me dizzy," Beverly said in as soothing a voice as she could muster.

"I don't want to sit down! I want you to explain how this could have happened! No, better yet, I want you to get the property owner on the line and tell him we'll sue him for every penny he's got if he pulls out this late in the game!"

"I'll call, but it won't make any difference," Beverly stated calmly.

"And why not?"

"Because he never signed our contracts, remember?"

Alexander thought about it for a moment. She was right. The old bugger had told him from the beginning that he had no interest in signing anything until all the pieces were in play. He was an old-fashioned man who insisted a man's word was his bond. While that was not usually the way Alexander did business, there was something about the man he couldn't help but admire and trust.

"Well, get him on the phone and tell him I'm willing to go higher if he—"

"He's not there," Beverly cut in.

"What? How do you know he's not there?" Alexander asked irritably.

Beverly rolled her eyes. "Alexander, if you don't sit down, I'm not telling you anything else."

Alexander shot his equally stubborn business partner a rebellious glare, knowing it didn't faze her in the least. Mumbling, he sat down hard behind his desk.

"Thank you." Beverly smiled. "There was a fax on my desk when I arrived this morning. It seems that the property owner, Mr. Solomon Carr, suffered a medical emergency of some type, which explains his lack of communication and why all business dealings have been left up to a close family member.

"The fax also gave his apologies, but he believes leaving things to the younger generation has been a long overdue move on his part. While he regrets pulling out so late in the negotiations, he says he has every confidence you will understand."

Alexander sat frozen for several seconds while

Beverly prepared for the storm she knew would follow.

"He's left it up to the younger generation?" Alexander asked, as if tasting the words on his lips.

"That's what he said," Beverly confirmed.

"A close family relative?"

"Yes, I believe the name is . . ." Beverly pulled out her Palm Pilot. After clicking the screen a few times, she nodded. "Jack. The name is Jack."

Alexander was up and pacing again. He placed a contemplative hand under his chin as he walked. "Younger generation . . . Jack . . . a male . . . must be the old guy's . . . son," he decided. "Set up a conference call with him. Preferably something in the evening, and tell him . . . tell him we were sorry to hear about his father, but are relieved to know he is doing better now."

He paused again. "Tell him we understand how swamped he must be with taking over his father's business affairs, but we would like to sweeten the deal by, say, ten percent."

Beverly gave Alexander a disapproving frown.

"Trust me. By the time he pays the extra fees for the new contracts and legal consultation, we'll get it back in spades," he assured her.

"Alexander, I'm not worried about recovering any financial losses right now," Beverly confessed. "I'm worried about *you*."

"Me?" Alexander repeated, surprised.

"Yes, you. Why are you so determined to purchase this ranch property? You said you were just going to sell it off by the acre to anyone willing to pay a high enough price."

"So?"

"So . . . since when do we buy land just to tear it apart, especially land as beautiful as this Oklahoma property?" Beverly asked, tossing a folder filled with photos of the ranch on his desk. She continued her query when he did not reply. "Alexander, you're not going to sell the property, are you?"

"What are you talking about? We purchase property all the time. It's what we do, remember?" he said offhandedly.

Beverly frowned. "We buy property, yes, but we also fix it up and sell it. That's how we make our profit. You can act as nonchalant as you want, Alexander, but I haven't seen any contractors' fees, maintenance agreements, or sales proposals on the table in regard to this property.

"This is also the first time you've shown an interest in a residential property. We buy corporate properties and you know it."

"What's your point, Bev?" Alexander asked, closing the folder and sliding it back to her without looking at it.

"My point is, you've been so distracted by something lately that your entire focus is off. You've been more than a little irritable and I know you well enough to recognize when you're up to something."

Alexander knew there was no use arguing with his business partner and longtime friend. She knew him far too well for him to deceive her. He sat back with a sigh.

"All right, I *have* been making a few changes, or at least trying to. I don't want to get into what I've been doing right now, but I promise to fill you in the moment I have more details."

"But I could help you if you'd just—"

Alexander shook his head. "Not this time, Beverly. I know you mean well, but this is something I need to do myself."

"Fine, but can I ask you one question before you shut me out?"

"I'm not shutting you out." When she didn't look any less concerned, Alexander nodded.

"I know you've been trying to get custody of your daughter for some time now, and I know the problem has been the amount of time you spend traveling with this job so you don't have a specific residence apart from a hotel penthouse. My question is this—are you trying to buy the ranch so you can provide a stable home environment for Shasta?"

"That's crazy and you know it," Alexander said before standing abruptly to rummage through a nearby filing cabinet.

"That's what I thought too at first, knowing how much you've avoided being anywhere near a ranch since your sister's death years ago. Yet that's the only reason I could come up with to explain your sudden interest in a private property, and a ranch no less. There has to be something more to it than just business. I mean, you won't even visit your parents because—"

"Don't try to analyze me, Beverly!" Alexander said angrily, slamming the file cabinet drawer closed. He immediately regretted the outburst. Turning toward her, he apologized. "I'm sorry," he groaned with frustration before returning to his chair. "Like you said, I've got a lot on my mind right now. I know you mean well, but I don't want to discuss this right now. Let's just focus on closing the deal, all right?"

"All right," Beverly reluctantly agreed. "But we're going to discuss this further the moment—"

"Excuse me, Mr. Hawkins, but your wife is here," the receptionist's voice interrupted from the intercom.

"Ex-wife," Alexander mumbled irritably. "What the devil does she want, Pam?" he growled, wondering if his day could possibly get any worse.

"I don't know, sir, she won't say."

"Tell her I'm busy."

"You'll see me now, Alexander," a familiar voice said into the intercom.

"Do you mind?" the secretary complained.

Alexander groaned.

Beverly walked to the door. "I'll get in touch with someone about the property and get back to you with a conference time and date."

Too frustrated to respond, Alexander nodded. He waited for Beverly to leave before hitting the speaker button on his desk phone. "Send her in, Pam," he grumbled, "but tell her she's only got five minutes."

"That's all I need," his ex-wife assured him before relinquishing the intercom to the secretary again.

Alexander took several long, deep breaths, exhaling each slowly. He knew he needed to be in total control of his temper before speaking to Lana. While they had been divorced for over seven years, Alexander feared he would never be fully over her.

Lana entered the office in her usual self-important fashion, dressed in Prada from head to toe.

"I don't know why you've been avoiding me, Alexander, but I won't be put off any longer," she stated haughtily.

The fact that he gave her a truckload of money in

addition to child support each month, and was still paying the exorbitant credit card bills she seemed to have no conscience about running up, was reason enough to avoid her, Alexander thought grimly.

"What is it this time, Lana?" Alexander inquired, sitting back before she issued her inevitable list of demands.

"Aren't you going to ask me to sit down?" she asked, as if hurt. When he did not answer, she sat opposite him at the desk. "It's been eight years, Alexander, darling. Honestly, one would think you would be over me by now." She crossed her long, slender legs.

Alexander swallowed, sitting back in his chair, hoping doing so would put him outside the view of her womanly assets. He remembered a time when just watching the woman walk sent chills up and down his spine. Truth was, it still did. He concentrated hard, thinking of the last bill she sent him from Gucci. He sobered instantly.

"We've only been divorced seven and a half years. Our daughter isn't quite eight yet," he reminded her. "And I'd love to be over you, Lana, but you keep sending me bills to remind me of your existence. Why you send them is beyond me. If memory serves me correctly, you remarried, which freed me of alimony. I pay nearly twice the child support necessary because I love my daughter. You, however, don't deserve the same privilege."

She ran a hand over her perfectly styled hair. "Well, can I help it if you feel guilty for divorcing me?"

"*I divorced you?*" Alexander growled. "All that shopping has ruined your brain, Lana. You were the one who left with that movie producer without even saying good-bye! You didn't even tell me you were pregnant with *my* child until weeks after you'd left. The only reason I couldn't get custody of Shasta was . . ." Alexander's words trailed off.

He didn't want to do this. Opening old wounds never got anyone anywhere, he reminded himself. Besides, he knew Lana's tactics. First beguile him and then agitate him. That way he'd be so frustrated he'd give in to her whims just to get her off his back. Well, they weren't married anymore, so the rules of engagement had to change. There was nothing she could manipulate him into anymore. She had no more firepower and she needed to know that.

Alexander took a deep, calming breath. "What did you want, Lana?" he asked, forcing himself to calm down.

Lana's expression changed to one of utter distress. This didn't faze Alexander in the least. He knew that not being able to find the right shoes to go with the right dress constituted panic and distress for his ex-wife.

"It's Shasta," Lana said with a sad but irritated sigh.

"What is it? What's happened to her? Is she all right?" Alexander asked desperately, sitting forward as if he'd been shot from behind.

Lana rolled her eyes skyward at Alexander's reaction. "There's no need for drama, Xander," she said glibly. "Honestly, I don't know why you let the girl get to you the way you do. She's spoiled enough as it is with you giving her everything she wants with absolutely no thought to me or how I'm getting along and—"

"What's happened to my daughter, Lana?" Alexander asked again, growing increasingly sick with worry.

"I was merely trying to express that I too have needs and—"

"Lana, the fact that you know I would never do anything to hurt a woman doesn't mean I'm not mildly tempted to wring your beautiful little neck right now if you don't tell me what's happened to my daughter."

Lana ran gentle fingers down the length of her slender neck. "You . . . you think my neck is beautiful?" she asked, ignoring what she knew was an empty threat, choosing instead to revel in what she took as a compliment.

What had he ever seen in the woman? Alexander wondered. He seriously suspected there was more empty space in Lana's cranium than there were brains, and if she didn't start giving him information soon, he wouldn't be responsible for his actions.

"She's fine, of course," Lana said, tiring of waiting for another compliment. "She's been kicked out of another boarding school."

Alexander visibly relaxed, letting a relieved sigh slip from his lips.

"The girl is as stubborn as you are. Not only did she refuse to dissect a frog in her advanced science class, but she sneaked into the lab before class and freed all the frogs, mice, and insects she could find, as well as poured every bottle of chloroform down the drain," Lana informed him. "The little imp probably could have gotten away with it if she hadn't inhaled some of the gasses. She passed out just outside the classroom. She's fine now but had a horrid headache for a few days."

Alexander smiled proudly. "That's my girl, stand up for what you believe in." He chuckled. "Good plan, but the execution obviously needed a bit more work."

"Oh well, I'm glad you're so pleased with the child because she's yours until I can find another school willing to take her, which will be quite difficult considering her rather unruly reputation. This is the fifth boarding school she's been expelled from in three years and word does get around, you know," Lana said worriedly.

"No problem. I can take her for about four days, starting two weeks from now," Alexander readily agreed.

Lana sighed. "I'm afraid that won't do. She will arrive on a plane this evening at precisely ten p.m. You will have to keep her for the summer, as I have plans," she said, standing.

"Are you insane? I can't take Shasta now," Alexander said, stunned by Lana's nonchalant attitude. "I fly to Georgia tomorrow to close a deal. Then I'm off to California and then Naples."

Lana stood. "You're always saying you want more time with your daughter, Xander. Well, this is the perfect opportunity for you to do just that," she said, walking toward the door. "As for your previous engagements," she added, opening the door, "you will simply have to cancel them."

"There's nothing simple about it, Lana. I—"

"Cancel everything, Alexander. I don't care how you do it, but see to it you are at the airport to pick up your daughter this evening. You'll have to keep her all summer because I have previous engagements that I simply cannot miss."

"Whoa . . . hold on!" Alexander said, attempting to get up from his desk, but finding himself entangled in phone, fax, and copy machine cords. He knocked over several folders on his desktop in his struggle.

"I already left the flight information with your secretary. Give Shasta a kiss from me, and I'll see you both in September. Toodles!" she said, before closing the door behind her.

"*September?*" he muttered, finally managing to free himself. He cursed as he picked the folders up from the floor, replacing them on his desk. This was only mid-May. "Lana!" Alexander roared before rounding the desk to open the door. "There's no way I—" he started, nearly colliding with Beverly in the process.

"We've got a small window of opportunity here, Alexander," Beverly said as she whizzed by him and into the room.

Alexander cursed, seeing the elevator doors close down the hall.

"I spoke to the old man and he said you were more than welcome to speak with Jack. He said he'd stand by Jack's decision. Only problem is that Jack won't negotiate over the phone. You'll have to fly out there."

"What am I going to do with her?" Alexander grumbled, rubbing his temples as he walked past Beverly to his desk.

Beverly frowned. "She divorced you, Alexander. The good thing about that is that you no longer have to *do* anything with her. Now, back to the situation at hand."

"I didn't mean my wife."

"Ex-wife," Beverly corrected.

"Ex-wife," Alexander growled. "I meant, what am I going to do with *Shasta*? She's been expelled from school."

"Again?" Beverly asked, both surprised and appalled. She threw up an apologetic hand when Alexander shot her an angry glower. "Sorry," she said, taking a seat.

"I'm supposed to pick her up from the airport tonight."

"Kind of short notice, isn't it?" Beverly asked suspiciously.

"Apparently her mother has other plans. Plans, I'm willing to bet, she made the moment she heard she'd have to have Shasta all summer."

"So you pick her up tonight?"

Alexander nodded.

"That's not so bad. How long do you have her? A week, two?"

"Until September when school starts again," Alexander answered. He looked up when Beverly gasped in surprise. "Exactly."

"Okay," Beverly said, finally able to shake off the shock. "Well, we can work with this."

Alexander sat up straighter as he watched Beverly take a turn at pacing the floor. She was an attractive woman with soft caramel skin that was as flawless as her intellect. They had met in college and gone into business together shortly after graduation.

"I got it!" Beverly said, coming to an abrupt halt. "You can leave Shasta with me while you fly out to tie up loose ends. I'll keep her until you get back from talking to Jack."

It took Alexander a moment to shift mental gears. "I appreciate the offer, Beverly, but I can't leave Shasta with you while I'm off doing business."

"And why not?" Beverly asked, insulted.

"You'd bore her to tears and you know it," Alexander said with a sincere smile. "She likes you, but let's face it, Bev, your idea of a fun weekend is going over real estate law and writing out new contracts while my daughter helps staple the papers."

Beverly was about to protest but knew he was right—at least partially. "Okay . . . so . . . we'll just have to compromise," she suggested.

"Compromise, how?" Alexander asked, unable to imagine what she would come up with next.

"Well, I'll fly to Cali, Naples, and anywhere else you were supposed to show up for closings, and you . . . you . . ." she stammered, trying to come up with a plan as she went. "Aha!" Beverly said, leaning to place both hands atop Alexander's desk. "You pick up Shasta tonight, then take her with you in a day or two when you fly down to Oklahoma to talk to Jack. Shasta will love it out there, I'm sure!"

Alexander shook his head dramatically. "I can't take her to Oklahoma with me. I have no idea how to keep her occupied while I'm trying to do business, and who knows how long it will take to talk this guy into selling? God," Alexander groaned. "I sure hope the country bumpkin isn't totally green when it comes to real estate . . . although that could be a definite plus for us."

Snapping out of his reverie, he continued with more important issues. "Besides, you know how bored Shasta gets. She's a seven-year-old child with the intelligence level of a college student."

"Don't do this, Alexander," Beverly warned. "Don't throw away a perfectly good opportunity to spend time with your daughter and to take a much-needed vacation."

Alexander thought about it for a moment. "Granted, spending time with my little girl would be more than worth it, but a vacation? Beverly, we're talking months, not a week or two."

"Alexander, we've been working together since college and I can't remember you ever taking a vacation. You and Lana didn't even go away for your honeymoon because you were here running things twenty-four-seven."

"We were just getting the business successful. I couldn't leave you here alone to handle things. It would have been too much for one person alone and you know it," Alexander said in defense of himself.

"That was true back then, but this is now. Alexander, it's been nearly ten years and believe me when I say I know what I'm doing. I can handle things around here just fine without you."

Alexander couldn't argue. His conscience wouldn't let him. He knew he wouldn't have been as successful as he was without Beverly. "I'd do it if it were possible, Bev, but—"

Beverly put up a hand to stop his excuses. She reached across the desk to press a button on Alexander's phone.

"Yes, Mr. Hawkins?" the receptionist asked from the other end.

"It's me, Pam," Beverly corrected.

"Oh, sorry, Ms. Ross."

"No problem," Beverly said in a rush. "Could you step in here for a moment please?"

Beverly ignored Alexander's quizzical gaze.

"Have a seat, Pam," Beverly instructed when Pam arrived. She waited for the young woman to get comfortable. "Correct me if I'm wrong, Pam, but don't I recall you having some college experience on your resume when you applied here two years ago?"

It was Pam's turn to look puzzled. "Yes," she answered suspiciously. "I majored in child psychology but . . ." She paused. "I was unable to finish my senior year."

"Why?" Beverly asked, handing Pam a glass of water.

Pam took a sip before answering. "My mother took ill, so I got a deferment while I helped out at home."

"Please tell me that your mother is doing much better and you were able to finish school," Alexander said, feeling guilty for not having been aware of her situation.

"I wish I could, Mr. Hawkins, but the truth is . . . my mother passed away from cancer two years ago. I took the job shortly thereafter because I needed the money to pay her medical expenses and funeral costs. I planned to go back to school, but I guess I . . . I lost the desire to do much of anything for a while."

"I'm sorry for your loss, Pam. I had no idea," Alexander said sympathetically.

"How could you have known? It wasn't exactly something I put on my resume. I was an emotional wreck when I started here, but Ms. Ross was very patient with me." Pam smiled gratefully.

"Why do I get the feeling you knew about all this, Beverly?" Alexander asked suspiciously.

"Because I did. Pam's grandmother attends the

church I go to. She explained Pam's dilemma and I told her to send her our way."

Alexander mulled the information over in his head. "What does any of this have to do with—"

"Pam should be back in school. She's had two years to grieve, which is a year more than necessary in my book. She should be focusing on her studies and getting her degree. She's a great secretary, but let's face it, it's not her chosen profession."

"True," Alexander agreed. "Do you still want to be a child psychologist, Pam?"

Pam brightened instantly. "Yes! Very much!" Her smile quickly faded. "I don't see it happening any time soon, however. I'm still paying off my student loans and my mother's medical bills. I can't afford classes on my own right now, but I hope to finish school someday."

Alexander shot Beverly an understanding glance. "Perhaps we could help each other, Pam. I've got a situation I think you could help me with and you've got one I know I can remedy."

"I'm afraid I've missed a step, Mr. Hawkins. What are you talking about?"

"I just found out I'll have my daughter for the next four months or so. She's only seven and a half, so I can't leave her in a hotel room on her own while I'm in meetings. I've also got a very lucrative deal in the works, which requires not only my attention but my presence as well."

It was obvious by Pam's expression that she did not understand where the conversation was leading.

Alexander took a breath and dove in. "I have to fly to Oklahoma and it might take me a while to close the current deal. I have no choice but to take my daughter with me, but I won't be available every moment of the day and believe me when I say my daughter requires just about every moment of my time."

Pam smiled. "I've met Shasta a few times, Mr. Hawkins, so I understand your dilemma. She's a very intelligent child and more than a little precocious as well."

"Indeed," Alexander agreed, taking no offense at Pam's observations. "I thought it might be nice as well if I turned this little trip into a lengthy but much-needed hiatus for a few months. The problem is that I would need someone to watch my daughter when I'm not there."

When Pam still looked confused, Beverly decided to step in. "What Mr. Hawkins is trying to say, Pam, is—would you consider flying to Oklahoma with him and his daughter as her au pair for a few months? He trusts you. Actually, we both do.

"In return, he'll pay all your expenses as well as take care of your mother's outstanding medical bills in addition to writing you a check to cover your entire senior year if you'll agree to go back to school in September to obtain your degree."

Pam inhaled sharply in surprise and disbelief.

"I know this is a lot to think about on such short notice but—"

"Yes!" Pam blurted out.

Both Alexander and Beverly looked equally surprised at the outburst.

Pam stood before them. "I—I trust the two of you completely," the twenty-four-year-old beamed. "My grandmother has told me a great deal about you, Ms.

Ross. I know about your church and community activities and I've even heard you speak at a few conferences for African-American businesswomen! I know all about your family and I have had a secret crush on your nephew, Anthony, for quite some time now," she admitted, embarrassed.

"I also know a lot about you, Mr. Hawkins. I've read every magazine article printed about you and how you and Ms. Ross started this place fresh out of college and built it into a multimillion-dollar money machine! I know you come from a humble background, though you never talk about it in public or during interviews. My grandmother says she knows your parents and—"

"We get the point, Pam," Alexander said with a chuckle.

"I'm sorry. I'm just so . . . yes! Yes! I'll help you with Shasta, Mr. Hawkins, and I will graciously accept your help with my situation as well!"

"Wonderful." Beverly smiled, trying not to laugh at the young woman's overly exuberant reaction. "The information you need to book hotel and flight arrangements is on my desk. Why don't you go get busy with that while Mr. Hawkins and I work out other details, okay?"

"Yes!" Pam chirped happily. She surprised them both with a heartfelt hug. "My granny is going to be elated!" she said before practically running out of the office.

"She's a good kid," Beverly said, sitting down as if exhausted by Pam's whirlwind excitement.

"You're not so bad yourself." Alexander smiled, patting Beverly's shoulder as he walked by her and to his desk. "You never cease to amaze me, Bev."

"Yeah, well, I'm just an amazing woman, Alexander. What can I say?" Beverly grinned.

"Ah, excuse me," Pam's voice interrupted over the speakerphone.

"Yes, Pam?" Alexander asked, feeling a slight headache coming on.

"Um, sir, I, ah—"

"What is it, Pam? Spit it out," Alexander coaxed.

"Well, sir, I was just about to book the arrangements for the trip, but, well . . ." Pam took in a deep breath. "I just want to make certain that . . . I said I trusted you and I do, of course . . . well, Sir, you need to know that while I'm booking a suite for you and Shasta, I'll be booking a separate one entirely for myself. Shasta may stay in either room at her leisure, but I just wanted to make it clear that . . . well . . . we won't be sharing anything except an occasional cup of coffee from time to time . . . sir," she finished nervously.

A small smile crept up the edges of Alexander's lips. "You are a gem, Ms. Pamela Benson," he acknowledged, "and I respect you far too much to attempt taking advantage of either your intellect or your kindness. Two rooms will be fine . . . and expected."

"Thank you, sir. There's one other thing," Pam said nervously.

"Yes?"

"I was thinking, since we're talking about an extended stay, perhaps it would be better for Shasta if I looked for a bed-and-breakfast as opposed to a stuffy hotel room."

"That's a marvelous idea, Pam. Go ahead and do that," Beverly answered for Alexander.

"Yes, ma'am," Pam said before clicking off.

"This is going to be interesting," Alexander said, shaking his head at Beverly, who, in his opinion, was enjoying his discomfort far too much.

Chapter Three

"Can I at least go over *there* and play?" Shasta asked her father, pointing to an inviting area just off the roadside.

Alexander looked out from under the hood of the smoking car, annoyed. "No. Stay close to me. There might be wolves or tigers or something out there," he warned, before using his jacket to fan the smoke.

"Dad, tigers are not indigenous to Oklahoma wildlife. While there are wolves and coyotes, the chances of them having a den anywhere near an open road like this are highly unlikely."

"I'll keep a close watch on her, Mr. Hawkins," Pam said reassuringly.

Alexander had almost forgotten Pam was there. The woman had a quiet spirit and a gentle disposition. Shasta took to her immediately and hadn't stopped chattering the entire trip thus far. Alexander was impressed with the amount of patience Pamela displayed in regard to his daughter's never-ending questions.

She also had a wonderful sense of humor. Alexander had already decided to become a surrogate big brother to her and she seemed not to mind in the least.

He groaned inwardly, realizing he would be as protective of her as he was of his daughter. *Great*, he thought, *just what I need, another woman to worry about.*

"Did you say something, Mr. Hawkins?" Pam asked innocently.

"I was just saying, fine, let Shasta play, but the two of you stay within ear- and eyeshot," Alexander warned, wondering how he was ever going to win an argument with two such strong-minded, intelligent females to contend with.

Putting down the hood, Alexander realized he didn't have a clue how to fix anything he had been staring at for the past twenty minutes. He made a mental note to schedule an auto mechanics class or two the moment he got back to civilization.

Wiping at his sweat-soaked brow, he looked up toward the blinding sun. Looking away, he said a silent prayer for help and was relieved when he spotted a pickup truck making its way toward them. He began waving his hands as he stepped into the middle of the narrow dirt road.

The pickup slowed, coming to a complete stop several feet away. Alexander watched as a tall, lean, Native American man with flowing gray hair stepped out of the truck. He was wearing a pair of dusty denim jeans, an odd pair of boots made from a material Alexander could not define, and a blue-jean shirt. The man pulled a weathered Stetson from the front seat and placed it carefully on his head before closing the truck door.

He didn't bother looking under the hood as he walked lazily toward Alexander.

"I think we ran out of water, or radiator fluid," Alexander said, offering the stranger his hand while trying not to sound completely incapable. "Thanks for stopping. The name's Alexander."

The man nodded, taking Alexander's hand with a firm grip. "Joseph," he said stoically.

For the first time in his life another human being impressed Alexander. He would have sworn he was beyond such a notion, but there was no denying it. Alexander felt himself in complete awe of Joseph.

The lines of the man's face reminded him of the old Indian chiefs whose pictures he had seen in his college textbooks. His face read like a map of experiences, while his ebony eyes seemed as sharp and clear as those of a man in his twenties. Alexander estimated his age to be closer to seventy.

"Where you headed?" Joseph asked.

"I'm trying to find a Mr. Jack Carr. He runs the 1850 Ranch somewhere near here. Ever heard of it?"

Joseph nodded.

"Could you tell me exactly where it is?"

"You're on it," Joseph informed him.

Surprised, Alexander took a closer look around him, turning to walk a large circle in the middle of the road as he did so. He had a hard time imagining that any one person could actually own land as lush and green as what he now took note of for the first time. He took in miles of fresh air and scenery that seemed far too natural and untouched to exist in this day and age. There was something almost mystical about its purity.

Returning to Joseph's side, he asked, "Are you telling me that Jack owns the creek down there, those hills, and everything right down to the blades of grass, plus some two thousand additional acres?" Alexander caught a dark, almost sad look cross the old man's eyes before it was replaced with an inexplicable pride that straightened his back.

"Can a man own the air he breathes?" Joseph asked. "Can he ever really own the mountains, hills, creek, or blades of grass?"

Alexander understood Joseph's point but wanted to lighten the mood. "Apparently you can if your name is Jack." He chuckled. Alexander cleared his throat at Joseph's blank expression. "Sorry."

"Main house and office are up yonder," Joseph said, pointing in a northeast direction.

Alexander sighed. "Well, no time like the present to get the ball rolling. Mind giving us a ride up there?" he asked, gesturing toward the area where Shasta was doing cartwheels while Pam sat beneath a tree watching her.

"Got an appointment?" Joseph asked, folding his arms across his chest.

"No, not exactly," Alexander admitted.

"Then I will give you a ride into town," Joseph said, turning to walk back to his truck.

Alexander cursed, before catching up with Joseph. "I need to go to the ranch, not town."

"No appointment," Joseph said, before trying to step around Alexander.

"Fine, then we'll walk," Alexander said stubbornly.

"The woman and child will come with me," Joseph said matter-of-factly.

Alexander tried his best to calm his increasing temper. "And why would they do that when they're perfectly capable of walking with me?"

"Takes three hours to reach on foot from here," Joseph said, making his way to the truck and starting the engine.

Stubborn was one thing, stupid was another thing entirely, Alexander told himself. He would not have his daughter or Pam stranded in the middle of Oklahoma because he would not do the reasonable thing by accepting a ride into town.

"Shasta! Pam! Let's go!" he called, opening the passenger-side door.

Shasta ran across the field with Pam close behind her. Alexander held the passenger door open for them. Pam got in first, followed by Shasta, who let out an excited and awestricken gasp upon seeing Joseph. Alexander squeezed in next, closing the door behind him as Joseph started the engine.

"Are you a real Indian?" Shasta asked Joseph, leaning across Pam's lap to get a better look at the stranger. "Well, of course you are, and I'll bet I know your heritage. You're Cherokee, aren't you?"

"Yes," Joseph answered proudly as they drove off.

"I read in a book that there are a lot of Cherokee Indians in Oklahoma." She studied the man carefully. "Are those real cowhide boots you're wearing? Did you make them yourself? Did you ever count coup? That's such a silly word, *coup*, and I wonder why they spell it c-o-u-p instead of spelling it like it sounds, k-o-o," she spelled quizzically. "I imagine there's no need to count coup anymore since they used to do it to show their bravery," Shasta stated sadly.

She looked up at Pam as she continued, "Whenever someone did something really brave, like touch an enemy during a battle, but chose not kill him, the braves would get feathers from the council as a reward. They used to do lots of brave things back then, but now there's nothing brave left to do."

"Are you certain?" Pam asked, smiling down at her young charge. "He just stopped to pick up three complete strangers. That seems pretty brave to me."

Shasta thought about it for a moment. "Yeah!" she agreed happily, but was frowning again soon after. "But who will give him a feather?" she worried.

"Now we wear our feathers on the inside," Joseph assured her.

"But how can—"

"Enough, Shasta. Give Joseph a break. Just enjoy the scenery," Alexander suggested.

"Yes, sir."

It wasn't long before Shasta's usual barrage of questions started afresh.

"Do I call your people Indians, or do all of you prefer to be called Native Americans?" she asked, sounding unsure of herself for the first time.

Joseph smiled. "May *I* ask *you* a question, Little Sparrow?"

"Yes, of course!" Shasta grinned excitedly.

"My people were here before this land was called America. Do you agree?"

"Yes," Shasta answered, disappointed at the easy question.

"If this is true, how then can we be natives of America? I am a native of the land, yet not a native of

America. Do you understand this?" Joseph asked patiently.

Shasta remained thoughtfully silent for several moments before answering. Suddenly a broad smile broke out on her face. "Yes. I understand. It makes sense to me now."

"Indian was a name given us long ago by a man who traveled to our land. It is a name most people know. Many of us prefer being called Indian, yet there are many of us who prefer the term Native American."

Shasta nodded. "I understand."

"If you seek a name for me, Little Sparrow, Joseph will suffice." He winked down at her.

Shasta tugged on her father's sleeve. Alexander bent low, allowing her to whisper in his ear, "He calls me Little Sparrow, Daddy. I think it's my new Indian name."

Alexander grinned. "It's a beautiful name, Shasta."

"Should I ask Joseph to give you a new Indian name too?" she asked, not wanting her father to feel left out.

"I think I might be too old to get a new name, pumpkin," Alexander whispered back, suspecting Joseph would probably name him Chief Moron of the African-American Tribe, if asked. "Why don't we let Joseph drive while we enjoy the scenery?" he suggested.

"Okay," Shasta agreed, but as usual, she soon asked half a dozen more questions of Joseph. To his credit, he answered every one. Like his daughter, Alexander absorbed everything said during the hour-and-a-half drive into town.

*   *   *

Closing the passenger door behind them, Alexander stood eyeing his surroundings with disbelief. He felt as though he had stepped back in time only to awaken in the midst of an old western ghost town, only there were people walking the streets. Most of the buildings looked ancient, and some were actually made of wood. The cars parked along the edges of wood sidewalks were old pickup trucks of various colors.

Several signs on the doors of the buildings had been painted in large block letters on wood platforms. There were no paved sidewalks, no asphalt or tar roads—not so much as a painted line in the middle of the street to separate traffic. Instead the roads were dirt. The sidewalks—where there were any—were made of worn wood, but somehow were still strong underneath.

Alexander couldn't help but do a double take at a horse tied to a hitching post not more than five feet from where Joseph had parked the truck. It too seemed a bit out of place with its well-muscled hindquarters and tall haunches. With its pure white skin and braided mane hanging proudly on either side, it obviously had been well cared for.

Alexander surveyed his surroundings once more. "My God," he breathed. "This isn't real."

"Your little one thinks it's real enough," Joseph said with a hint of laughter in his voice.

At his words, Alexander snapped out of his trance, looking about him for Shasta. Not seeing her anywhere, he looked at a near frantic Pam, who had obviously been so caught up in her surroundings that she too had lost sight of Shasta.

"It's okay, Pam. She does this all the time,"

Alexander said in an attempt to keep the young woman from getting hysterical, which it appeared she was only a hairbreadth away from doing at the moment. "You check that way, and I'll go down here. Something probably just caught her eye and she—"

Pam was gone before he could complete the sentence.

After several unfruitful attempts to locate his daughter, Alexander was just about to panic when Joseph put a firm hand on his shoulder while pointing with the other to a small bar and grill two stores away.

Alexander entered, stopping abruptly at the door after spotting Shasta sitting at a counter. He exhaled, relieved.

"Did real cowboys used to eat here?" Shasta asked a woman sitting on a stool next to her. "I read that back in the olden days they didn't serve Indians in places like this. Is that true? Have you lived here long? Is that a real cowboy hat you're wearing, or do you call it a cowgirl hat since you're a lady? How come you—"

"That's enough, Shasta," Alexander said firmly as he approached. "Leave the nice lady alone," he warned, lifting his daughter off the stool and setting her on her feet.

"It's all right, I have one at home just like her," the woman said, chuckling.

"She's far too inquisitive for her own good and sometimes . . ." Alexander stopped short upon looking at the woman for the first time. Today seemed to be the day for one awestricken moment after another. He knew he shouldn't, but couldn't help but stare.

Her flawless mahogany complexion gave off an almost ethereal glow, while her piercing gray eyes startled him as she sat watching his stunned reaction to her. He immediately got the sense she was used to it. The sharp lines of her face, perfectly chiseled cheekbones, and strong chin seemed familiar to him somehow.

She stood, stepping away from the counter. Alexander momentarily admired her hair, which fell in large, unruly black ringlets as it rested just short of her breasts. The ebony color and softness reminded him of a raven's soft wings. His gaze continued down a slender neck, past full breasts, to a small waist, amply round hips, and legs so long he had trouble swallowing.

She wore an unremarkable pair of brown leather boots, old Wrangler's jeans, a white button-down cotton shirt with the first three buttons unbuttoned, and a red bandana tied in a knot around her neck. He caught the glimpse of a turquoise bracelet around her slender wrist when she leaned across the stool to retrieve her hat. She stood slowly, placing it on her head.

Alexander suddenly felt as though time had frozen. His heartbeat quickened, his knees nearly gave way beneath him, and he sensed something stronger than the obvious physical attraction. An electrical charge seemed to flow between them and Alexander felt something stir deep in his soul.

He watched as the woman knelt regally before Shasta.

"If you get bored during your visit, you are more than welcome to come by the ranch. My daughter is seven, and I'm sure she'd love to meet you. Just ask anyone in town how to get to the 1850 Ranch, and they'll be able to get you there or . . ." The woman stood to reach into her back pocket. "Here's my card. Just give me a call if you want to come out, and I'll send someone to pick you up."

A slender hand reached out, retrieving the card from the woman before Shasta could take it. The woman looked up to see Pam take a protective stance beside Shasta before gently nudging the girl behind her.

The woman gave Pam an understanding nod. "Enjoy your trip, little lady." She winked down at Shasta with a tip of her hat before turning.

"Just a moment!" Alexander said before the woman could leave. "Did I hear you say you work at the 1850 Ranch?" he asked hopefully.

The woman raised a suspicious eyebrow at him. "Are you the child's father?"

"Yes, I am." Alexander extended a hand to her. "I am Alexander Hawkins. This is Pamela Benson, and this," he said, bringing Shasta out from behind Pam, "is my inquisitive daughter, Shasta."

"Pleased to meet you," the woman said, shaking his hand and then theirs.

"Our car broke down just outside the ranch, and I was wondering if you wouldn't mind giving us a lift up there," Alexander said, charmingly.

The woman took a moment to study Alexander carefully before answering. She liked what she saw. She liked it very much indeed. He was of a dark complexion, with strong, sharp features. He was well muscled, but not in a way she was accustomed to. The men she saw every day on the ranch had hard, strong bodies from the rigors of daily chores.

This man, however, had muscles of a less-cut nature. She supposed he'd spent hours at the gym working out every day or at least several times a week. Yet he was sexy with his now-dusty fashionable shoes, black slacks, and white dress shirt with sleeves that he wore rolled up around his biceps. His gold watch had diamonds around the square face, which sparkled beautifully when she shook his hand.

A nice package to be certain, she had to admit, but it was the stranger's eyes that held her attention most. They were an interesting mix of hazel with tiny specks of gold dancing mischievously around the pupils. He reminded her of something caged and untamable, and it was obvious he held his obstreperousness close in check.

One word came to mind like a whisper: *dangerous.* Yes, she decided, the stranger with the untamable eyes was somehow dangerous. The hairs on the back of her neck stood on edge as the blood warmed in her veins.

She fought the recognizable feelings stirring within her, unwilling to acknowledge or accept them. There had been only one man in her life that had made her heart skip a beat and her throat go dry. Though her husband had been deceased for nearly eight years now, Jacqueline recognized passion's stirrings within her.

She inhaled sharply in an effort to free herself of the undeniable connection between them. Visually, he was a stranger to her, but her soul cried out with familiarity and desire. She squelched the barrage of emotions, feeling suddenly as though she had betrayed Bryce's memory.

She forced herself back to the moment. "Why are

you going to the ranch?" she asked suspiciously, placing the thumbs of both hands in the front pockets of her snug-fitting jeans.

Alexander thought the action sexy, though he chided himself for thinking so. "I need to speak with Jack," he answered, noting an odd expression cross the woman's face before quickly disappearing.

"About what?"

While Alexander thought the woman attractive, he was not about to stand in the middle of the run-down bar and grill being interrogated by her. It would be one thing if she was someone of importance, but she looked to him to be nothing more than Jack's secretary, at best.

"It's business," he answered guardedly.

"What kind of business?" she asked, nonplussed by his obvious annoyance with her inquiries.

"Look, I've been doing business with the owner, Solomon Carr, for several months now and I have the old man's permission to speak with his son," he said, trying to sound as polite as possible through his irritation. "I don't mean to be rude, miss, but I'm not at liberty to discuss the details with anyone but the young man himself."

Alexander frowned at the sniggers he heard from several of the patrons seated nearby. While he thought it odd, he wasn't in the mood to be interrogated. He'd had a brutally hot and frustrating day thus far and wanted only to meet Jack, set a business meeting, and then check into the bed-and-breakfast as soon as possible.

"Look, I hate to impose on you like this, but if you're going in that direction we could really use a lift. Hopefully this guy, Jack, will have enough sense to snatch up my offer and send me on my way. It's not like I'd planned to spend more than an hour discussing it with him," Alexander stated.

"I hear Jack's got a pretty good business mind. I'm sure if there was any interest in your offer you would have been contacted by now," the woman said, turning to walk away.

"Wait!" Alexander said, taking hold of her arm to prevent her exit. He was dumbfounded by his action, knowing it had less to do with wanting to get to the ranch and more to do with not wanting her to leave his presence. He released her immediately.

"Please, you don't understand. I've got to get up there to make him an offer that I'm sure will impress even a country bumpkin like him," he blurted out and then regretted the words immediately. Why had he said something so foolish? *The woman is turning my brain to mush!* he thought desperately.

Alexander heard several insulted gasps and grumbles behind him. He turned to see three very large, angry-looking men coming toward him. He was further surprised when Joseph put a firm hand on his shoulder, squeezing so hard the area went instantly numb. "What the—"

The woman put both hands up, one toward Joseph and the other toward the approaching men, all of whom stopped in their tracks, to Alexander's great relief. He rubbed his shoulder as he spoke.

"I meant no disrespect, miss, but—"

"Joseph will bring the three of you to the ranch," she informed him, heading for the door. Alexander heard the old Indian say something in his native tongue, which, judging by the tone, suggested he wanted to do nothing of the kind. The woman turned, narrowed her eyes at him, and spoke in his language. Alexander was relieved when Joseph nodded.

She was gone without having looked back.

"Come." Joseph waved with obvious rancor.

Nodding for Pam to follow, Alexander took Shasta's hand before following him out.

At the ranch, Joseph pointed to a small, run-down building. "In there," he said before walking away.

Once inside, Alexander was more than a bit perturbed that no secretary sat at the small front desk. "Watch her," he told Pam as Shasta inquisitively searched the room for something to pique her interest. "I'll be back in a moment."

Pam nodded.

Alexander walked down the hall and entered a room. He was surprised to find the woman from the restaurant sitting in a chair behind a desk.

"Is Mr. Carr in?" he asked, looking around the room.

"Mr. Carr and his wife are on vacation," the woman informed him. "Have a seat."

Alexander sat, cautiously. He was becoming increasingly guarded when in her presence, not knowing what he would do or say next. "Yes, I realize that, but I was referring to his son, Jack. We had business, remember?" he asked.

"What business do you have with Jack, Mr. Hawkins? And please do not tell me it's private. Either you speak to me first or I'll have you thrown off the ranch." She hoped her words sounded convincing and hated the renewed heat coursing through her at seeing him again.

"I was in negotiations to buy this place from the owners. I invested a lot of time and effort in the process. Mr. Carr . . . Solomon Carr, that is . . . had agreed on a specific price, which by the way was more than fair, but then he took ill. I received a fax stating that his son, Jack, was taking over and that I was welcome to come here and speak with the man. The fax also stated that the owner would agree to whatever Jack chose to do."

Alexander forced himself not to look at her full, pouting lips.

"Because we were so far into the negotiations, there are several fees that have accrued. I would much prefer closing the property deal, in which case those fees would be forgiven."

"Jack will never sell this place," the woman stated flatly.

"Really?" Alexander asked, coming back to his senses after her adamant statement. "Then I hope he's got money to burn, because I can keep him tied up in court costs and legal fees until his little trust fund is completely wiped out. He'll have to run off to Daddy in Europe, or wherever the devil the old man is."

"I see. Would you excuse me a moment, please?" the woman asked, not giving him time to answer as she stood to open a window behind her desk. She leaned out, giving Alexander an extraordinary view of her backside. "Thomas!" she called loudly. "Come here." She closed the window and reclaimed her seat.

"Did Mr. Carr sign anything?" she asked, looking at Alexander through passionately defiant eyes.

"Not exactly. However—"

"Either he did or he didn't," the woman said, crossing her arms in front of her ample breasts.

Alexander stood in challenge. "Just who the devil are you anyway?" he insisted.

The woman stood, walking to stand directly in front of Alexander. "Jacqueline Renee Carr." Then, taking one step closer until she and Alexander were nearly toe to toe, she added, "But my friends call me . . . Jack."

Understanding dawned on Alexander's mortified face. It was official. He was having the worst day of his life. On the other hand, things couldn't possibly get any worse. He told himself that until a tall African-American man entered the office in response to Jacqueline's summons.

Alexander knew he was about to be ushered off the ranch, but the thought didn't bother him much because he knew this was only the beginning. He would be back, and eventually, whether she knew it or not, he would be back . . . for her.

Chapter Four

"I need to speak to Cory right away," Jacqueline said into the phone. "I don't care what he's doing! Tell him that if he doesn't take my call, he'll lose our business, which is something he can't afford to have happen. Yes, I'll hold."

Jacqueline sat back in her father's chair while she waited. She had been running things pretty smoothly for a week now and so far things had been going reasonably well. There were a few minor incidents of people trying to get over, but that was to be expected, she told herself.

Everyone knew the 1850 was under new management and that Jacqueline had been put in charge. She expected to be challenged and, like her mother, even welcomed a good mental and strategic battle or two, but she drew the line at being taken advantage of.

"Yeah?" an irritable male voice grunted from the other end of the phone line.

"You delivered the wrong feed again, Cory," Jacqueline informed him, trying to keep her voice as diplomatic as possible. "I'd greatly appreciate it if you would be kind enough to have someone pick up the—"

"That's the best I can give you, Jack. Take it or leave it," Cory said stiffly.

"What do you mean it's the best you can give me? Cory, you sent me low-quality feed that I wouldn't give a dog! This is completely unacceptable. I want the same quality feed you were sending to the ranch when my father was here, understand?"

"Yeah, I understand," Cory answered. "Then you need to pay what you owe, and then we can schedule a new delivery."

Jacqueline was caught off guard by Cory's pronouncement.

Cory sighed heavily. "I hate to do this to you, Jack, but I don't have much choice. Your father should have settled the debt before he took off. He should have left you with a clean bill. This puts both of us in a bad situation. I can't send you what you need, and you can't keep your herds fed the way they should be without quality feed. I'm really sorry to do this to you but, again, I don't have a choice."

"How much?" Jacqueline asked, almost afraid to hear the answer.

"You folks owe me just over two thousand."

"Two thousand . . . dollars?" Jacqueline managed. "That's impossible! My father would never have allowed a debt to accumulate that high!"

"I've got his signed markers sitting right here in front of me. You're more than welcome to come in and look them over anytime," Cory said before hanging up.

Jacqueline sat with the phone in her hand for several moments before hanging up. How could this be? How could her father have incurred such a debt and why hadn't he told her about it before? Something wasn't right and she was going to find out what it was.

Jacqueline walked to the corral where several ranch hands busied themselves with the horses. She watched, enthralled, as Joseph approached a skittish mare. Raising a hand slowly, he whispered something as he took stealthy steps closer. The horse whinnied, prodded the ground, and shook its head, but eventually calmed.

"We haven't seen you out here for a while," a tall brown-skinned man said as he leaned lazily against the wooden posts.

"I've been busy with paperwork," Jacqueline said, keeping an eye on Joseph.

"You know what they say about all work and no play," the man said with a half-playful smile.

"Yeah, it's how people make money and lots of it," Jacqueline stated, in no mood to be playful. "Tell Joseph I went to check on some business in town. I don't know how long it will take, so tell him not to hold dinner for me," she said, before walking away.

"Hey, Jack!" the man called after her.

"What is it, Ian?"

Ian took his hat off before speaking. "I j-just wanted to say, w-well, that I know things are about to get tough for you, but I-I'm here if you n-need me."

"Thanks," Jacqueline said, trying to turn away, but Ian caught her by the arm.

"Don't turn into one of those old sp-spinster

women who rot away on the inside because they d-didn't take the time to find happiness or l-love," he stuttered nervously before releasing her arm.

Jacqueline knew Ian had had a crush on her since they were children. While he had grown into a sweet, hardworking, and handsome man, he would never come close to what she'd found and lost in her husband. "I've known happiness and I've experienced love, Ian. You don't need to worry about me," she said gently before offering him a friendly smile and walking off hurriedly.

Ian stood staring after Jacqueline until she disappeared around the side of the house.

"It'll never happen," a male voice said from behind Ian. "She wants you about as much as she wants the cattle to contract mad cow disease."

"We'll see," Ian answered, knowing how Dusty and several of the other ranch hands found humor in his hopes that Jacqueline would someday look in his direction. "W-we'll just s-see," he stuttered, before walking back to the corral.

Jacqueline got in the pickup truck, slamming the door hard behind her. What the devil was going on? she wondered. Her father was one of the most responsible men she knew. It wasn't like him to forget to mention such a huge debt. She tried to calm herself but was unsuccessful as Ian's comment invaded her mind.

What had Ian meant, *I know things are about to get tough for you?* She wanted to believe he meant he would be there to help *if* things got tough for her, but somehow knew his words were more warning than concern.

Jacqueline checked her watch. It was nearly one o'clock. She would have to hurry if she was going to be on time to meet Jasmine when she got home from school.

After the hour-and-a-half drive, Jacqueline parked the truck downtown deciding to walk rather than drive the last three blocks to the feed store. After passing several shops and giving her usual greeting to the store owners, she began feeling uneasy.

"Good afternoon, Mrs. Brown, how are you today?" Jacqueline smiled, stopping to look through the clothing racks outside the woman's store.

"Fine," Mrs. Brown answered curtly before going inside.

Continuing her stroll, Jacqueline paused to say hello to an old family friend. "Hello, Mr. Baker. How's business today?" she asked, running a hand over a beautiful handcrafted leather saddle.

"It'll do," he answered before grabbing his cane and hobbling to the back of the store.

"Must be the heat," Jacqueline decided before exiting the store.

Arriving at the feed store, she was quickly ushered to the back office.

"Have a seat, Jacqueline," Cory said, motioning to the chair opposite his cluttered desk.

Jacqueline frowned suspiciously, unable to recall a time her childhood friend had called her anything but Jack.

"Here's the folder with the markers," Cory said, leaning forward to hand her a thick brown folder stuffed with papers.

Jacqueline took her time thumbing through the information. Once done, she began again, hoping, praying there had been a horrible mistake she had overlooked.

"It's accurate," Cory assured her. "I've been supplying your ranch with feed for ten years now and my father was doing it long before that."

"I see," Jacqueline said, noting the dates, which went back some twenty years.

"I'm sorry you had to find out this way, but I just can't afford to keep supplying you folks with the best feed I've got and not getting paid for it. I'm taking too much of a loss."

"I understand," Jacqueline said. "No, actually, I don't. How could this have happened? How could he let the debt accumulate for so long and to such an extent? Why didn't he tell me? Did my mother know about . . ." She stopped, seeing her mother's signature on a sales receipt. "I don't understand this at all."

"We all had a few tough years there, Jack. We've suffered drought, storms that flooded the pastures, turning anything of use into mush, pestilence, disease, and a million other things that make it near impossible to keep a herd alive. By the time you put out money to reseed or fix damages, there's nothing left."

"No! I don't accept that. There's got to be a mistake here. This can't be right!" she insisted. "Besides, you said the debt was two thousand dollars, and these receipts are in excess of five."

"I forgave as many of them as I could," Cory confessed. "Look, maybe I can go over it again and see if there's anything else I can—"

"No," Jacqueline protested, pulling out her checkbook. "I'll pay what we owe."

"But—"

"I don't know why my father didn't tell me about this, but now that I'm responsible for the 1850, its debts are up to me," she said, taking a pen from Cory's desktop.

"Jacqueline," he pleaded.

"Don't worry, Cory, things will be tough for a while but not impossible. This is only a minor setback."

"But you don't understand—" Cory started.

"I understand enough to know that we don't need to be in debt to anyone," Jacqueline stated, writing out the check.

"But—"

"No buts," Jacqueline said with pride. "The 1850 won't be in debt to anyone."

"But, Jack," Cory said, putting a hand over hers to prevent her from writing. "The 1850 is in debt to just about everyone."

At that, Jacqueline looked up, shocked. "Wh-what are you saying?" she asked, mortified.

"I'm saying that I'm not the only one who's been giving your family markers and I'm not the only one who has decided to call them in." Cory hated having to break the news to her, but he didn't want her to be caught off guard when folks started knocking on her door during the weeks ahead.

"Are you telling me that there are other businesses here in town that we owe large sums of money to?"

Cory remained silent.

"Of course you are," Jacqueline realized suddenly. "That certainly would explain a lot." She stood, pacing the floor near the desk.

"On the way here I kept getting the sense that people were avoiding me, and the ones that weren't seemed almost . . . angry about something. Now I understand. They think we've no intention of paying them back."

"Look, Jack, if there's anything I can do, just name it."

"Can you get hold of the business owners we owe money to and have them meet me at the ranch on Friday evening, say around seven or so?"

"Yeah, I guess so, but what—"

"Just do it, Cory. You make sure you're there as well. Tell folks if they're not at the meeting, I'll assume we have no debt with them. Would you do that for me, please?"

"I'll round 'em up," Cory assured her.

"Good," Jacqueline said before opening the door. "I'll see you then."

Jacqueline exited Cory's office. After closing the door behind her, she leaned heavily against the wall. She didn't understand what was going on. How could things have gotten so out of hand?

She inhaled deeply, adjusting her hat on her head. There was one more stop to be made and she refused to make it looking flustered. This was nothing more than an odd situation and she had been trained to handle odd situations, she reminded herself. She exited the feed store with renewed confidence as she headed for the bank.

*   *   *

"Next!" an older, stout woman called out.

Jacqueline's feet felt like lead, but she managed to move them, slowly.

"Well, hello, Jack!" The woman smiled. "What can I do for you today?"

Jacqueline willed herself to maintain control. "I need to make a withdrawal," she said, lifting her chin as she spoke. "Here's my account number."

Looking down at the withdrawal slip, the teller blanched visibly before turning concerned eyes on her customer. "But that's fifty thousand dollars, Jack."

"I'm aware of that. Now type it into your little machine there and give me my money please," Jacqueline said, straightening her back stiffly.

"But—"

"Just do it!" Jacqueline insisted before catching herself. "I'm sorry. I don't mean to be rude, but I'm in a bit of a hurry, so could you please just put the transaction through?" She tried to smile but knew it wasn't very convincing.

"Is there a problem here?" the bank manager asked, coming to stand behind the teller.

"Good afternoon, Benjamin. There's no problem here. I was just about to make a withdrawal, that's all," Jacqueline explained.

Benjamin looked at the withdrawal slip. His eyes widened and then quickly narrowed on Jacqueline. "Would you mind stepping to the side and joining me in my office for a moment, Jack?" he asked, not giving her time to respond before moving away from the teller.

Jacqueline gathered her things before following him. Once inside the office, she sat opposite his desk.

"What's the problem, Benjamin?" she asked irritably.

"No problem. Or at least not one we can't handle," Benjamin answered. "Would you care to tell me why you need so much money?"

"No, actually I would not."

Jacqueline saw the corners of Benjamin's mouth turn up, though she would not have classified the action as a smile.

"I realize you've been given the ranch to run in your father's absence, Jack, but do you think it's wise to run off, first chance you get, spending every dime in your trust fund? Seems a bit irresponsible, don't you think?"

Jacqueline bit her tongue to keep from responding. She had known Benjamin since grammar school. She could barely tolerate his arrogant posturing then, and she realized she had even less patience for it now.

"Why do you want to take the money out of the bank, Jack?" Benjamin pushed.

"I wasn't aware that I needed to discuss my banking transactions with you, Ben."

"I am the manager of this institution, Jack. All final decisions rest in my hands. I have the last word on what is and is not to be approved, and at the moment I can see no reason to approve this transaction. If you want to change my opinion, I suggest you start explaining yourself," Benjamin suggested with a smug expression on his face.

"Insensitive ass," Jacqueline said under her breath.

"Excuse me?"

"I said, since you asked . . ." she lied. The last thing Jacqueline wanted to do was explain her situation to anyone, especially Benjamin. But if there was one thing she had learned from life on the ranch, it was that a person had to do whatever it took to keep things running. Sometimes that meant digging heels deep in the dirt and gritting teeth until the job got done.

She inhaled deeply before speaking. "Apparently my father forgot to mention a few debts that needed to be paid. It is my intention to pay them now," she said, trying to sound as nonchalant as possible.

"Fifty thousand dollars worth of debt?" Benjamin asked with a chuckle.

Jacqueline wanted to reach across the desk and slap his arrogant face. The ogre was gloating. He knew it, and so did she.

"Ben, I don't know how much we owe, but—"

"I can assure you your family owes a lot. Or so I've heard."

"Look, I don't want to waste your time with my problems. Can I just have my money so I can get back to the ranch, please? We're in the middle of preparations for the rodeo and I need to be there to make certain everything—"

"Why don't you just sell the place?"

"What?" Jacqueline said, shocked.

"You've got money trouble, and I happen to know of a few people who would be interested in buying the old place at a respectable price. Keep your money, Jack," Benjamin coaxed as he slid the receipt across his immaculate, organized desk. "I'll call a few friends."

"No!" Jacqueline protested. "I mean, no, thank you," she said, managing a small smile. "I appreciate it, Ben, but I prefer to handle this myself. The ranch is in good shape and I'm certain things will be all right after I take care of the debts. I've called a meeting at my place Friday night for anyone to whom we are obligated. I'll pay what's owed and things will be fine."

"A meeting?" Benjamin asked curiously. "And anyone your family owes may attend?" he repeated thoughtfully. "How . . . interesting."

"Yes, I'm sure it will be," Jacqueline agreed. "Now if you'll just sign my withdrawal slip, I'll be on my way."

Jacqueline could almost see Benjamin's wheels turning, and that, she knew, was never a good sign.

"I really don't think that's a good idea, Jack. I think maybe I should—"

Jacqueline was on her feet in an instant. "You know, Ben, I really don't care what you do or don't think is a good idea. Now, I've been pretty patient with you up to this point, but I'm tired, I'm hungry, and completely out of patience, so here's what's going to happen. Either you initial my withdrawal slip or I'm going to make a special trip to your house where I might just *accidentally* mention the fact that you were spotted leaving the strip bar with Essie Booker several times last month, and from what I hear, she's not the only woman that's had you dancing after dark.

"Now, I can't say for certain, but I'd be willing to bet you've depleted your own trust fund as well as any money left you by your father after his death ten years ago, which means you need Lorraine at this point a whole lot more than she needs you."

Jacqueline could almost hear Benjamin's heartbeat quicken as she returned to her chair, crossing her legs in the process. "No rush. Take your time. Give it plenty of thought."

Benjamin had had the good sense to marry money. Lorraine's family had been in politics since the town was first established. Her father was the state senator; her brother, the mayor; her mother was about as active as her political husband; while Lorraine had been pushing for a judgeship.

She was an attractive woman, who knew both her sexual and her political power, and had no problem wielding both at her leisure. It was common knowledge that Lorraine ruled her household the same way she did a courtroom: with complete autonomy.

"So what's it going to be, Ben?" Jacqueline asked, already knowing the answer. She smiled when he signed the form. "Thank you," she said, standing as he handed it to her.

"Essie and I are just friends. She was having a bad night and, well, all the girls and I are friends and I'm certain Lorraine would understand that. I just don't want her upset by anything someone may have *mistakenly* perceived," Benjamin said, stumbling.

"Mmm," Jacqueline said, retrieving her withdrawal slip and opening the door.

"You know, Jack . . ." Benjamin waited for Jacqueline to turn around. "I'm really not the kind of person you'd want as an enemy."

She knew he was right. Like his father before him, Benjamin had made a name for himself by being the city's toughest financier. What he didn't already own, or couldn't coerce someone into selling somehow got burned to the ground or never lasted long due to low sales or insurance issues.

He was running his own potter's field, and to date, there wasn't a George Bailey in sight.

Jacqueline was not about to back down now, however. She smiled as she spoke, though she made certain her voice matched his in threat and sincerity. "Nor am I, Benjamin. Nor am I," she said before exiting the room and closing the door behind her.

"See you Friday," became the annoying comment of the day as Jacqueline passed the shop owners on her way back through town. It always amazed her how fast news traveled in a small town, especially her small town. She decided to stop by the soda shop for a cool glass of lemonade before heading back to the ranch. She needed to calm down before making the hour-and-a-half drive. Jacqueline placed her order and then sat back to relax.

It wasn't long before thoughts of Alexander made a stealthy intrusion in her thoughts.

Why had she reacted to him the way she did? Sure he was handsome, well built, and single, but he was also there to take her ranch away if he could. And why wasn't that cute little girl of his in school? Jacqueline wondered if the attractive young woman with them was the girl's mother but realized the child was too old to be hers. Perhaps Alexander had roped himself a lovesick college student whom he could drag about the country and had somehow talked her into looking after his daughter.

Wouldn't that be just like a rich man? Jacqueline thought with disgust. Perhaps his young Pygmalion was tutoring his daughter. How convenient, she mused. No matter. She couldn't have cared less what

Mr. Alexander Hawkins did with his girlfriend. It didn't matter to her one bit. Jacqueline soon wondered why, then, she was thinking about the man at all.

"I thought about offering a penny for your thoughts, but as contemplative as you look, I think offering a quarter per would earn me a small fortune in no time."

Jacqueline started at the sound of Alexander's voice. She knocked her glass over the side of the table, but Alexander managed to catch it before it hit the floor. She grabbed a handful of napkins, wiping furiously at the soaked tabletop.

"Sorry, didn't mean to scare you," Alexander apologized as he helped clean up the mess.

"I wasn't scared," Jacqueline said tersely.

"Startled then?"

"Oh, just . . . go away," Jacqueline urged, in no mood for Alexander's annoyingly charming company.

"Now, is that any way to treat a stranger in town?"

"It's been three days since you made your offer, Mr. Hawkins. I turned you down flat. Why are you still lurking about?"

"Lurking has such a negative connotation to it, Ms. Carr," Alexander said, sitting down opposite her at the table. He motioned to the waitress, who came over instantly. "Two more . . ." He looked at Jacqueline.

"Lemonade," she said, realizing she wasn't going to be able to get rid of him.

"One Pepsi, one lemonade . . . and add two burgers and two orders of fries." He smiled at the young waitress. She hurried off to fill the order.

"Give me a break," Jacqueline said, rolling her eyes.

"What?"

"Why don't you just slip her your room number at the B-and-B and get it over with?"

"I was just being friendly. Can I help it if I'm a nice guy?" Alexander smiled impishly.

Jacqueline couldn't help but smile as well. "I'll bet you gave your mother all kinds of trouble when you were a teenager." She chuckled. She watched Alexander's expression change from playful to painful in the blink of an eye. She made a mental note not to mention his mother in the future . . . if there was one.

"So, how did you know I was staying at the bed-and-breakfast?" Alexander asked, moving the condiments to the side to allow the waitress to place the plates and drinks on the table.

"Are you kidding?" Jacqueline asked, taking a bite of a fry. "This town is so small you can't so much as sneeze without everyone knowing who did it."

Alexander laughed and Jacqueline liked the sound of it.

"I'm sorry about the other day. I was rude and there is never an excuse for that. I should have spoken with your father myself. If I had, the entire situation could have been avoided. I know you'll never believe this, but I'm really a nice guy. It's just that I'd had a really tough day and traveling with a precocious child is never easy and then the car broke down and Joseph refused to take us to the ranch and . . . you're not going to help me out here by forgiving me any time soon, are you?"

"I'm having far too much fun watching you squirm," Jacqueline admitted, but then flashed him a gorgeous smile. "Don't sweat it. What's done is done," she said, standing. "It's too bad we had to meet under such disagreeable circumstances, Mr. Hawkins. I get the feeling, had things been different . . ." Her words trailed off. "I appreciate the apology, and for that, lunch is on me." She reached into her back pocket and pulled out a money clip. She put a twenty on the table in front of him. "Have a safe trip back to the city," she said before exiting the soda shop.

Alexander sat staring after her in disbelief. She was talking far too fast to interrupt and he got the distinct feeling even if he'd managed to get a word in edgewise, it wouldn't have mattered. He sat back, stunned and rejected.

"Can I get you anything else?" the attractive young waitress asked with a coy smile.

"No, I believe I'm done for the day," Alexander answered.

"Have a nice day then," the waitress said, disappointed, though she made certain to take the money from the table.

Alexander exited the soda shop determined to rethink his nice guy strategy. He would handle the situation the way he handled anything else he wanted. He would be tenacious and thorough. The problem was, he couldn't figure out which he wanted to pursue more, Jacqueline or the 1850.

Chapter Five

"I don't know if I can do this, Cookie," Jacqueline said as she plopped down on a kitchen chair.

Cookie patiently wiped her hands on her apron. The short, rotund woman with the smiling eyes rubbed Jacqueline's back soothingly as she spoke.

"You'll do just fine, Jack. Don't let the townspeople scare you out of doing what needs to be done. Now, pick your chin up off that floor and get out there and handle your business. Besides, it's pouring down rain outside, so not many will show up, I'd wager."

Jacqueline was just about to thank Cookie for the helpful pep talk when the kitchen door flew open.

"I th-think half the t-town is in th-there!" Ian stuttered frantically.

"Calm down, Ian, or turn around and hightail it out of my kitchen," Cookie grumbled.

"S-sorry."

"Grab that platter of steaks and put them out on

the living room table. Tell everyone Jack will be there momentarily."

Ian followed her instructions and was gone without saying another word.

Cookie turned toward Jacqueline, who looked ready to hyperventilate if she didn't destress, and soon.

"Stand up," Cookie ordered. Jacqueline obeyed. "Good. Now, take a deep breath and let it out slowly. You've dreamt of running the ranch and handling ranch business since you were a kid. Did you think it would be all peaches and cream?" Cookie waited for Jacqueline to shake her head.

"Of course you didn't. So this is just a bump in the road, a glitch of sorts, nothing you can't handle, right?" Jacqueline nodded, though she wasn't certain she agreed. "Good, then take yourself out there and set those greedy so-and-sos on their ears!"

"I'm on it," Jacqueline said with a determined smile before exiting the kitchen.

She surveyed the crowd of townspeople sitting in her living room. Several expressions were cold and harsh, while others appeared sympathetic. She didn't know which of the two she resented more. She didn't want anyone feeling sorry for her, nor did she want to argue about her father's past debts.

"Thank you all for coming," she said, forcing herself to smile as she sat down in a chair opposite the small card table Ian had set up for her. "I apologize to those of you who have suffered through hard times, knowing we owed you a great debt, and I thank you as well for your patience. As you know, my father has left me in charge of the ranch as well as anything connected to it. What I would like to do is—"

"I still got chores to do at home, little girl, so let's get to the point of this. You owe us money, now we're here to collect," someone yelled from the back of the room.

"Oh, shut up, Pierce! Let the girl speak!" Mrs. Brown said from the corner.

"I don't see why I have to. I'm speaking for everybody in here. We've spent years listening to her father's long-winded speeches, and I'm not about to spend a few more listening to hers, so get on with it!" the man insisted.

"Why, you weathered old windbag. I ought to—" Mrs. Brown started.

"No, it's all right, Edna." Jacqueline smiled reassuringly. "Mr. Pierce is right. He shouldn't have to wait another moment for his debt to be paid. No one should. So let's get down to business." Jacqueline nodded to Ian, who was sitting nearby.

Thumbing through several ledgers, he nodded, pulling one out from the bottom of the pile. Handing it to her, he winked, wishing her luck.

"How much do we owe you, Mr. Pierce?" she asked, motioning the man forward.

"Exactly three thousand two hundred sixteen dollars and forty-nine cents," he said before joining Jacqueline at the table.

Jacqueline smiled nervously. "All right then. May I see the markers please?"

"Yep. Got 'em all right here," Mr. Pierce said proudly. "Every last one of 'em."

Jacqueline took the papers. Looking over them,

she began flipping through her ledger simultaneously.

After ten minutes of impatient waiting, Mr. Pierce
huffed loudly. "What are you doing?" he asked
Jacqueline, who offered no reply as she read another
marker and then checked her ledger. "What the
devil is she doing?" he asked, turning to face the others in the room. Several offered confused shrugs.

Turning back to Jacqueline, he prepared to let
loose a verbal tirade but was prevented from doing so
when she spoke.

"Ian," she said, sitting back in her chair, "please
give Mr. Pierce six dollars and twenty-three cents."

"Cash or ch-check?" Ian asked, prepared to do either.

"Good question," Jacqueline admitted. "Would
you like that in cash or by check, Mr. Pierce?" she
asked, looking up at the confused man.

It took him a moment to find his voice. "Wh . . .
what the blazes are you trying to pull here, Jack?" he
roared. "Your father owes me—"

"Yes, I heard you the first time, Mr. Pierce, but I'm
afraid once your debt to my father is deducted from
his debt to you, the balance due is only six dollars
and—"

"There's no way in Hades your people only owe
me and mine six bucks," Mr. Pierce assured her
loudly. "You'd better check that again, girlie!" the
irate man insisted.

"Certainly," Jacqueline agreed. After another few
moments of calculating, she gasped. "Goodness!
You're right, Mr. Pierce. My calculations were indeed
incorrect. You have my sincerest apologies! We do
owe you more than I had at first suspected."

"There, you see?" Mr. Pierce said proudly, giving an approving glance to his friends sitting nearby.

"In actuality we owe you . . . *seven* dollars and twenty-three cents. I apparently forgot to carry the one," Jacqueline stated with mock embarrassment.

"The girl has lost her mind!" Mr. Pierce roared. "God save us from our children!" he said with a dramatic roll of his eyes. "How do you come to that conclusion, missy?"

"If you'll calm down I'll be more than happy to explain it to you, sir."

Mr. Pierce groaned but calmed slightly.

"Your first marker is from . . ." Jacqueline sorted through the papers on the coffee table. "June first, 1989, for six hundred dollars," she said, showing him the marker.

"That's right, your father needed the down payment on a small tractor. I lent it to him, son of a gun never paid me back."

"I see. Well, altogether we owed you quite a bit of money. However, when you factor in that just three months after you loaned my father the money for the tractor, he in turn paid your house note, which was . . ." Jacqueline checked the black ledger. "Four hundred thirty-six dollars even. In addition, a week later he paid your son's hospital bill after he crashed your truck. That bill totaled three hundred seven dollars and sixty-two cents.

"Let's see what else we have here, shall we?" Jacqueline asked, picking up another marker from the table.

"In 1991, you lent my father seven hundred dollars to fix the roof on our stable, but two months later he loaned you nine hundred dollars to buy your first Angus bull yearling. And then in nineteen . . ."

On and on it went until Jacqueline had balanced out her father's account with Mr. Pierce. The man left the house with exactly seven dollars and twenty-three cents and more guilt than he could handle.

"Who's next?" Jacqueline asked, feeling only slightly more relaxed.

"I suppose I am," Mrs. Annie Pearl said, as she came up to the coffee table with her list of debts. "I've never borrowed money from anyone in my whole life, dear, so there should be no reason you can't pay the seven hundred sixty-two dollars your father owes me."

Jacqueline could nearly see the horns sprouting from her head. "Please sit down," Jacqueline offered. Twenty minutes later, Ian handed the humiliated woman a check for forty-seven cents.

"I-I hadn't realized it was your ma who paid my hospital bill all them years ago," Annie said tearfully. "Old Doc Brown just told me it was taken care of and not to worry about it none. I didn't know . . . I'm sorry, Jack, dear. You keep the money. I couldn't possibly take a dime from ya."

"It's all right, Ms. Annie," Jacqueline said soothingly. "I'm just sorry you had to find out this way. Now, please take the money and we'll call it even."

"Oh, but I couldn't. I'm so ashamed," Annie confessed.

"You can and you will. Otherwise you'll cause me to disgrace my mother's name by not paying you a debt she owed. Here you go. Take it . . . please," Jacqueline persisted.

The old woman took the check, holding it close to her heart. "Bless you, Jack," she said, before leaving the house with her head hung low.

The situation continued much the same way until well after midnight. Jacqueline handed over money to anyone to whom it was owed. Most debts were small, but there were a few it hurt to pay. Mr. Clemens, a now elderly horse breeder, collected close to thirty thousand dollars for two of the 1850's prize horses, which the old man had bred specifically for Solomon.

There was Mrs. Miller, who collected just over five thousand dollars for creating the stained glass windows for the attic that Leila loved. Each made-to-order window had been handcrafted and etched in fourteen-karat gold.

There were other legitimate debts that Jacqueline was more than willing to pay. Several townspeople who were owed large amounts graciously offered to take only half what was owed, though Jacqueline felt compelled to pay the entirety.

After the last debt had been paid, and all the guests seemed to have finally left, Jacqueline tucked the remaining money away in the safe before closing and locking the doors for the night. She sighed heavily, leaning against the wall.

"That . . . was amazing."

Jacqueline jumped at the deep male voice. She watched as Alexander rose slowly from a chair in the back of the room.

"What are you doing here?"

"I was curious," Alexander admitted. "Word was, you were going to make good on your father's debts tonight. Anyone with an outstanding debt from him was supposed to show up and collect. Free money, I believe they were calling it."

Jacqueline frowned. "Yeah, well, show's over. You can leave now."

Alexander laughed. "I'm willing to bet their heads will still be spinning in the morning."

Jacqueline couldn't help but smile proudly. "Yeah, I don't think they saw that one coming."

"You've got a beautiful smile. You should show it more often," Alexander said. He noticed her tense immediately. Jacqueline opened her mouth to say something he was certain would be dismissive, but he didn't want to give her the chance.

"Can I give you a hand with some of this?" he asked, folding up his chair and doing the same to a few others.

"I don't need your help, Alex. It's late, you should go."

It took Alexander a moment to comment. He was too surprised by hearing himself referred to as Alex. He'd always thought himself too serious a person to be given a nickname of any kind, though his ex-wife had been known to call him Xander just to get on his nerves.

Hearing Jacqueline call him Alex heated his blood.

"Is something wrong?" Jacqueline asked, collecting paper plates from around the room.

"No, nothing at all," Alexander lied.

"No one's ever called you Alex before, have they?" Jacqueline asked, looking at him curiously.

Alexander shrugged. "Not exactly."

"They either have or they haven't."

"Then no, I suppose no one ever has," he admitted.

"It's probably because you're so uptight."

"I may be many things, Ms. Carr, but I can assure you uptight is not one of them," Alexander said, insulted.

Jacqueline sighed. "If you say so. Look, it's late and I've got to clean this mess up before I turn in, so if you don't mind . . ." she said, nodding toward the door.

"No problem. I'll give you a hand," Alexander offered, completely ignoring the gesture as he began folding more chairs and placing them in a corner. He busied himself with other tasks as well, knowing Jacqueline watched him carefully. He stopped when she came to stand directly in front of him.

"What are you doing here, Alex?" Jacqueline asked, narrowing her eyes at him as she placed one hand on her hip.

Alexander swallowed hard at the look of her. The woman was all long lines and vivacious curves in just the right places. He cleared his throat before speaking. "Gathering paper products," he finally managed, holding up a stack of used paper plates and cups as proof.

"No, I mean, what are you really doing here?"

"I told you, I'm—"

"Sit down," Jacqueline insisted, taking the items from him and placing them on the coffee table. She waited, collecting her thoughts and trying to decide how best to get her point across.

"What I mean is, why are you still in town? You know I won't sell the ranch. If you're waiting for me to go bankrupt, it will never happen, so you can forget it. You seem like an intelligent man and the kind of guy who knows when to cut his losses and walk away. So, again I ask you, Alex, why are you here?"

"Since you're so fond of questions, I have one for you," Alexander said. "Why are you being so stubborn about selling this place? You're forgetting that I was in the middle of negotiations with your father about the sale of the 1850 when his health took a sudden turn and things got sidetracked.

"Think about it, Jacqueline. If your father was smart enough to get rid of the ranch, and he left it to you, then why can't you see your way clear to follow his lead?" Alexander leaned back patiently as he awaited her answer.

"It hasn't been proven that you were talking to my father about the sale of the ranch. He has never mentioned any negotiations or even hinted that he wanted to get rid of the place. Just the thought of it goes against everything I've ever known to be true about my father."

"You don't think I've made this up, do you?" Alexander asked, hoping she wouldn't force his hand by requesting paperwork he knew he could not produce.

"I think you were talking to someone about the ranch, Alex. I'm just not positive it was my father. In any event, why can't you just walk away? There are plenty of other ranches out there for sale, I'm sure."

"Yes, there are. However, none offer what this one does. You've got the richest soil, the best location, and plenty to work with here."

"Alexander, the 1850 is more than just land, cattle, horses, and buildings. Every inch of this place holds old memories that can't be factored into a sale price."

"Really?" Alexander said dryly. He wasn't interested in old memories. He was interested in making
a few new ones for himself and his daughter.

"Yes, really," Jacqueline said, realizing he wasn't
taking her seriously. She decided to try a more relat-
able approach.

"The people walking around here doing chores
every day are more than just paid ranch hands,
Alexander. They're family. They were either born
here or they were brought here from one of the boys'
or girls' homes not far from here. I know everyone's
name upon sight.

"I can tell you when Toni lost her front teeth after
trying to rope her first steer, and how much it cost to
have them replaced with implants. I can bring you to
the spot where Dusty proposed to his wife ten years
ago, and I can show you which tree my great-grand-
mother knelt beside when she gave birth to my
grandfather Joseph.

"When you step outside that door tonight, it isn't
just land beneath your feet, it's history, our history,
and there's not a person living here who wouldn't
give his last drop of blood to keep it that way," she
concluded.

Jacqueline sighed, picking up more paper items
from the coffee table. "Even if I were to sell this place
to someone, it would be to someone who could survive out here, not to a man who not only wouldn't
last a summer, but wanted to sell the place off for
parts."

Jacqueline heard Alexander's quick intake of breath.

"What, does it surprise you that I know who you
are and what you do? We get newspapers and magazines as well as cable television out here in Hicksville,

U.S.A., Mr. Hawkins. Besides that, most of us are computer literate. All the information I wanted was only a Google search away. Now, if you'll excuse me," she said, making her way toward the kitchen, "I have work to do."

Alexander followed her. "What makes you think I want to sell the property?" he asked curiously.

"Because that's what you and your partner do, isn't it?" she said thoughtfully, throwing the paper goods into the garbage. "What I can't figure out is why you're interested in the 1850."

She turned to face him. "You and your partner buy corporate buildings and factories. You've even been known to purchase large vacant lots and sell them to people wanting to build strip malls or office complexes. The 1850 doesn't fit the bill, Alex, so why all the interest?" Jacqueline asked, standing only inches from him now.

Alexander looked away guiltily. He took a step back, but Jacqueline took one forward. The woman was relentless, he thought, and if he didn't get out of there soon, his entire plan would go under and he'd never get the property.

"You're right, I should go."

"Why are you after my ranch, Alex?" Jacqueline persisted.

"It's just business, Jacqueline. My partner and I thought it would be a nice way to branch out. You know, explore new territory and all that."

"You're not a very good liar," Jacqueline said. Finally tiring of Alexander's avoidance, she stepped away from him, turning her back to him. "Fine, just go. You can see yourself out."

"I don't know why you find this so confusing. This ranch is an amazing find. I don't think you realize—"

Jacqueline swung around quickly. "What did you just say?" she asked.

"I was saying that I don't think you realize—"

"No, before that," she said, cutting him off.

"I don't know why you find our interest in the 1850 so confusing?"

"After that," Jacqueline said, approaching him again.

The woman was as tenacious as a predator, Alexander thought. She wasn't just asking him questions, she was practically stalking him now.

"The ranch is an amazing find?"

"Yes, that!" Jacqueline said, pointing an accusatory finger at him.

"Where's the mystery?" Alexander asked, confused.

"The word *find* suggests you were seeking or looking for something. What were you looking for, Alexander?" Jacqueline asked suspiciously.

"I don't know what you're talking about, Ms. Carr," Alexander said as he exited the kitchen for the living room.

Jacqueline stopped him halfway across the room. "You know precisely what I'm talking about, Alex. Properties that are for sale are listed just about anywhere you look, newspapers, cable, Internet, on billboards, they're literally all over the place.

"But properties that aren't for sale, the places people have no intention of selling, have no need of advertising. Those are the properties one has to *find*. Tell me something, Alex. How many other ranches did you seek out and what was it about the 1850 that made you so determined to pursue it?"

Alexander felt a headache coming on. He tried stepping around the persistent woman, but she wouldn't let him.

"Jacqueline, this is crazy. I didn't seek anything. You're reading too much into what I said and it's confusing you," he said, rubbing his temples.

Jacqueline decided he was definitely hiding something, and she sensed that she was getting close to figuring out just what it was. However, he looked about ready to collapse. She backed off slightly.

"Sit down, Alexander," she said, concerned. "I'll get you something for your headache. If you keep rubbing your temples like that you're going to wear dents in the sides of your head."

Alexander smiled tiredly. "I'll be all right. Look, I'm sorry about the intrusion. I shouldn't have come. It doesn't matter how or why I found this place. The fact is, I did. Here," he said, pulling a small envelope from the inside pocket of his Armani jacket. "Wait until I'm gone, then sit down and take a look at what's inside. You already know where I'm staying. I'll wait for your call. Good night, Ms. Carr," he said tiredly before leaving the house.

Jacqueline set the house alarm before turning out the lights. She would clean up tomorrow, she decided. Right now all she wanted was a long hot bath and a good night's sleep.

She was halfway up the stairs when her curiosity got the best of her. She lazily opened the envelope Alexander had given her. Unable to see what was written on the paper inside, she entered the bathroom, turning on the lights. She began reading with little enthusiasm.

Ms. Carr,
*   This is just a first offer. Take it under considera-*
tion. It might seem a little low, but I am no rancher, so
I'm not certain how much the cattle, horses, buffalo,
and other livestock would procure in today's market.
This is just a guesstimate. Looking forward to hear-
ing from you soon.
Alexander Hawkins

Jacqueline turned the page knowing no matter how high the offer, it wouldn't come close to what the 1850 was worth to her.

Her scream woke everyone in the house.

Chapter Six

"Take your time, Jazz," Jacqueline called to her daughter from opposite the corral fencing two days later. "Thatta girl! Feel Pepsi's cadence, don't force the movements."

She watched proudly as Jasmine threw her leg over the large mare's neck to ride sidesaddle, never breaking the horse's stride. "Be patient, love. Pepsi will let you know when she's ready," she called nervously.

"That's a big horse for such a little girl."

"What are you doing here, Alex?" Jacqueline asked, without taking her eyes off her daughter.

"Business of course," Alexander said, resting his elbows on the fence.

"We don't have any business to discuss," Jacqueline assured him as she stepped up on the lowest wood beam. "Easy," she called to Jasmine, who had managed to get both feet atop the saddle of the still galloping horse. "Feel the cadence, darlin'."

She watched her daughter bring herself effortlessly to a standing position atop the horse, reins in hand. "Thatta girl, Jasmine, excellent," she praised.

"I left a proposal with you a couple nights ago. I was hoping your lack of response was because you were so impressed by the figures you wanted to see me in person to discuss it, so here I am." He smiled handsomely.

To say she was impressed by the offer was putting it mildly, Jacqueline mused. The figure he had written down was well into the millions. While she had always considered the 1850 priceless, he had done an excellent job in coming close. It had taken Cookie, Ian, and several others to calm her after reading the proposal, but she wasn't about to tell him that.

"I told you the 1850 isn't for sale, Mr. Hawkins. Now, as you can see, we're pretty busy here, so please go away."

Alexander was beginning to understand Jacqueline. He noticed that she called him Alex whenever their conversation was casual and free of stress, Alexander when her temper was rising, and Mr. Hawkins when he was getting on her absolute last nerve. He smiled, feeling oddly relieved to know he at least had some effect on her.

Not wanting to push too hard, too fast, he remained silent as he turned his attention to Jasmine. He was shocked to see the child standing erect atop a large white mare. He recognized it as the one Jacqueline had mounted outside the bar and grill the day he arrived.

"That's a bit dangerous, don't you think? I mean, shouldn't someone be standing alongside her in case she falls or something?" Alexander asked, worried.

"And why is she standing on top of a fully grown horse in the first place?"

"She's going to be in the junior trick-riding competition at the rodeo this year."

"But what if she falls? She's pretty high up there and could get hurt pretty badly."

"If she falls, she'll pick herself up, dust herself off, and start again," Jacqueline answered. "Use your hips, Jasmine! Stay centered. Remember to breathe long, even breaths. Thatta girl," she encouraged.

"But what if she breaks something?"

"She won't."

"But what if she does?"

"She won't," Jacqueline repeated irritably. "Don't look down when you reach for the rope, Jazz. It throws your balance off," she called out, turning her full attention back to her daughter.

Jasmine nodded, refocusing her attention and bringing her head up as she again reached for the rope tied at her waist, without looking this time. Grasping it in her right hand, she swung it expertly to the side of the horse until she could get the animal to move at a faster pace. She then brought the rope high above her head, where she swung her arm in larger circles.

"Don't force it, Jasmine, just wait. Let Pepsi see the rope. Let her get used to the flow," Jacqueline called.

"She's not going to—"

Before Alexander could finish the question, Jasmine brought the rope down in large circles encompassing both her and the horse. Pepsi whinnied, but didn't break her stride. Jasmine brought the circle of rope up, and then down again, in an amazing display of coordination and control. Alexander watched, as much impressed as he was terrified for the girl.

"Amazing," he said, without realizing he had even spoken. Though awed by Jasmine's riding abilities, Alexander was relieved he had left Shasta with Pam to visit the town's small but impressive historical museum. Had his daughter been with him to see Jasmine riding and doing stunts, it would have been just a matter of time before she began pleading for lessons herself. Alexander frowned, knowing he would never consent to such a thing.

"Yes, she is," Jacqueline agreed, bringing Alexander back to the present.

They watched Jasmine in awed silence for several moments until she brought the rope back up and over her head, then back to the side where she skillfully gathered it, replacing the tie at her waist. She rode, still standing, with arms outstretched.

"Jasmine . . . what are you doing?" Jacqueline asked, alarm sounding in her voice. Her daughter did not answer as she closed her eyes. "Jasmine don't you dare!" Jacqueline insisted as she climbed another rung on the wooden fence.

Still Jasmine stood atop the mare perfectly still with outstretched arms and closed eyes.

"What is it?" Alexander asked. "What is she going to do?"

"Shh," Jacqueline said, quieting him.

Alexander watched both mother and daughter closely. It was obvious Jasmine was preparing to do another trick. She reminded him of a gymnast just before going into a routine.

"Please, Jasmine, don't do it," Jacqueline whispered, clutching the fence in front of her.

Alexander watched as several people appeared to crowd around the corral. They too turned their full attention on Jasmine. Joseph climbed the fence with an agility that surprised Alexander considering the man's years.

Finally, Jasmine opened her eyes, took in a deep breath, bent her legs at the knees, and with a great heave up and over, managed to flip her body backward.

Alexander held his breath, shocked at the stunt that would have been successful if Jasmine had landed a bit more gently on the saddle the way she had intended. Instead, she dropped forcefully atop Pepsi's hindquarters, startling the horse completely and causing it to bolt.

The result happened so quickly no one had time to react as Jasmine went flying, landing hard on the ground, knocking the wind out of her in the process.

Alexander was halfway over the fence when Jacqueline grabbed the back of his shirt, pulling him back down.

"No!" she insisted, holding him there with a vise grip as she watched Joseph tend to his great-grand-daughter.

"Is she all right? Is she okay? What if she broke something? And why aren't you out there helping her? She's *your* daughter, for God's sake!" he growled.

Jacqueline shot him a glare so intense Alexander immediately grew silent.

Turning her attention back to Joseph and Jasmine, Jacqueline gave a relieved sigh when her grandfather nodded quickly before helping the child up. It was obvious Jacqueline had been nearly overcome with fear for her daughter.

Alexander tried to apologize for his accusatory comment. "Jacqueline, I'm sorry. I didn't mean to suggest—"

Jacqueline turned on him. "Follow me," she said with pursed lips and furrowed brow. Alexander tried to speak, but she had already turned her back to him and walked away. Looking around, he was surprised to find all eyes on him. The looks of anger and contempt staring back at him convinced him that his safest course of action was to follow Jacqueline.

Once inside the office, Alexander closed the door, fully intending to smooth things over. "Look, I'm sorry for—"

"Sorry?" Jacqueline shot back before he could finish. "Don't you *ever* question my judgment when it comes to my daughter, Mr. Hawkins. Both your arrogance and your ignorance could have gotten my baby killed out there!"

Arrogance? Ignorance? Killed? The words swirled around Alexander's head accusingly. "But—"

"But nothing! While I did not want Jasmine to attempt the trick, once I realized she was determined, there was nothing I could do. If I had jumped the fence and run toward her I would have spooked the horse, which in response would have thrown her violently. Likewise, if I had let you jump the fence and run toward her after she fell, you would have startled the horse and she would have been trampled. Have you ever seen the look in the eye of a startled animal, Mr. Hawkins?"

A horrifying memory from the past momentarily gripped Alexander's mind. He shook his head to clear it before finding a nearby chair to sit down in until his pulse slowed.

"You could have gotten my daughter killed out there today, Alexander. Do you understand that?" Jacqueline asked.

"I'm . . . I'm sorry, Jacqueline. I certainly didn't mean to put Jasmine's life in danger and I should never have questioned your judgment. Challenging you in front of the ranch hands wasn't exactly the wisest thing I've ever done either." He smiled vaguely.

Jacqueline eyed him carefully. He suddenly appeared tired, as if the experience had drained him emotionally. She took a step toward him and then kneeled in front of his chair. She placed a gentle hand on his knee as she spoke.

"Perhaps I shouldn't have gone off the way I did. You're just a city boy, a tenderfoot with no clue what rules exist on a ranch, and besides, you were just trying to be helpful. You don't even know my daughter that well, but you were willing to risk your safety to ensure hers. That is as commendable as it is appreciated, Alex." She managed to smile.

"Yeah, well, some rescue that would have been, eh?" Alexander smiled in return. "I'd probably have gotten both of us killed."

Jacqueline stood, laughing. "Nah, Joseph would have saved Jasmine."

"Thanks," Alexander said dryly as he too stood. "Do you realize we've argued every time we've met? Why do you suppose that is?" Alexander asked contemplatively.

"Probably because you're here to steal what's mine, Alex," Jacqueline answered.

"Steal?" Alexander was surprised by her choice of words. "I've never stolen anything in my life. I'm a businessman. I make deals. I don't steal. You'd know that if you would take the time to hear me out and maybe get to know me better." He smiled handsomely.

"You want my ranch, Alex. That's all I need to know about you. It really doesn't matter how much money you offer, you will never get the 1850."

"Ease up, Jacqueline, I want the ranch, not your firstborn," Alexander stated in an effort to lighten her mood. He didn't think he'd ever met anyone as serious as Jacqueline. And she called him uptight?

"No, Alex, you want my lifeblood. You don't get it, do you? This land, these people, the buildings, the cattle and horses, they're a part of me. They're a part of my history. The 1850 is who I am and someday it will be part of who my daughter is and her children after her.

"Nothing's changed since the last time we spoke, Alex. You're wasting your time showing up unannounced at every turn, and if you don't stop I'll be forced to ban you from the grounds."

"But it's just property, Jacqueline. It can be bought and sold just like everything else in life."

Jacqueline was about to protest his words but realized there was only one way to make him understand. "Come with me, Alexander," she said, walking toward the door.

"Where?"

Jacqueline turned. "I can't explain. You'll just have to trust me," she answered before exiting.

Alexander followed Jacqueline out of the small office, across the property, and into the main house. Once inside, he admired the western motif. The house was a spacious three-level home built in keeping with the rustic log cabins of the 1800s. Alexander was familiar with the style.

"Impressive," he said, admiring a glass-enclosed rifle case that housed several different firearms. He noticed an old musket complete with powder pouch among the collection.

"My father's pride and joy." Jacqueline smiled. "This way, Alex," she said, opening a door at the end of the hall.

Alexander followed her in.

"Whoa!" he exclaimed upon seeing what awaited them.

Jacqueline stood in the center of the room, smiling proudly. "Come on in and meet the family, Alex."

Alexander was immediately impressed by the surroundings. The large room consisted of solid oak walls that nearly shone from being waxed to perfection. Each wall was covered with photographs and other antique items. While normally this would not have seemed unusual, the majority of the photos were black and white, some with frames and some without.

Jacqueline patiently introduced Alexander to generations of her family dating as far back as the year 1850. On one wall Alexander saw slaves, pioneers, farmers, preachers, doctors, lawyers, parents, children, and individuals so old their faces seemed made of old shoe leather. Some of the photos were so old and weathered by time that they looked more like old etchings than photographs.

"That's Ezekiel Carr." Jacqueline beamed as she pointed to an aged photograph of a man dressed in overalls, standing next to a plow horse in the middle of a field. "He was a freeman who worked a very small plot of land down by the lake in the 1800s. He was eventually able to purchase the plot in 1850. He built a small two-room cabin on the property and lived there all his life.

"He eventually married and had ten sons." Alexander raised an eyebrow at the mention of such a brood. "When his youngest, Sampson, grew up, he stayed on the property. He became a very successful blacksmith who saved most of his earnings until he eventually added a few rooms to the small cabin and purchased more of the surrounding land. He named the place the 1850 in honor of the year the original grounds were purchased.

"Both the original land and my great-great-great-grandfather's cabin are still part of the 1850 today. We lost Sampson's cabin to a tornado back in the early 1900s, however."

"That's amazing," Alexander said, appreciating the shared history and a bit awestricken in spite of himself.

They continued the tour and Alexander stopped before a picture of several Native American children with their hair cut short, wearing shoes and regular clothing. While they looked out of place, he admired their expressions of bold determination and sheer defiance.

The third wall was covered with framed letters from family members and newspaper clippings. Jacqueline read several rodeo and birth announcements, declarations of freedom and war, and lists of those who died in them. The weaponry displayed impressed him.

"You can hold them if you'd like," Jacqueline offered.

"Are they . . . authentic?" he asked, breathless, as his eyes darted back and forth between a Civil War sword and scabbard, a flint-bladed bone knife fashioned in the traditional Native American style of the times, a pearl-handled pistol, and two bow and arrow sets, one with Native American markings and the other clearly African.

Alexander stretched out his hand toward the African quiver. It was obvious he wanted desperately to pluck an arrow from it, but he didn't dare. Jacqueline watched as he lowered his trembling hand to his side.

The fourth wall held antique blankets and quilts along with shelves for antique cooking utensils and other items.

Jacqueline pointed to a quilt so large it nearly took up a quarter of the wall. "Do you know what this is?"

"It's a quilt," Alexander answered, admiring the workmanship.

"Yes, but do you know what kind of quilt it is?"

Alexander shook his head.

"This is called a Freedom Quilt," she informed him. "It's a map my great-great-great-grandmother, on my father's side, made for her husband and children. She was able to escape from the plantation she had been born and raised on down in Georgia.

"She chose to go alone because she didn't want to risk her children if she got caught, nor did she want to endanger her husband. Before she left, she made this quilt and gave it to her master's wife. That way her daughters could see it and learn the way to freedom. The mistress was clueless, of course, thinking it nothing more than a pretty blanket for her bed."

"I understand," Alexander acknowledged, "but

how did they read it? There are no street names or times or dates."

"Ah, now that's the interesting part. You have to start at the plantation," she said, pointing to a carefully placed patch with a plantation etched on it. Alexander nodded. "Well, you always move in the direction of the sun, so you would go from the plantation to this patch here," she said, passing several pictures of animals, and stopping at a picture of a saw, "and from there you would go . . ."

On and on it went until Jacqueline had explained the entire flight to freedom.

"That's downright ingenious," Alexander said, impressed.

He walked slowly around the room, alone, this time taking in every detail with renewed respect and admiration. "You're right," he said, returning to Jacqueline's side. "This isn't just a ranch. It's . . . something more. Covered wagons, rifles, beaver hats, authentic buffalo coats . . . My God, Jacqueline, this place is amazing!"

"So you understand now? You'll go back home to Manhattan or wherever you came from and leave us poor country bumpkins to our home and history?" Jacqueline asked hopefully. She frowned when Alexander did not answer.

"This is all so . . . incredible. You know, with a little work and a lot of money, you could easily turn this place into . . ."

Jacqueline looked at Alexander. She couldn't define the look that came over his face. "A historical working ranch? That is what you were going to suggest, isn't it?"

How could he have been so stupid? Alexander

chastised himself. In all the excitement and awe he'd forgotten he wanted the ranch for himself and Shasta. Giving Jacqueline tips on how to improve the ranch and make it more equitable wasn't part of the plan.

He suddenly felt like the enemy. If he got what he wanted the entire history of the 1850 would be not only changed but lost. If he walked away from the ranch, he'd lose something more valuable—his daughter.

"Actually, it's been my life's dream to turn this place into something everyone can enjoy. It's not just a matter of my family roots. This place is a part of Oklahoma history. It is my belief that it should be shared," Jacqueline said as the two walked toward the door.

"Is that why there are boards, planks, and more wood than you can shake a stick at lying about outside? You're trying to renovate the buildings?"

"Yes and no. Like I said, the goal is to get this place approved as a historical working ranch. In order to do that, there are certain things I have to do. Those things cost money and lots of it," she explained, closing the door behind them as they walked down the hall and back outside.

"What you see out here are preparations for this year's rodeo. We host one every year. This is going to be the biggest one yet. The money will go toward renovations on the ranch and the buildings on the south grounds."

Alexander looked around him. Again it touched him how beautiful the land was, and looking at Jacqueline made him understand what she'd meant earlier. The land was indeed a part of her. She looked radiant as she stood, talking about the 1850.

"How much money will it take to get the place approved?" he asked, wondering where on earth the question had come from.

Jacqueline tensed slightly. "I think I've shared all I care to with you, Alex. How much or by what date, and other issues facing me, are my business alone. I was simply trying to show you why I'd never give up the ranch."

"You do have a plan though, don't you? I mean a plan for turning this place into a historical working ranch."

"I tried to talk my father into it, but he didn't quite get the vision," Jacqueline said sadly.

"That's fine, but isn't this place yours for a whole year? At least that's what the word around town is. Why don't you just do what needs to be done and deal with your father later?"

"Yeah, like that'd happen." Jacqueline laughed until she realized Alexander was serious. "It sounds good in theory, Alex, but the truth is my father would never allow it and all the Carrs who came before him would probably roll over in their graves to say the least."

"But it's *your* dream, Jacqueline. If there was ever a time to—"

"I appreciate your verve, Alexander, but even if I were to attempt to turn this place into what I want, it would certainly take longer than a year. We're talking at least five years worth of renovations alone if we budgeted it right. Not all of us are millionaires, you know."

"I became a millionaire by taking chances, Jacqueline. If I see something I want I go after it with a vengeance until I get it," Alexander informed her.

Neither the words nor the connotation was wasted on Jacqueline. Her breath caught in her throat and a fiery heat turned circles in the pit of her stomach. It was a reaction she was becoming far too familiar with whenever Alex was present. "Well, it's been a busy day and I've got to get up early, so you should get going."

"Subtle," Alexander droned in response. "Thanks for sharing your history with me, Jacqueline," he added before getting in his rental truck.

"I didn't do it to be kind, Alex. Let's just say it was my way of educating you about a few things. Now, you have a safe trip back to Manhattan or wherever you came from. I'm sure you've got a cozy little life set up for you back East with your cute little girl and that gorgeous young girlfriend of yours. You focus on that, and I'll focus on the 1850, okay? Good-bye." Jacqueline smiled, before closing the truck door and walking away.

Alexander smiled as he watched the cocky woman walk back into the house. He tried to remember the last time anyone had dismissed him so completely. This was the first.

"It won't be quite so easy to get rid of me, Ms. Carr," Alexander mumbled as he turned the key in the ignition. For the first time in his life, he suddenly wasn't certain what the best course of action would be. He felt the makings of a plan beginning to form in his mind.

Half an hour into his drive back to town, Jacqueline's words echoed in Alexander's ears. *And that gorgeous young girlfriend of yours.* She thought Pam was his girlfriend? And had he detected a bit of tension in her voice when she said the words?

Alexander wondered why women always jumped to conclusions. Perhaps he wouldn't mind so much if they at least came to a correct one every now and again.

Chapter Seven

"Dad!" Shasta screeched upon seeing her father enter the soda shop. "Isn't this place the greatest?" she asked, running to take hold of her father's hand. "Come on! We have a booth over here!"

"All right, calm down. I'm coming." Alexander laughed. He allowed Shasta to pull him to a booth where Pam patiently awaited them. He sat down with concern. "Are you okay?" he asked, knowing his daughter's ability to wear a person down.

Pam smiled. "A little worn around the edges, but otherwise fine."

"We saw the most amazing things today, Dad! We saw a real live covered wagon and we got to walk around inside an authentic log cabin from the early 1800s! They actually disassembled it from one place and reassembled it inside the museum. It was so amazing! All the original stuff is still there! You have to come with us tomorrow to see it, okay?"

Alexander watched his exuberant daughter as she

spoke. She was so excited she could barely sit still. It was good to see her happy and he knew it would be impossible for him to give her up to her mother when September rolled around. For too long he had fought a losing battle with the courts. He was beyond ready to have his baby girl with him on a daily basis.

"So, Dad, will you come?" Shasta asked hopefully.

"Of course I will." He smiled, hugging his daughter. "Let's order, shall we?"

Half an hour later the threesome arrived at the bed-and-breakfast. Shasta had pooped herself out and was practically walking in her sleep.

"Would you take her upstairs and get her ready for bed?" Alexander asked Pam.

Pam nodded tiredly. "Sure. Is it okay if I put her in the room with me tonight? We've got to be up early for our trip to the 1850."

"You're going to the 1850 tomorrow? Why?" Alexander asked with obvious distress.

"Would you rather we didn't go?" Pam asked.

"I . . . well . . . I'm not sure I want Shasta around that kind of environment. A ranch can be a pretty dangerous place for . . ." Alexander paused. "I'm just not sure I want her near a ranch, that's all." He made a mental note to get rid of every horse on the grounds the moment he purchased the 1850.

Pam sighed, knowing there would be no living with Shasta for the remainder of the trip if she didn't get to go to the ranch.

When they'd bumped into Cookie and Jasmine at the soda shop late in the afternoon, Pam was relieved that Shasta had found a new friend. The two girls talked for nearly an hour. Before leaving, Jasmine begged Pam to bring Shasta to the ranch the next day.

"Well, I suppose we can preempt the inevitable temper tantrum if you go with us to the museum tomorrow morning instead of in the afternoon. I'll look through the brochures in my room to see what else I can find to keep her mind busy and her time occupied," Pam stated.

"We'll figure something out, but for now get her tucked into bed. I'll be up after a while. I have some business to take care of," Alexander said, distracted.

"Take your time, Mr. Hawkins. You have your own room, remember?" Pam smiled nervously.

"I know, Pam. And how many times do I have to tell you I didn't bring you here to ravish you, for goodness' sake. I would never . . ." Alexander wasn't about to spend the next ten minutes trying to reassure Pamela. He would have to let his actions, or lack of them in this case, speak for him. "You know what? Just take Shasta upstairs. I'll see you both in the morning," he said, sitting down on the antique sofa.

"Good night then," Pam said before taking Shasta upstairs.

Alexander relaxed for several moments before reaching for the phone on a nearby coffee table. He dialed O on the rotary phone and then waited patiently for someone to answer.

"This is Marge, how can I help you?" a woman said, yawning.

"I need to make a long-distance call, please."

"Long distance to where?"

"New York City." He gave Marge the necessary information and then waited patiently for someone to answer.

"Hello?"

"Hey, Bev, it's me."

"Alexander! How are things in Oklahoma?"

"Things are going okay here, but I need a few favors. There's something I want to look into, but I don't have the resources I need on my end."

"Sure. Just hold on a sec while I figure out what the devil I did with my Palm Pilot." Beverly was back on the phone within moments. "Okay, shoot."

Alexander gave Beverly the information she needed to get the tasks done.

"I'd ask why you need this kind of info, but I know you'd just give me the brush-off so I won't bother."

"You are wise beyond your years, Beverly Ross," Alexander said dryly.

"Well, can you at least tell me how Shasta and Pam are making out? Are they loving the laid-back country life, or are they champing at the bit to come home?"

"Shasta is soaking it up like a sponge. She loves everything about the place and hasn't stopped reading and asking questions since we got here."

"I knew she'd enjoy herself! And what about Pam? How's she adapting?"

"I'm not sure. It's only been a few days and she's always so quiet that I can't really tell what she's thinking or feeling. She's great with Shasta though, very patient and protective."

"I wouldn't worry about Pam. She's young but she's got a good head on her shoulders," Beverly assured him. "And what about you? How are you adjusting? Is Verona, Oklahoma, a place you can put down roots, and have you talked our boy Jack into selling the property yet?"

"Actually, *our boy* turned out to be a woman. She's the old man's daughter. Her name is Jacqueline Carr. They call her Jack for short. She seems to know what she's doing in regard to running the ranch, unfortunately. She's a single mother and an only child.

"The old man had a heart attack, so he and the wife decided to do some traveling overseas or something. Jacqueline's running things in their absence, and so far as I can tell, she's doing a good job of it. The ranch hands seem to respect her as well. She's quite an amazing woman, actually," he concluded. Alexander thought they had been disconnected when Beverly did not respond. "Bev? Are you there?"

"Uh-huh . . . yeah, I'm here," Beverly answered.

"Is everything okay?"

"So, have you spent much time with Jack . . . I mean Jacqueline?" Beverly asked innocently.

"Not as much as I'd like, but—" Alexander was surprised at the admission. "Don't go getting any crazy ideas, Beverly. This is business, nothing more!"

"Did I imply otherwise?"

"I know you well enough to know what you're thinking whether you voice it or not," Alexander complained.

"Likewise." Beverly chuckled.

"I'm serious, Bev!"

"Oh, don't get your panties in a bunch, Alexander. If the sparks are flying between you and Jack, I say let them fly. You've been single for seven and a half years already. It's about time someone rekindled passion's embers within you."

"Passion's what?" Alexander choked out. "Don't

be ridiculous! I haven't the time for romance or the need for passion. I'm here to get the ranch, remember?"

"Trust me, Alexander. If there's anyone in the world who needs romance and passion, my friend, it's you. As far as getting the ranch is concerned, go ahead and get it. Who's stopping you? I'm only suggesting that as long as you're there, why not get the ranch *and* the girl?"

"Good-bye, Beverly," Alexander said, his tone thick with exasperation.

"Oh, that's cold. You're hanging up now? Don't you want to know how business is going?"

"Business is going just fine, I'm sure. You sound too happy for there to be a problem," Alexander stated confidently.

"Okay, you've got me on that point, but do me a favor, would ya?"

"What?"

"I don't doubt that you'll do what's best for Shasta. Just promise me you'll do what's best for all parties concerned, Alexander. You're a good man and God knows you deserve some happiness. If this woman can give you that, then pull out all the stops to make it work, all right?" Beverly asked, hopefully.

"I'll locate a fax machine in the morning and send you a blank fax so you'll have the number. Send everything the moment it's ready. Good night, Bev."

Beverly gave an exasperated sigh. "Good night, boss."

Alexander retired to his room but sleep evaded him. He showered, brushed his teeth and hair, donned a pair of shorts, and relaxed in a chair on his balcony. While he never slept more than four or five hours a night, he knew he wouldn't get that much tonight.

The harder he tried to get Jacqueline and the 1850 out of his mind, the more thoughts of both invaded him.

What was it about her that made his pulse quicken and his blood heat up like a smitten schoolboy? She was attractive, but so were a million other women, yet he reacted to none of them the way he did Jacqueline.

She was intelligent, humorous, determined, strong-willed, a loving mother, a trustworthy daughter, and if the way the ranch hands worked around the ranch was any clue, she was also one heck of a rancher.

Alexander groaned as he rubbed his temples. He had to stop thinking about the woman before he went crazy. If he was going to spend the rest of the night thinking about Jacqueline, he was determined to make it a beneficial endeavor.

He would work on a plan to separate the woman from the ranch. While he liked Jacqueline well enough and thought her daughter to be a darling little girl, Alexander knew getting his daughter full-time was all that would matter in the end.

After several hours of deep contemplation, Beverly's words invaded Alexander's mind, *promise me you'll do what's best for all parties concerned, Alexander.*

How on earth was he supposed to do what was best for everyone and why the devil should he care about anyone but himself and Shasta? With the money Jacqueline would make from the sale of the house, livestock, horses, and other items, she would be wealthy beyond her dreams.

Why won't the stubborn woman just take the money and run? Why can't she just . . . Alexander knew what had to be done. It would mean taking a huge risk, but he suddenly realized nothing else would do. He picked up the phone again.

Marge answered after several rings. "H-hello?" she said sleepily.

"Hello, Marge. It's Mr. Hawkins again. I need to place a local call this time, please."

"Time? What time is it anyway?"

"It's six o'clock in the morning."

"Well . . . all right. What's the number?" Marge crooned, responding to Alex's sexy voice.

"I don't know."

"You don't know?" Marge asked with disbelief.

"I'm afraid not, but you do."

"Hello?"

"I'm so sorry to wake you at this hour, Jack, but I have a rather insistent caller on hold," a flustered Marge said into the phone.

"Oh God! Is it my father? Is he all right?" Jacqueline asked, terrified.

"No, no, nothing like that! The caller is a Mr. Alexander Hawkins. Shall I put him through?" There was a long pause while Marge awaited an answer. "I knew this was a bad idea. I'll tell him to ring you again later in the day."

"It's fine, Marge, I wasn't asleep anyway."

Jacqueline listened as several clicks invaded the silence.

"Jacqueline?"

"Alexander? Is everything okay?"

"Everything's fine. I'm sorry to disturb you at this

hour, but I had to get you before your day got started."

"Well, you've succeeded. How can I help you?"

"I was wondering if . . . well . . . I thought if you weren't busy, maybe . . ."

"You were bold enough to call my home at this hour, Alex. It's a little late to get all shy and boyish on me. What's up?" Jacqueline prodded.

"I was wondering if you and Jasmine would care to join Shasta and me for the day. Shasta wants to show me the museum and a few other places in town. Your daughter invited her to the ranch for a few hours, but I thought since it's supposed to be another gorgeous day, why not go for an early evening drive and a late dinner instead? That is of course if the two of you aren't busy. It's a Saturday so I was hoping Jasmine didn't have any school engagements." Alexander waited nervously for an answer.

"That's . . . very sweet of you, Alex, but as I said, we've been pretty busy over here with preparations for the rodeo. I can't walk away for a full day."

"Come on, Jacqueline, live a little. The ranch will do fine. You're the boss, delegate responsibilities and enjoy the day with your daughter. I promise to show you a good time."

"Well, I can't leave the ranch, but perhaps you and Shasta would like to spend the day here on the 1850. I can have Cookie provide us with a lovely afternoon picnic basket and we can eat on the west grounds where there's less construction going on. Does that sound all right to you?"

"Sounds great, what time should we be there?"

"We'll be in town at nine to pick up Jasmine's new saddle. There's no sense putting more mileage on your rental car, so we'll swing by and pick the two of you up. Can you be ready by nine-thirty, or is that too early for you city folks?"

"We'll be ready," Alexander answered dryly.

"Great, but I do have one question."

"Fire away."

"Why are you excluding Pam?" Jacqueline asked pensively.

Alexander knew what she really wanted to ask: *Isn't Pam your woman, and if so, why are you leaving her behind tomorrow? Did the two of you break up?* "I'm not excluding her, I just don't want—"

"Good, then make sure she's ready in the morning as well. We'll see the *three* of you then. Good night, Alex." Jacqueline wasted no time hanging up.

Alexander followed suit, wondering how he was going to show Jacqueline a good time when he didn't know his way around town yet.

Still not sleepy, he stepped outside and sat down. Alex leaned back in his chair looking up at the sky. It had been a long time since he'd witnessed one of Oklahoma's greatest treasures and he wasn't about to miss the show.

Alexander watched the pastel colors of dawn dance a majestic waltz across the early morning sky. He smiled believing there was nothing more beautiful than an Oklahoma sunrise or sunset except perhaps a Texas one. He allowed the wildflower-scented air to refresh him. For the first time in his life he believed the old adage, there's no place like home. He hadn't realized until that moment how much he'd missed it.

Chapter Eight

"Well, who is he and what exactly do you know about him?" Cookie asked as she began filling a large picnic basket with food.

"I already told you who he is. His name is Alexander Hawkins," Jacqueline answered.

Cookie thought for a moment until recognition dawned. "Just be careful, Jack. Word is he's here to buy the 1850 and he'll do whatever it takes to get it," she warned.

"I know," Jacqueline admitted sadly. "But today isn't about the 1850, Alexander, or me. It's about the girls getting together and having fun."

"Hmm, like I said, be careful," Cookie reiterated.

Jacqueline rolled her eyes in frustration. "I will. I promise."

"And one more thing, Jack."

"Yes?"

"Try to have a little fun yourself."

Jacqueline laughed. "I don't even know if I remember how to have fun, Cookie, but I can promise you that I'll try."

Jacqueline rolled her eyes when the phone rang. "See what I mean? There's always something else to do."

"It's a Saturday morning, for Pete's sake. Who could be calling this early?" Cookie complained as she filled small containers with potato salad.

"I'll get it," Jacqueline said, answering on the third ring. "Hello?"

"How's my girl?" a booming male voice asked exuberantly.

"Dad! Hi! I'm great! How is . . . where are you two this week anyway?"

"Scotland," Solomon groaned.

"Wow, I know Mom is thrilled!"

"She's having a good time all right. She's a little disappointed that the men aren't walking about in skirts like they do on the commercials, though. I told her that would be like Joseph walking around the 1850 in nothing more than a loincloth and headdress!"

Jacqueline couldn't control her laughter. "You sound great, Dad. I'm so happy the two of you are enjoying yourselves."

"You don't sound so bad yourself. How's my grandbaby? How's the ranch and how are the preparations for the rodeo coming along?"

"Jasmine is fine, though she gave us quite a scare the other day when she tried adding a back flip to her trick-riding routine and missed her mark."

"She's okay of course," Solomon said, completely certain that his granddaughter was fine. "The girl's made of tougher stuff than most!"

Jacqueline shook her head. "You're too much, Dad." The way her father bragged on his family's strength and heritage, Jacqueline wouldn't have been surprised if Solomon claimed their bloodline could be traced back to the birth of Christ himself. "Yes, Jazzy is doing just fine." She chuckled.

"What's happened to my grandbaby?" Leila asked worriedly in the background.

"Nothing, everything's fine, so quit your worrying, woman."

"I want to speak to Jack," Leila protested. "I can ask her myself."

"There's nothing to ask. The child's fine, now go look for some more kilt-clad men or something while I talk to my daughter, for heaven's sake," he said with a playful chuckle.

"Give me that phone, old man," Leila insisted, taking the phone from her husband.

Again Jacqueline laughed. "Well, it's good to see the two of you are still madly in love."

"Jack, dear, how are you? How's my grandbaby?" Leila asked worriedly.

"I'm fine, Mother, and so is Jasmine. She had a slight mishap the other day, but she's fine now. How's Scotland?" Jacqueline asked, attempting to change the subject before her mother booked a flight home to check on Jasmine herself.

"It is quite lovely, really. It has an almost mystical quality to it and—"

"Mama, Mr. Hawkins said I could take Shasta down to the lake if it's okay with you," Jasmine said, coming up behind her. "He said he'd wait down by the corral for you. So, can I, Mama? Can I take Shasta to the lake?"

Jacqueline cursed inwardly. "Yes, baby, go ahead. Tell Mr. Hawkins I'll be right there," she whispered, holding one hand over the phone.

Please, God, don't let my mother have heard that! Jacqueline pleaded before returning to the call.

"Anyway, she got winded by the fall, but other than that she was fine." Jacqueline hoped she sounded casual.

"Well, I'm glad she's all right. Um, Jack, dear . . ."

"Yes, Mother?"

"Just who precisely is Mr. Hawkins?"

"Hawkins?" Solomon said in the background. "Wasn't that the name of the young man who was trying to buy the ranch?"

"Yes, I believe it was," Leila answered. "Oh dear. Jack, you're not thinking about—"

"No, Mother, I'm not thinking about selling the ranch to Mr. Hawkins or anyone else," Jacqueline assured her.

"So, are you and Mr. Hawkins—"

"No, I am not dating, sleeping with, or bearing Mr. Hawkins's young, Mother. We've never been out on a date, never kissed, and never held hands. We've never even been in the same room for more than fifteen minutes. . . ." Jacqueline paused. "Okay, there was that one time when I showed him the family gallery, but other than that we haven't—"

"You showed him the family gallery?" Leila asked with disbelief.

"She did what?" Solomon echoed.

"She showed Mr. Hawkins the family gallery," Leila repeated.

"What? Let me talk to her," Solomon insisted.

"No, Solomon. This is between a mother and her daughter. Now go away."

"It'll be between Mr. Hawkins and my shotgun if he so much as—"

"Pipe down and let me talk to Jack," Leila insisted. "Now, Jacqueline, dear, you must be careful. I know it gets lonely on the ranch, but—"

"Hold on a minute, Mother, Cookie is just dying to talk to you." Jacqueline shoved the phone at Cookie before grabbing the picnic basket and heading for the door.

"But what do I tell her?" Cookie asked, but Jacqueline was already gone.

"Sorry for the delay," Jacqueline apologized, coming to stand beside Alexander.

"No problem at all." Alexander smiled before returning his attention to the horses in the corral.

"They're beautiful, aren't they?" Jacqueline asked.

"Yes, they are. Hard to believe such graceful animals can be so deadly."

Jacqueline thought that an odd thing to say. "Yes, but that's only if the rider doesn't know how to handle the horse, in which case they shouldn't be anywhere near one, let alone riding one."

"So you think your horse would never hurt you?"

"I've had Pepsi since she was born. We know each other's ticks very well. She would never hurt me and vice versa," Jacqueline said with confidence.

"Horses aren't human, Jacqueline. Unlike us, they are slaves to their instincts. It doesn't matter how much you think you know your horse, given the right circumstances, she would turn on a dime. She wouldn't mean to, but she'd hurt you, or even kill you if you were the only thing standing between her and what she perceived as safety."

Jacqueline was surprised by the conviction registering in Alexander's voice. "Alexander, did something happen to—"

"Let me carry that," Alexander offered, taking the picnic basket from her. "Lead the way," he said, stepping aside to let her pass.

Jacqueline was tempted to pursue her questions. Horses weren't the only ones with instincts, and right now hers were telling her there was more to Alexander's observations than guesswork. Now, however, was not the time to discuss it.

She smiled. "Follow me."

"You'd swear they were long-lost sisters the way they've been carrying on." Alexander laughed.

"I know and I'm happy for it." Jacqueline chuckled as they watched the girls splashing around in the lake. Jacqueline checked her watch. "They've been at it for nearly two hours already."

"This certainly beats spending the day in a stuffy museum."

"I agree," Jacqueline said, forcing herself to look away from him. She didn't know how anyone could look so completely edible while sitting on a picnic blanket and dressed in Armani from head to toe, but Alexander was pulling it off marvelously.

She inhaled deeply, calming herself before she did something crazy like kissing him senseless. *I wonder if that would constitute fun in Cookie's book,* Jacqueline mused. *Lord knows it would in mine. Get a grip, girlfriend. The man already has a woman, remember? And just where is Pam, anyway?* she wondered.

"Speaking of agreements, I thought it was understood that Pam was to come along today."

Alexander laughed. "Not exactly the smoothest transition ever made, but I'll explain anyway."

Jacqueline smiled. "Thank you."

"I heeded your request and asked Pamela to join us today. She accepted and left the B-and-B this morning saying she wanted to find suitable clothing for today's outing.

"She told me not to wait because she still had the card you tried to give Shasta that day at the grill. She said she'd call for a ride when she was ready."

Jacqueline wasn't sure if she believed him or not.

"You can trust me, Jacqueline."

"Says you, Alex."

Alexander gave a hearty laugh. Jacqueline liked the pure male sound of it.

"I saw Pam while I was waiting for you. Seems Cookie sent some guy to pick her up from town earlier. I think she likes him because they were standing pretty close to one another at the corral, and I felt like I was intruding when I spoke to them. They looked like two guilty teenagers when they turned to greet me."

"Did you get the name of the man Pam was with?" Jacqueline asked curiously.

"Yeah, it was . . . Ian."

"Well, I'll be," Jacqueline said, both surprised and thrilled.

"Is there a problem? Should I be concerned?" Alexander asked protectively.

Jacqueline put a calming hand on Alexander's shoulder. "Everything's fine, Alex. Pam couldn't be in better hands . . . or more deserving ones for that matter."

"There's no part of Pamela that should be in Ian's or any other man's hands," Alexander growled.

"Will you relax, Alex?" Jacqueline chuckled. "Pam is a grown woman. She can take care of herself, and besides, Ian is the quintessential gentleman. She's safe with him, I promise."

Alexander stopped his posturing while he weighed his options.

"Jealous much?" Jacqueline mumbled and then hated herself for feeling the way she did; she quickly realized she was also jealous.

"Jealous? Why would I . . ." Understanding dawned and Alexander sat down. "Jacqueline, I was hoping Pam would explain our situation to you. I didn't think you'd believe me if I tried to."

"Try," Jacqueline encouraged.

"Pam is Shasta's au pair."

"Au pair?" Jacqueline repeated.

"Yes, that's a person who looks after—"

"I know what an au pair is, Alexander."

"Sorry. You had a rather confused look on your face."

"That's because I was wondering why you didn't just refer to her as your daughter's nanny, for Pete's sake!"

Alexander laughed. "Sorry. It's just that for me, the word *nanny* brings forth images of a cranky old woman in her seventies with a white nurse's cap."

"Or the dog from *Peter Pan*," Jacqueline threw in.

"What dog? Peter who?" Alexander asked, completely confused.

"The dog from *Peter Pan* was named Nanny, wasn't it? You were telling me what the word *nanny* brought to mind for you, and I was just saying that . . . You

An Important Message From The ARABESQUE Publisher

Dear Arabesque Reader,

I invite you to join the club! The Arabesque book club delivers four novels each month right to your front door! It's easy, and you will never miss a romance by one of our award-winning authors!

With upcoming novels featuring strong, sexy women, and African-American heroes that are charming, loving and true… you won't want to miss a single release. Our authors fill each page with exceptional dialogue, exciting plot twists, and enough sizzling romance to keep you riveted until the satisfying end! To receive novels by bestselling authors such as Gwynne Forster, Janice Sims, Angela Winters and others, I encourage you to join now!

Read about the men we love… in the pages of Arabesque!

Linda Gill
PUBLISHER, ARABESQUE ROMANCE NOVELS

*P.S. Watch out for the next Summer Series **"Ports Of Call"** that will take you to the exotic locales of Venice, Fiji, the Caribbean and Ghana! You won't need a passport to travel, just collect all four novels to enjoy romance around the world! For more details, visit us at www.BET.com.*

A SPECIAL "THANK YOU" FROM ARABESQUE JUST FOR YOU!

Send this card back and you'll receive 4 FREE Arabesque Novels—a $25.96 value—absolutely FREE!

The introductory 4 Arabesque Romance books are yours FREE (plus $1.99 shipping & handling). If you wish to continue to receive 4 books every month, do nothing. Each month, we will send you 4 New Arabesque Romance Novels for your free examination. If you wish to keep them, pay just $18* (plus, $1.99 shipping & handling). If you decide not to continue, you owe nothing!

- Send no money now.
- Never an obligation.
- Books delivered to your door!

We hope that after receiving your FREE books you'll want to remain an Arabesque subscriber, but the choice is yours! So why not take advantage of this Arabesque offer, with no risk of any kind. You'll be glad you did!

In fact, we're so sure you will love your Arabesque novels, that we will send you an Arabesque Tote Bag FREE with your first paid shipment.

* PRICES SUBJECT TO CHANGE.

YOU'LL GET 4 SELECT ROMANCES PLUS THIS FABULOUS TOTE BAG!

ARABESQUE

Visit us at:

know what? Let's just forget I even opened my mouth," Jacqueline said, mortified at her immature response. "Sometimes I am such an idiot," she mumbled under her breath.

She immediately busied herself with preparations for lunch.

Alexander took the paper cups from Jacqueline, placing them off to the side. He held her hand firmly as he spoke. "The dog's name was Nana, not Nanny. And I thought what you said was cute, not idiotic." He smiled.

"But the way you looked at me . . . and then you acted as though—"

"I'm a twenty-nine-year-old adult male, Jack. Admitting I know the characters of a Disney movie doesn't exactly come easy."

"So what made you fess up, or were you just taking pity on me?"

"When I thought about it I realized that some of my most treasured moments have been spent lounging around on the living room floor having Disney marathons with my daughter. I would hope when she's grown she could look back on those days with pride.

"I figured I couldn't expect her to be proud of something I wasn't willing to admit to when given the opportunity. And yes, I thought it much more chivalrous to throw you a life preserver than watch you sink." He chuckled.

"Oh, you—" Jacqueline tried to throw a paper cup at him, but he took it from her.

Without warning he leaned forward, kissing her lips softly.

He intended the kiss to be brief, but she smelled

as sweet as warm honey and her full lips tasted of the fresh strawberries she had been snacking on. He couldn't help but kiss her again. He moaned in response to the intoxicatingly delicious taste of her warm tongue.

Jacqueline's resolve melted. This was the kind of man Greek myths were made of, tall, well built, and able to kiss a woman senseless. A breathy sigh escaped her and she felt Alexander's warmth moving away. She put a hand behind his neck, pulling him possessively closer.

Alexander followed her brazen lead by putting an arm around her waist, pulling her so close she was nearly sitting in his lap.

A million thoughts coursed through Alexander's mind, but not one of them was coherent.

The kiss ended and the two sat staring at one another.

"Is it just me, or is the earth spinning?" Alexander asked, stretching his arms out behind him and leaning back.

"If not the earth, then at least my head," Jacqueline reasoned. "Intoxicating," she breathed. "I wonder if . . ."

"If what?" he asked, lying down on his back.

"If that was a fluke or if all of your kisses sizzle like that," she said boldly.

Alexander opened his eyes in surprise. He didn't have to ask Jacqueline if she wanted to find out for herself, because the smoldering look in her sparkling gray eyes told him she did. He sat up, fully intending to begin the experiment, when his daughter's excited chattering interrupted him.

He forced himself to look away from Jacqueline

and focus on Shasta, who was running toward him full speed. She threw herself across his lap, claiming victory.

"I won, I won, I won!" Shasta yelled excitedly.

Jasmine reached the blanket, falling at her mother's side. "She's . . . too . . . fast!" she said between gasps.

"See, Dad, I may not have long legs like Jazzy, but I have speed and power. I may be compact, but I pack a big punch!" Shasta giggled.

"Indeed you do," Alexander agreed, silently thanking the Lord that he had seen her coming when he did and was able to protect himself from his daughter's careless limbs.

The girls chattered and ate while Jacqueline did her best to avoid Alexander's hazel eyes, which were increasingly beginning to resemble thick, warm brandy.

"May I have the butter, please?" Alexander asked, unwrapping an ear of corn.

"Tub . . . or squeeze?" Jacqueline asked sexily.

"Squeeze," Alexander answered, his voice thick and strained.

Their fingers touched, and held. The look in Alexander's eyes bespoke passion beyond Jacqueline's wildest imaginings. His inward struggle for control was obvious as his hand shook slightly beneath hers.

Jacqueline drew her hand back as if touching a hot flame.

Alexander was up and making a beeline for the lake before anyone could stop him. "I'm going for a swim!" he called over his shoulder as he went.

"But you still have your clothes on, Dad!" Shasta said, giggling at her silly father.

It was too late. Alexander dove in the lake like a man on fire, which Jacqueline knew wasn't far from the truth metaphorically. She covered her mouth to keep from laughing. She knew he had chosen the only way possible to calm his fevered libido.

"Can we go too, Mama?" Jasmine asked, ready to abandon their food for fun.

"No, sweetie, I think it's time to let the grown-ups swim for a while."

"Then why don't you go in with him?" Shasta suggested.

"Yeah, go swimming, Mama! You never have any fun. Look at Mr. Hawkins. He's splashing all over the place! I'll bet he can teach you how to have fun if you just ask him," Jasmine prodded.

Jacqueline was almost positive there were a great many things Alexander could teach her. "Maybe next time, girls. For now, let's just let Mr. Hawkins enjoy the lake by himself for a while, okay?"

"Yes, ma'am," both girls said sadly, in unison.

Half an hour later found the girls back in the lake, and Jacqueline waiting for Alexander. She had used her cell phone to call up to the house to have Thomas bring down a towel and change of clothes for Alexander.

She checked her watch and then stole a look in the direction of the trees where he had gone to change. Her breath caught in her throat when he finally walked toward her.

She blinked several times to make certain she was really seeing the image coming at her. He looked amazing. He was dressed in a pair of jeans that seemed tailor-made just for him.

A desirous sigh escaped Jacqueline's full lips when Alexander turned around, heading back to the trees. The view of his tight round glutes was nearly her undoing. He retrieved his wet clothes and shoes and again walked toward her. The tightness of his T-shirt bespoke pecks, biceps, and triceps matched only by the visible lines of his washboard abs. She recognized the snakeskin boots as the pair she had given Thomas a few Christmases ago. Jacqueline's heart skipped a beat when Alexander topped off the look by putting on a white Stetson hat.

She continued watching him, realizing suddenly that this was a man who was no stranger to this type of attire. Every movement Alexander made confirmed her suspicion. The look on his face, the swagger in his walk, and the confidence he evoked all screamed one thing: natural.

There was obviously more to Alexander Hawkins than he was letting on. Jacqueline began wondering if she wanted to know bad enough to find out.

Alexander reclaimed his spot on the blanket across from Jacqueline.

"Better now?" she asked, putting everything back into the picnic basket.

"I don't know what I would have done if we weren't near a lake after that kiss," he admitted with a sexy smile.

Neither the words nor the feeling behind them was wasted on Jacqueline. "Alex, we have to talk."

Alexander put up a hand to stay Jacqueline's words.

She turned to see what he was looking at. "Damn!"

she grumbled as a huge monster truck drove toward them.

When the engine stopped, Ian jumped down effortlessly from the vehicle. He gave a handsome smile as he rounded the front of the truck.

"Ian, how many times do I have to tell you not to drive that monstrosity on the—"

"Sorry, Jack!" Ian said, approaching them. "Ian McAllister." He extended a friendly hand toward Alexander.

"Nice truck." Alexander smiled, unable to help himself. While he personally had no use for a vehicle that huge, he inwardly envied Ian's ability to drive one.

"Thanks! If you get some time later, maybe I'll let you take her for a spin."

Alexander grinned. "It'd be my pleasure. Though I might require a few lessons first."

"What lessons? You just get in and start driving! You don't have to worry about hitting anything because this baby rolls over everything like butter," he said, beaming.

"Really? And what kind of engine—"

"Ah, excuse me, gentlemen," Jacqueline said, interrupting them. "Ian, what are you doing here and why are you driving that thing here by the lake? I've told you a million times that it's too dangerous a vehicle to have around the children who play here."

"I know, and I'm sorry, but she—"

"She? Ian, tell me you're not trying to impress—"

The passenger-side door opened and Ian's attention was diverted. He made his way quickly toward it. Reaching up, he motioned for the occupant to jump out. When she did, Alexander's smile faded instantly.

"Pam? What the hell—" Alexander started.

"Hello, Alexander . . . I mean, Mr. Hawkins," Pam said. "Good afternoon, Ms. Carr," she added with her usual bright smile. "I've been looking forward to meeting you. Ian has told me so much about you." She shook Jacqueline's hand.

"Hello, Pam, and please, call me Jack. Would you care to join us? There's plenty of food left."

"Thank you, but no. I'm just here to drop these folders off for Mr. Hawkins," she said, turning her attention back to Alexander. "Wow! You look—"

"What the devil are you doing in that truck?" Alexander asked, still stunned by her appearance.

"Ian gave me a lift. I told you I'd call here for a ride when I was ready. Don't you remember?" Pam asked innocently. "When we're done here he's offered to show me around the grounds and then we're going to dinner in town. We were hoping it would be all right if we took the girls with us. Ian was telling me about a quaint little drive-in restaurant where the waitresses actually Rollerblade up to your car with your order, just like they did back in the sixties!" she said excitedly. "I thought Shasta might like it."

"I'll take my pickup truck, not this monster, of course," Ian added.

"There's no school tomorrow, so I thought a sleepover might be in order as well," Pam hinted to Jaqueline and Alexander.

Jacqueline smiled. "I know the place. You'll love it, I'm sure, and yes, Jasmine may go and she can sleep over as long as it's all right with Althea. She's the owner of the B-and-B."

"Oh, I know, and she's a very nice woman. We met when I signed us in. I'll be sure to ask her permission first." Pam turned to Alexander. "Will that be all right with you, Mr. Hawkins?" she asked hopefully.

Alexander hesitated.

"The girls will be in good hands, Alex. I told you, Ian is a good man. You can trust him," Jacqueline promised.

"Shasta may go as long as you promise not to let her out of your sight, Pam. You know firsthand how quickly she can get sidetracked and walk away from you," Alexander said sternly.

Pam nodded. "I understand. Here are your files and I'll go collect the girls," she said, handing Alexander several folders.

"Is it all here?" he asked, skimming through the folders quickly.

"Everything except the info on the banker. Ms. Ross said your instincts were definitely correct, but she needs more time to gather the appropriate information. She also asked me to find out just how far you were willing to go."

Alexander looked up from the folders. "All the way," he said gravely.

She smiled. "Yes, sir, I'll tell her. Have a good day, Jacqueline."

Alexander and Jaqueline watched Ian and Pam head down to the lake.

"Amazing," Jacqueline mumbled.

"What?"

"He didn't stutter. Not once."

"He stutters?" Alexander asked, unable to recall.

"Not anymore, apparently."

Alexander handed Jacqueline the folders. "I'll go check on the kids and talk to Ian while you look these over," he said, turning to walk away.

"Alex, what are these?"

Alexander didn't stop or turn around. Jacqueline knew his mind was on his daughter and her safety for the moment.

"I can assure you that Shasta will be fine. Relax, Alex," she called after him.

Alexander turned abruptly and walked back to her. "Tell me something, Jacqueline. What will you be doing while I'm down by the lake?"

Jacqueline looked away guiltily. "R-reading these files," she answered.

"Hmm, and what will you do *before* you start reading the files?" he persisted.

"All right, all right. I'll use the cell phone in my bag to call the B-and-B to tell Althea that Jasmine will be staying with Pam and Shasta tonight and I'll ask her to keep an eye on her as well. I'll make sure it's all right with her. If all goes well, I'll call up to the house and have Cookie prepare Jasmine's overnight bag and a few treats for the girls as well," she confessed.

Alexander nodded. "Now, you live here and everyone knows you and your daughter, but you're still going to make all those calls and preparations for one overnight trip. So why should it be abnormal for me to have a word with Ian, man to man, so I can explain how important it is that both my daughter *and Pam* arrive safely and unaccosted at the B-and-B no later than eight p.m? My daughter is as precious to me as yours is to you."

Jacqueline nodded. "Fair enough," she answered.

"Now, make your calls and check out those files. I'll be back shortly."

Jacqueline watched Alexander walk away. He was

too good to be true, she thought. She wondered how he'd managed to stay single for so long after his divorce. He was intelligent, handsome, witty, muscular, a caring father, and . . . She paused. "He wanted to take her ranch from her," she reminded herself.

She took out her cell phone and began dialing.

Chapter Nine

Alexander sat down opposite Jacqueline on the blanket. He watched her as she read over the remaining few pages in one of the folders.

What was it about her that made him feel so comfortable? he wondered, leaning back against a tree. He tried taking his mind off her by surveying the surroundings. The sky was a flawless clear blue with not so much as a passing cloud. He watched a pair of hawks flying overhead.

"Alexander . . ."

"Yes?"

"I can't believe you managed to accumulate so much information in such a short amount of time. I only just told you about—"

"I can't take the credit," Alexander confessed. "My partner, Beverly Ross, did the leg and phone work. I simply told her what I needed and she came through for me."

"Well, she's amazing," Jacqueline said in awe. "I've

been trying to get some of this information for nearly five years now, but I couldn't get through the bureaucratic red tape. This is amazing!" she added, near tears.

"You said it was your dream to turn the place into a historical working ranch. Well, now we can turn your dream into a reality," Alexander said confidently.

Jacqueline was silent for a moment. "Alexander, I appreciate what you've done, but—"

"What now, Jacqueline?" he asked, exasperated.

"I can't accept your help. It comes at too high a cost."

"What cost? I'm talking about a business partnership, nothing more."

"Really? Then why did you say we?" Jacqueline asked.

"When did I say we?"

"You just said, now *we* can turn my dreams into a reality. Alexander, I've already told you I won't give you the 1850. Nor will I share it. The land and everything on it has been in my family for more generations than—"

"Yeah, I know the history. You showed me, remember? Look, Jacqueline, I'm not asking for the deed, I'm trying to help you."

Jacqueline opened her mouth to speak, but Alexander continued talking.

"Don't ask me why, because I wouldn't be able to explain it. Granted, my original intent was to buy the 1850 out from under you, but that was before—"

Before what? Alexander wondered. Before she captured his heart with that amazing smile of hers? Before he realized how much the ranch really meant

to her and her family? Before he saw firsthand how
caring and protective a mother she was, or did he
mean before she had stolen his heart with one kiss?

"Alexander, are you all right?" Jacqueline asked,
concerned.

He honestly didn't think he'd ever be all right
again. "All I ask is that you think my proposal
through. Look over the information again tonight.
Just know that I'm here if and when you're ready to
get serious about your plans," Alexander said, walking toward the house.

Jaqueline watched him walk off, her attention riveted on the firmness of his lean body. She hadn't
been this excited about a man since Bryce had died.

She sighed in frustration, knowing that there was
no way to keep Alexander in her life. If she was honest with herself, Jacqueline knew she wanted him. And
he wanted her ranch. As much as he tried to convince her otherwise, that was what Alexander was really after, but no amount of wooing or courting was
going to change her mind this time. Plus, there was
something odd about Alexander that Jacqueline
couldn't put her finger on just yet.

There was no way she could get involved with a
man she couln't fully trust.

Jacqueline shook her head, knowing she had to
do what was best for the 1850. That meant when it
came to Alexander Hawkins, she was better off without him.

It had been a week since Jacqueline had last seen
or heard from Alexander. While she was grateful he
was not a spiteful man and continued encouraging

Shasta's and Pam's soda shop meetings with Jasmine and Cookie, Jacqueline refused to sit around fawning over a man she had only just met and would probably never see again. She poured herself into preparing the ranch for the upcoming rodeo. She had slacked off shamelessly to handle old debts and laze around the pond like a lovesick schoolgirl.

Having her focus back on track gave her a renewed sense of pride and satisfaction. Every morning she reminded herself that she didn't have time for romance or complicated relationships.

Jacqueline pulled a bandana from her pocket to wipe the sweat from her brow. She had spent the better part of the day riding around the ranch, checking on the progress of the seemingly endless rodeo preparations. She smiled, satisfied that things were going according to schedule.

The contractors had nearly finished the new booths and gift shops. Several of the women from town walked around the south grounds a few miles from the ranch, choosing where they wanted to set up booths to sell their crafts at the rodeo.

An array of vendors, as well as the heads of nearly every safety organization in the city, walked in chaotic circles, checking everything from space availability to electrical surge protection. To the untrained eye, the cacophony of workers and vendors resembled a disorganized melee, but Jacqueline understood the process and was glad to see everything falling into place.

"I've been riding around the west grounds for the past two hours looking for you, Jack!" Thomas complained as he drove his Jeep up to her. He slowed his approach in an effort not to spook Pepsi, who looked about as tired as a horse could look.

"Easy, girl," Jacqueline said in a soothing voice as she stroked the side of Pepsi's neck to calm her. "I was there most of the morning. Did Ian and the guys get the stalls assembled yet?" she asked, prodding Pepsi closer to the truck.

"Most of them, far as I could tell." Thomas frowned, vacating the vehicle.

"What do you mean most of them? They've been at it for hours already. I'd better go check on them," Jacqueline said, frustrated.

"Hold on there a minute, Jack!"

"What is it, Thomas?"

"Those stalls have to weigh at least two hundred pounds each. They're made of pure metal and—"

"I know how much they weigh and what they're made of. I ordered them myself, so what's your point?"

"My point is that it's at least one hundred degrees out here, Jack, and the men are working as fast and as hard as they can under the circumstances. Not only that, but how fast can the job get done when you keep sending messages about new tasks you want done every two hours?" Thomas took off his hat to wipe his forehead with his sleeve.

"We know what you want done, Jack. Just trust the men to stick to the schedule. When the rodeo rolls around in six weeks, we'll be ready. It's not just your reputation on the line, you know, it's ours too," he informed her.

"I realize that, Thomas, but—"

"You're driving them too hard, Jack. Come on now, just look at your horse. She's about ready to keel over if you don't take her to the stable, wash her down, and give her some oats and water."

Jacqueline looked down at Pepsi's sweat-soaked coat. Parts of her looked as though she had been bathed in soapy water but not rinsed. She was mortified at her own neglect. She dismounted immediately.

"I—hadn't realized . . ."

"I know. That's why I came out here to talk to you. We all know you've got a lot on your mind with wanting to please old Sol and your mother too. We know where the profits from the rodeo are going, but if you keep working yourself and us the way you have been, nothing will matter because in the end, there won't be anyone else to help run it . . . we'll all be in the hospital with pulled muscles and heat stroke," he said, laughing.

"All right. Tell the boys to call it a day. The sun will be down in half an hour anyway. I'm going to walk Pepsi to the stable, so I'll be in late. Tell Cookie I—"

Thomas snapped his fingers. "That's right. Cookie said she needed to see you A.S.A.P."

"What about?"

"Don't know but she seemed pretty irritated. She told me to tell you to hightail it up to the kitchen, pronto. Unfortunately that was about two and a half hours ago . . . sorry," Thomas apologized.

"All right, well, she'll have to wait until Pepsi and I get there," Jacqueline reasoned.

"Here, I'll take the horse, you take the truck," Thomas suggested, taking the reins from her and handing her the keys.

"Are you sure?" she asked, knowing *she* wasn't.

"We'll be fine," Thomas assured her. "It's just horseflesh, Jack. It's not like I'm moving to Wyoming with Jasmine or something."

"Ha-ha, very funny, Thomas," Jacqueline said, getting in the truck. She had to admit it felt good to rest her back against the seat. After she'd ridden Pepsi all day, her muscles were practically screaming.

Jacqueline opened the kitchen door just enough to peek inside. She wasn't certain of Cookie's mood and she was too tired to get involved in an argument.

"Well, are you going to stand there with your head poking out like a baby kangaroo or are you coming in?" Cookie asked.

"Sorry," Jacqueline groaned, entering and making her way to the table where she took a seat. "What's up, Cookie?"

"Sometimes I swear, I don't know whether to hug you or turn you over my knee," Cookie lamented. She placed a tall glass of lemonade in front of Jacqueline as she spoke.

"A hug gets my vote." Jacqueline smiled tiredly before taking an unladylike gulp of the refreshing beverage. She moaned as the icy feeling ran a trail from her throat to her stomach. "God, that tastes good!"

"You'd have tasted it earlier if you'd stopped long enough to eat breakfast or lunch today."

"So that's what this is about, then? You're upset because I missed my meals?" Jacqueline smiled. "Don't worry, Cookie, I have a pouch full of your deliciously dried and cured beef strips in my saddlebag."

"Don't try flattering my culinary skills, Jack. Your body needs more than that in the course of a day," Cookie informed her as she pulled out several pots and pans.

"I'm fine, Cookie. And . . . what are you doing?"

Jacqueline asked, loud enough to be heard over the clanging of pots.

"You go get yourself relaxed down at the barn or something while I cook something up for you. Just see to it you stay away from all that construction equipment outside. Knowing you, you'll think the men aren't working fast enough so you'll start assembling things on your own. You are definitely your father's child," Cookie said, only half jokingly.

"Did Ian bring Jasmine back from town yet?" Jacqueline asked, vacating her chair.

"No, he called to say the girls wanted to catch a movie. I told him it would be fine, but I think he already knew that, or he'd have called your cell phone to ask you himself when I told him you weren't here."

"No problem." Jacqueline nodded. "Ian and Pam sure are spending a lot of time together lately. That makes every night this week, doesn't it?"

"It's about time Ian stopped fawning over you long enough to focus on someone more attainable," Cookie commented as she filled a pot with water.

"Hey! I'm attainable," Jacqueline protested.

"Not for Ian, you're not. Now if you want to talk about your Mr. Hawkins, that's a whole 'nother story. Seems to me you started missing meals, working yourself and everyone else to death, and sporting an attitude right around the time he stopped visiting the ranch."

Jacqueline was genuinely surprised by Cookie's observation. "He's not *my* . . . anything. He wanted the ranch. I told him no. There's nothing left for us to discuss and therefore no need for him to visit. I didn't really like him anyway."

Cookie chuckled. "You sound like a pouting child,

Jacqueline Renee Carr. Everybody knows you two had the hots for each other, especially that day at the lake when he wore those marvelously tight jeans and that . . ." Cookie cleared her throat and refocused her attention on the task at hand.

"Just go on down to the barn and take a look at your horse or something and leave me to my cooking. Be back in one hour, Jack, or I'll send someone out to find you," she warned.

Jacqueline exited the kitchen, wondering why Cookie would send her to the barn. She was usually yelling at her for spending too much time there.

Jacqueline willed her mind to un-busy itself. She was tired and her thoughts weren't making any sense. She would spend some time brushing Pepsi, shower, and then grab a bite to eat. By then Jasmine would be home, she estimated. She would spend some quality time with her daughter and then get some much-needed sleep.

Chapter Ten

Alexander wasn't sure what to expect when he'd knocked on the door of the main house. He'd spent the past week hoping she would call. When she didn't, he decided to stop waiting to hear from her and go find out what she thought of his proposal now that she'd had time to think about it. When he was greeted by Cookie and then sent down to the stable with the caution that dinner would be ready in nearly fifty minutes, he was shocked but pleasantly surprised.

He stood quietly at the stable entrance watching the mesmerizing sway of Jacqueline's hips as she stroked Pepsi's neck with one hand while brushing her gently with the other. She was humming a sweet, lilting melody that calmed even his uneasiness.

He was glad to catch her with her guard down and somehow knew he was witnessing one of the rare moments she ever did so.

Alexander leaned against the door frame, cringing when it made the slightest protest against the weight of him. The horse eyed him, whinnying its protest and stomping its hoof at the intruder.

Traitor, Alexander thought. A startled Jacqueline turned around at the sound.

"Need a hand with that?" he offered, trying to sound nonchalant.

"How long have you been standing there?" Jacqueline asked, irritation ringing like a bell in her tone.

Long enough for my body to crave every inch of yours, he wanted to say, but thought better of it. "Not long," he offered instead.

"What do you want, Alex?" Jacqueline asked before turning back around to brush the mare.

"You'll brush all the natural oils out of her coat if you don't let up pretty soon," he said, beside her now.

Jacqueline frowned. "And how would you know that?"

Alexander stiffened. "I—suppose—I . . . heard it, along with a million other facts that Shasta has been learning since we got here."

"I see," Jacqueline said, though she didn't believe him. *Great. More secrets.* Just what she didn't need at the moment. She wanted to ask him why he thought horses were so deadly and why he looked so damned at home in ranch clothes, and now she wanted to know how he knew about a horse's coat and oil. She knew he would find a way to avoid answering her, so she decided to leave the subjects alone.

"Can we talk?" Alexander asked, leaning back against Pepsi.

"About what, Alex?"

Alexander reached out to stay Jacqueline's hand.

Taking the brush from her, he placed it on a nearby bale of hay.

"I wanted to know what you thought about the proposal, but right now you're driving me mad," Alexander stated honestly.

Jacqueline raised an eyebrow at him. "Believe me, it isn't intentional."

"I thought it was just a physical attraction at first, but . . . there's something else."

Jacqueline sighed with resignation. "I—I don't know exactly what it is either, Alex, but . . ." She looked at him and he could see the passion and confusion in her eyes. "I want to know what it is or at least what there could be between us, but, Alexander, you can't have the ranch and no matter what you do or say, I'll never be so into you that I risk the 1850. Can you understand that?" she asked, hoping he could.

"I understand that you're scared, but then, so am I. I came here to get the ranch. Hell," he said, chuckling, "I totally expected to have been back in Manhattan by now. I certainly didn't expect to feel this way about you, Jacqueline, or the ranch itself. I know what I feel and what I want," he told her before leaning in to kiss her.

She backed away. "Alexander, maybe we should wait until we both know how we feel and—"

"I've done all the waiting I'm willing to do, Jacqueline," he said, walking over to close the barn doors.

"Wh-what are you doing?" Jacqueline asked nervously.

Alexander offered no response as he took Pepsi's reins and led her into a stall. He made certain he bolted the outside door before walking back toward Jacqueline.

"But she belongs in the stable. It's across the—"

"She'll be fine where she is. Won't you, girl?" Alexander turned back to look at Pepsi, whose large neck and head extended well over the stall door. Jacqueline felt both shocked and betrayed when Pepsi tossed her head up and down.

Alexander continued his advance toward Jacqueline.

"Alex, what's gotten into you? What are you doing?" she asked, backing away from him until her back was pressed firmly against the wall.

Alexander stopped inches in front of her. Without speaking he reached out, taking a handful of her ebony hair. She watched dumbfounded as he leaned in, inhaling deeply.

"You smell like summer," he said sexily.

"I smell like . . . Alex . . . what are you talking—"

He pressed his lips to hers before she could finish the sentence.

Jacqueline's confusion was instantly pushed out of her mind. She suddenly wondered how she would have made it through the rest of the evening without being this close to him. She willed herself not to think, not to move or even breathe. She wanted only his touch and the passionate kisses she had secretly been longing for.

Alexander needed to know if his memory of Jacqueline's touch and kiss was real or imagined. He'd spent the past week hoping she would call or visit. When she did neither he began thinking that perhaps the passion he'd felt was one-sided, that maybe Jacqueline felt nothing when they kissed at the lake. But it was clear to him now, as she pressed herself against him, moaning with desire, that the feeling had indeed been shared.

He backed away, breaking the kiss. He looked down into her beautiful eyes while he gave them both time to catch their breath.

"I—I thought you'd never come again," Jacqueline said, leaning forward to trace kisses down Alexander's neck.

"I was waiting for you to call," Alexander breathed, trying to control himself.

Jacqueline leaned back against the wall again. "City girls call, Alex. Country girls, well, we wait." She smiled. "We don't rush things and we never choose the easy path."

"Mm," Alexander mumbled, "I should have remembered that." He chuckled.

"You're just a city boy. You're used to fast cars and fast women," she teased. "How could you remember something you never knew?"

Alexander tensed slightly at the question.

"Don't worry, Alex. I'll teach you what you need to know," she promised.

He grunted deep in his throat. "Fortunately for you, I'm a fast learner," he said, before kissing her again.

Alexander slid his hand boldly beneath Jacqueline's shirt. He moved his hand up the length of her waist and side. He then maneuvered to her back, where he artfully unfastened her bra. Jacqueline's throaty moan was all the encouragement he needed to take both of her hands by the wrist, raising her arms high above her head. He then held them there with one hand.

He looked down into her passion-glazed eyes. "I want you, Jacqueline," he said hoarsely.

"I'm yours, Alex," she managed between heaving breaths.

Alexander needed no further prodding as he traced kisses down her neck and full breasts. Without releasing her arms, he used his free hand to massage one full breast before bending down to suckle her greedily.

Jacqueline cried out in pure pleasure as electrifying shock waves ran through her body like time-released passionate charges.

Alexander lifted her into his arms. Jacqueline trailed kisses up and down his neck as she slid her hand inside his shirt to run a warm hand over his nipples. He growled sexily at the sensation.

"The loft?" he asked, nodding toward the stairs leading up to the hayloft.

"The loft," Jacqueline responded. She waited for him to release her. She kissed Alexander with all the unspoken longing she harbored as she instinctively slid her hand beneath his shorts seeking what she so desperately needed. Finding it, she held him in her hand, massaging firmly.

Alexander grunted almost painfully. He reached down, pulling her hand up, freeing himself in the process. "Do that again and we won't make it to the loft. I'll take you right here in front of God, the horses, and anyone else who should happen in. And, Jacqueline . . ." he said, breathing hard.

"Yes, Alex?"

"I don't know if I can be gentle with you. I—it's been a long time." He visibly struggled for control. "I need desperately to be inside you," he managed.

Jacqueline felt her knees go weak. "I don't believe I've ever needed anyone or anything as much as I need you or . . . this," she confessed. "And, Alex . . ."

"Yes?"

"Don't be gentle."

Alexander nearly took the stairs two at a time. They were both naked and lying atop their clothing on the hay before either could recall having undressed.

Jacqueline spotted a small package hanging out of one of Alexander's pockets. She picked up the pair of shorts, removing the prophylactic from within. "Shall I?" she asked, but didn't wait for him to answer.

"Very impressive, Mr. Hawkins," Jacqueline commented, rolling the latex down his length. She worried about whether or not she would survive making love to such a well-endowed man.

She looked up to find Alexander smiling at her. "Trust me," he said, offering her a smile of his own.

"Alexander—"

"Shh," he said, kissing her lips softly.

Jacqueline closed her eyes as she stood naked before him, not because she was embarrassed but because she wanted to memorize the image of him, the sound of his voice, the scent of him, and how good it felt to be wanted by a man like him.

Alexander dropped to his knees before Jacqueline. He held her close, his muscular arms around her waist. "Come here," he said, pulling her down gently. She obeyed. He let his eyes roam freely over her body. To him she was perfection with her full breasts and pert nipples, and while her stomach was not flat, it was nearly so. He ran a hand over a long scar at the base of her stomach. He recognized it as a cesarean section. He gently pushed her hand away when she tried to cover it up. He bent low, kissing the angry scar and causing Jacqueline to moan hotly.

Alexander slid his hand between her muscular thighs, seeking what every inch of him desired. He stroked the soft nub gently and then with more fervor until Jacqueline begged him to take her.

"You're beautiful," he said, not wanting to rush the moment. He slid his fingers inside her and she pressed herself greedily against them.

"Alex! Please!" she cried out.

"In a second, love. I want to cherish the mom—"

Jacqueline wrapped both legs around Alexander. She used her powerful thighs to flip him onto his back. She smiled at his shocked expression as he now lay beneath her.

"We have Pepsi to thank for these thighs," she said, chuckling. "She's a stubborn horse who only responds to power."

"Remind me to send her a bag of oats in gratitude." Alexander grinned up at her.

Jacqueline rose up just enough to situate herself in a desirable position. Alexander groaned as she lowered herself slowly and completely, surrounding him in her warmth.

She didn't wait for him to collect himself before moving up and down with increased intensity.

"Jacqueline! God help me, you have to slow down and . . . baby . . . stop gripping me . . . like . . . that. . . ."

"Like what?" she asked with mock innocence. "Like . . . this?" she inquired, tightening muscles she hadn't used since . . . She wondered if she had ever used the muscles she was using now while married to Bryce. She pushed the thought from her mind, choosing to focus on the amazing man lying beneath her.

"Jacqueline . . . if you don't ease up, woman, I'm going to—"

Alexander's words were cut off as the barn doors swung open noisily.

"Mama! Cookie said I could show Shasta my—" Both Jasmine and Shasta froze.

"Well, where are they?" Shasta asked.

"I don't know. Cookie said they would be in here.'

Both girls looked around, checking each stall.

"Mama, are you in here?" Jasmine called.

"Damn," Alexander grunted as Jacqueline quickly rolled off him. "You trying to kill me?" he whispered.

"Dad? Is that you? I think the sound came from up there," Shasta said, pointing at the loft.

"Up there?" Jasmine asked. "There's nothing up there but stored hay."

"Let's check it out," Shasta suggested excitedly.

"I'll be down in a m-minute, Shasta. Stay there," Alexander called shakily as he searched for his clothes.

"Dad? Are you okay? You sound . . . weird," Shasta called from the bottom step.

"I'm . . . fine. Now go back to the house and I'll be there in a . . . Damn it!" Alexander cursed, hitting his head on one of the beams as he struggled to get dressed while in a crouching position. Jacqueline giggled and then covered her mouth.

"Mama? Is that you?" Jasmine asked suspiciously.

"Yes, Jazzy. I'm here, now go back to the house."

"What are you doing up there, Mama?"

Jacqueline could tell her daughter's voice was getting closer to the ladder. She searched her brain for an acceptable response for being caught in the loft with Alexander. She felt like a guilty teenager.

"Do you remember last week at the lake when you suggested I ask Mr. Hawkins to teach me how to have fun?" Jacqueline asked, trying to sound as casual as possible while fumbling with her bra straps.

"Yes," Jasmine answered, confused.

"Well, I asked him and he's . . . teaching me."

Alexander rolled his eyes. Jacqueline shrugged in response.

"Cool! Can we play too?" Jasmine asked.

"No!" both adults yelled at the same time.

"What kind of game is my dad teaching you?" Shasta asked, obviously unconvinced.

"Uh . . . uh . . ." Jacqueline stuttered.

"Hide-and-seek," Alexander answered for her.

It was Jacqueline's turn to roll her eyes.

"But aren't you supposed to play some place where you have lots of room to hide?" Shasta asked.

"Okay, so I'm a little rusty," Alexander admitted. "Now go back to the house and we'll be there in a moment," he added sternly.

"Yes, sir, but, Dad . . ."

Alexander gave an exasperated sigh. "Yes, Shasta?"

"I'm telling!" she said before running toward the door.

"Telling what?" Jasmine asked, hot on her heels.

Jacqueline chuckled. "That little girl of yours is far too smart for her own good."

"Smart has nothing to do with it. This just makes me wonder what she's been exposed to when she's with her mother," he said bitterly.

Jacqueline didn't want Alexander's mood to be ruined by the incident. Fully clothed now, she straddled him. "I wouldn't mind being exposed to you again sometime soon." She grinned.

Alexander kissed her. "How about tomorrow night at the B-and-B?"

"Mm . . . can't," Jacqueline said with a sigh. "I've got too much to do. The rodeo preparations have been keeping me pretty swamped. I pretty much pass out at the end of the day and besides, everyone knows me at the B-and-B. I might as well walk around town with a sign stuck to my forehead that says *hello, everyone, I've been having sex with Alexander Hawkins!*"

"Would that be such a bad thing?" Alexander asked. "People knowing, I mean."

"For you, no. For me, most definitely."

"I see," Alexander grunted as he stood.

Jacqueline didn't think he did at all. "Making love to you was one of the most fulfilling and touching things I've ever done in my life. It's not that I don't want to be seen in public with you, nor am I ashamed of what we just did," she assured him. "But I can't risk hurting my daughter or my family by being labeled fast or loose. Can you understand that?" she asked, silently praying he could.

"Yes," he said after a long breath. "But that doesn't mean I have to accept or like it, damn it."

"Come on. Let's go get something to eat," she coaxed, making her way down the ladder.

"Mm, something smells good!" Jacqueline said dramatically as she and Alexander entered the kitchen.

Cookie shot her a daunting glare. "Girls, how would you like to help Pam and Ian make the posters for the rodeo?"

Shasta beamed. "Sure!"

"Okay!" Jasmine chimed in.

"They're in the living room. Tell them there's extra markers and paint in the cellar next to the storm shelter if they need them."

Jacqueline and Alexander sat down opposite one another at the table after washing their hands.

Cookie waited patiently for the children to leave.

Jacqueline leaned forward, motioning Alexander to do the same until he was within earshot. "Hold on to your butt," she whispered.

Alexander didn't have time to ask what she meant.

"Just what were the two of you thinking?" Cookie asked accusingly.

She waited for an answer, but neither offered a response. "I see, so now you have nothing to say. I'll just bet the two of you weren't at a loss for words when you were in the barn!"

"Actually, words weren't necessary for—" Alexander teased.

"Don't you dare get smart with me, young man. I'm more than three times your age . . . and weight, for that matter . . . and I won't settle for disrespect!" the plump five-foot-four-inch woman stated.

"Yes, ma'am. I apologize," Alexander said as he stood. He bent low to give Cookie a warm hug and loud kiss on the cheek.

She shrugged him off. "You young folks today are so full of charm that you don't think you need common sense." Cookie's eyes widened with worry. "And you," she said turning her full attention on Jacqueline, "what on earth would possess you to tell that sweet little girl you were playing hide-and-seek with her daddy?"

At that both Jacqueline and Alexander nearly fell out of their chairs with laughter.

"Oh, so this is funny to you, eh?" Cookie frowned, but neither of them was listening as they were both too busy holding their stomachs at Cookie's hilarity.

"Well, fine, then! Fix your own plates!" she said before exiting the kitchen in an indignant huff.

"That was an amazing meal," Alexander said, sitting back and pushing his plate away.

"But you didn't finish your steak." Jacqueline frowned as she finished the last of the food on her own plate.

Alexander laughed. "I'm stuffed!"

"Wimp."

Alexander stared in amazement at Jacqueline's clean plate. "Where do you put all that food? I think your plate was packed higher than mine, yet you ate every morsel."

"Hey, I've been out on the open range from sunup until sundown for the past seven days straight. This was the first good meal I've had all week. Besides, I've got a very high metabolism," she joked.

He shook his head. "So you said you were waiting for me to call you. Does that mean you read the proposal along with the other information I gave you last week?" he asked with trepidation.

Jacqueline wiped her mouth on a napkin and then sat back as she mulled the question over. "Alex, I told you, I've been so busy that I—"

"What about all those hours spent out on the open range?" Alexander queried. "Are you trying to tell me you didn't spend any of that time contemplating—"

"Okay, okay, so I thought about it, but it isn't that simple. Alex, entering a partnership with you as the financier and me in charge of all major decisions and such, I have to admit, sounds good on paper, but I just don't know."

"You don't know what, Jacqueline?"

"If I can trust you," she blurted out.

"That's a legitimate concern," Alexander admitted. "But it doesn't change the fact that I came here for the 1850 and then changed my mind after—"

"Yes, Alexander, it counts, but I just can't shake the feeling that there's more to you than you're letting on."

"What do you mean?" he asked nervously.

"I don't know exactly. It's just that there have been times when I've thought you were holding something back from me. Like I said, I'm not sure what, but how can I enter into a business partnership with a man I don't fully trust?"

"Simple," Alexander said with a shrug. "People do it every day. I even do it. You just have to check your facts, make certain all your information is legit, and if everything is as it should be, you go for it. Besides, it's not like I'm asking you to enter into a verbal agreement. My lawyers drew up all the paperwork. Have your lawyer take a look at them. I'm on the up and up, Jacqueline."

"My father's lawyers already looked at them."

Alexander couldn't hide his surprise. "And?"

"And . . . they found everything was as it should be."

"Then why won't you . . ." Alexander didn't want to keep going over the same questions. He tried to think of a way to convince Jacqueline he could be trusted.

"Did you trust me when we were together in the barn earlier?"

Jacqueline raised an eyebrow at him. "That's not fair, Alex. That wasn't about contracts, that was about . . . passion."

"It was about trusting me with your most valuable possession, Jacqueline. You trusted me with your heart."

Jacqueline blinked twice. "We're both adults here, Alexander. I shared my passion with you, but I would never and could never give you my heart."

She'd shocked him again. Did the woman ever say the expected? Alexander wondered. "But we . . . or at least we started to—"

"Alexander, my heart was never an issue. Look, let's not talk about that right now. The fact is I already signed the contracts. I was just waiting for you to come. I'll get them for you before you leave. There were a few changes that needed to be made, but I'm sure you'll have no problem with them.

"So," she said, smiling, "how about you give me a call on my cell phone sometime tomorrow and we'll set up a time to meet and discuss our plans for turning the 1850 into a historical working ranch?"

"So you were willing to make love to me, but it never involved your heart?" he asked, obviously perplexed.

"Alex, this isn't the time," she said again.

"I'm sorry, Jacqueline, but you're going to have to explain it to me. This isn't making any sense. You'll make love to me, and now you tell me that you'll be my business partner, but you won't give me your heart? How does that work?"

"Alex, one thing has nothing to do with the other. You said yourself that business partners don't necessarily—"

"But we made love . . . or at least started to!" he reiterated. "I'm sorry, I didn't mean to get so upset."

"Alexander, when we were together earlier, did you offer me or even think about offering me your heart?" Jacqueline asked, turning the tables on him.

"Hell, woman, I'd have given you my heart, my mind, my soul, and my bank account numbers if you'd wanted them!"

Jacqueline chuckled. "Seriously, Alex."

"I am serious, Jacqueline. My heart and my libido are connected."

"If that were true, then that would mean you haven't been with a woman since your divorce from Shasta's mother . . ."

"Seven and a half years ago," Alexander finished for her.

Jacqueline's heart raced as she sat stupefied by the suggestion. "Are you telling me that until me, you hadn't been with a woman . . . any woman, anywhere . . . in seven and a half years?"

"That's precisely what I'm telling you," Alexander admitted, "and could you please not look so horrified by the information? It's not like something was wrong with me," he grumbled.

"Alex, I was with you in the barn, remember?

Trust me, I *know* there's nothing wrong with you. But how . . . what . . ."

"I was too busy trying to make enough money to support my ex-wife and child to even think about another woman. Once I had things the way I wanted them, or the way I thought I wanted them, I pretty much occupied my time between work and getting my daughter. Lana and I slept together once or twice after she left me, but that was it."

"Getting your daughter?" Jacqueline inquired. "What did you mean, between work and getting your daughter?"

"It's getting late. I'd better get Shasta," Alexander said, standing.

"Alex, I'm sorry. I didn't mean to sound so—"

"Look, what it boils down to is that I can't offer a woman my body without also giving her my heart," he confessed. "I'm a twenty-nine-year-old grown man with a daughter to raise, a business to run, and a life to live. I'm sorry, Jaqueline, but I'm not looking for a one-night stand or a summer fling!"

Alexander immediately regretted saying the words the moment they fell from his lips. *I'm beginning to sound like a woman,* he lamented. What the heck was going on? Wasn't the woman supposed to be the sensitive one, crying when she felt spurned? And wasn't he, at six feet three inches tall, supposed to be the one brushing her off? He needed to clear his head before he said anything else he'd regret later. He needed a good stiff drink and a good night's sleep. Perhaps tomorrow he'd be himself again.

Chapter Eleven

Jacqueline exited the house in the morning to gray skies and more wind than she would have liked. Having watched the news the night before, she expected a few scattered showers, but nothing close to what her instincts told her would be an all-out storm.

She hurried to the stable to ready Pepsi for another long day. As she approached, she could hear the unsettling whinnies and prods of the horses inside.

"They've been like this since sunup," Thomas said, raising his voice to be heard over the increasingly loud wind.

Jacqueline nodded, pushing the stable doors open. "They know something's up."

"There are no tornado warnings for this area, but channel six just posted some for surrounding areas. It could be only a matter of time before we get hit, Jack," Thomas said worriedly.

"Get everybody up and working. I want the stalls

secured, and have a crew work on stabilizing the bleachers we set up last week. Make sure someone herds the bulls, but keep them separate from the cows! And—"

"I'll take care of it, Jack, don't worry," Thomas assured her before running outside to his truck. He began beeping the horn relentlessly. As if by magic, doors started opening and closing simultaneously around the entire ranch. Both men and women poured out onto the grounds. Anyone strong enough and old enough made his or her way to Thomas.

After saddling and mounting her horse, Jacqueline maneuvered her way through the crowd. She did a double take when she spotted Alexander talking to Ian and Thomas near the truck.

"Listen up, people!" Jacqueline said at the top of her voice. "Things are going to get pretty ugly around here over the next few hours. Hopefully, all we have to do is make it to sunset and then things will calm down. But," she said, not wanting them to get too comfortable with the notion, "we all know what the weather does in Oklahoma, don't we?"

"It does whatever the hell it wants!" Someone in the crowd yelled.

"That's right! So let's hope for the best and—"

"Prepare for the worst!" the crowd finished for her.

"Ian! Patrick! Lamont! Gather some men and round up the bulls. We've had half a dozen new calves born since spring. We can't afford to lose even one!" The men nodded in understanding and agreement.

"Dustin, Travis, and Kyle, check the fencing along the east gate. . . ."

Jacqueline continued giving orders until everyone had something to do. "Okay, people, let's get this party started!" she exclaimed.

Alexander watched Jacqueline with an observant eye. Her leadership and total control of the situation impressed him, but he sensed the tenseness in her voice as well. He watched as she prodded Pepsi toward him.

"What are you doing here, Alex?" she asked, concerned.

"I saw the sky this morning and knew things were going to get ugly. Knowing how worried you've been about the preparations for the rodeo, I figured you might need an extra hand."

"Where are Shasta and Pam?"

"Inside with Cookie and Jasmine. I thought they'd be safer here than in town," Alexander confessed.

"You're right about that. I sometimes think we've got more storm shelters around here than we have people to fill them. As for any help you can offer, I don't mean to be rude, Alex, but I think it would be safer for a city boy like you to stay inside where it's safe. I can't afford to be worried about your safety at a time like this. I've got too much at stake."

Alexander smiled. "Ian mentioned that he was a few men short and could use a hand securing the bull pens. Thomas also mentioned needing an extra hand rounding up the cattle."

"This isn't a movie, Alex. This is dangerous work and I don't want you getting hurt. Now go inside before—"

"I know what I'm doing," Alexander stated firmly.

"You're from Manhattan, for God's sake, Alex, how could you possibly—"

"Trust me, Jack."

Had he just called her Jack? He never called her Jack. What was he playing at? Jacqueline wondered. She searched his eyes carefully. He exuded confidence and an unshakable iron will. Trust him? She was beginning to think she didn't even know him.

"Fine. Help Thomas wrangle the horses. You'll find saddles and everything else you need in the—"

"I've already done that," Alexander said before hurrying over to a mammoth black-and-white-spotted stallion.

Jacqueline recognized the brooding horse as her father's. No one had ever been able to get near it, let alone ride it, but Solomon. She was just about to yell a warning to Alexander when he mounted the horse in one swift movement. She watched, both impressed and terrified, as he kicked the horse into a gallop to catch up with Thomas's truck.

"If he makes it through this in one piece, I'm going to kill him," Jacqueline said, knowing for certain now that Alexander was keeping more than just one secret from her.

Jacqueline helped some of the men disassemble canopies that had recently been set up to shelter rodeo attendees in case of rain when the time came. She knew they would not be heavy enough to shelter them from a strong storm like the one they were about to face.

"Zack, help me roll this," she said over the din. "Leah, Dale, tie the ends of this tarp once we've closed it. Please, we must move quickly before—"

The rain started in an angry downpour before

Jacqueline could complete the sentence. Within moments the ground was saturated with puddles of mud so thick her boots sank into it like bricks.

"Hurry!" Jacqueline urged. "All right! Good job, people, now take the rest of these down." She pointed to a dozen others. "Stay focused and move quickly. Those rods are made of metal! We've got to get them down before any lightning strikes." Everyone moved quickly.

"Jack!" Ian called from behind her.

Jacqueline turned, surprised to see him standing there. "I thought I told you to—"

"We've got problems, Jack!"

"What problems?" She stood, leaving the rest of the crew to finish rolling the tarp. She suddenly felt soaked to the bone.

"The storm's worse on the other side of the ranch," he informed her.

Jacqueline looked up to see black clouds looming menacingly over the north skies. "We should be all right, there's no one near the lake and—"

"Joseph is and so are his men," Ian said, but a loud clap of thunder and the electric crackle of lightning muffled his voice.

"But I didn't send anyone over there!" Jacqueline protested. "What the devil is . . . Who did you say was there?" she asked, wondering who would be bold enough to go off on their own, and for what purpose?

"Joseph," Ian said, pensively. "Joseph and his crew are there."

"What is my grandfather doing out here in this kind of—"

"He insisted, Jack. We tried to talk him out of it, but you know Joe! He does what he pleases."

"Well, tell him and his crew I said to get back to the house! We need them there in case—"

"There's more, Jack." Ian waited until the thunder stopped shaking the sky before speaking. "Lightning struck and it's on fire. The whole lake area," he yelled over the sound of rain and wind. "Some of the men got out, but—"

"But what? Ian—what?" She grabbed his shirt collar in terror.

"We can't find Joseph. He's still in there. Jack, I don't think he's going to make—"

Jacqueline released Ian, mounted Pepsi, and headed for the ranch before Ian could catch his breath.

She couldn't believe her eyes when she arrived at the lake. Black smoke wafted through the air like an angry army. Red and orange flames licked at trees like a serpent's tongue, devouring everything it touched.

"Dear God!" she said with disbelief as the sight momentarily stunned her. She snapped out of it quickly when Thomas rode up beside her.

"Jack!" Thomas called, trying to calm his horse and get it to move closer to Jacqueline. It refused to obey, obviously terrified by the fire. "You're too close!"

"Get Ian and anyone else who has a winch on their truck. Tell them to fell the trees over there. I'll need a clear path!" she said, pointing farther down to the left where the fire had not yet reached.

"But—"

"Do it now, Thomas!" she yelled, leaving no room for discussion. She watched him speed away.

Turning back to face the flames, Jacqueline stared at the scene before her. She quickly estimated the safest point of entry. She rubbed Pepsi's neck gently, leaning forward as she spoke.

"That's our Joseph in there, girl," she said in a low, even tone. Pepsi whinnied, prodding the ground impatiently. "We'll not lose him to an unexpected storm or a few measly flames, will we?" she stated rather than asked. Pepsi reared up on her hind legs in response. Jacqueline prodded the huge animal forward.

After several moments of searching, she was beginning to lose hope. "Grandfather, where are you!" Jacqueline called as tears mixed with thick black smoke burned her eyes. A burning branch fell from a tree, landing inches from Pepsi's hooves. The horse reared unexpectedly and Jacqueline hit the ground. While she was grateful for the soft mud to cushion her fall, she cursed when the horse bolted away, running wildly from the flames. She stood, brushing herself off. She began coughing as she went deeper into the area.

"Get out of here!" Alexander called from the bottom of a small ridge.

"Alex?" Jacqueline managed. She spotted him kneeling beside someone at the base of a small incline.

"Grandfather!" she screamed, half running, half sliding as best she could given several downed tree limbs and flames that bellowed every time the wind picked up.

"He's unconscious," Alexander informed her when she finally got to them.

Jacqueline was horrified to see her grandfather's

condition. He was pinned at the waist by a downed tree, yet she was grateful it was only a sapling.

"I can't get it off him. The rain has flooded the lake and it's overflowing." Alexander nodded to the left of them. Jacqueline's eye's widened with the realization that they were now in a ditch. She spotted several places where water had begun caving in the mud around them. "I'll stay with him. You . . . go get . . . help!" he said, coughing.

"I'm not leaving either of you! By the time I got back, the sides of the ridge would have caved in and you would both have already drowned or been buried alive!" Jacqueline protested.

Alexander knew her words were true. "We've got to roll this off him. You dig, I'll pull!" he yelled, grabbing a still unconscious Joseph under both arms.

After several tries, they accomplished their task. "Thank God!" Alexander exclaimed, winded by their efforts.

"We've got to get him out of here. The fire is getting too close!" Jacqueline warned.

Alexander looked up to find her words all too true. They were now in the center of a muddy ravine surrounded on all sides by trees set ablaze with fire and smoke so thick they would have choked to death had it not been for the easterly wind and pouring rain. He inwardly cursed the situation, knowing there was no way out.

The two shared a helpless look momentarily.

"I—I don't know what else to do," Jacqueline said, her voice barely audible over the noise. "Even if we made it to the lake, the water would probably be boiling by now."

Alexander was about to say something when the

ground began to shake violently. *There are no earthquakes in Oklahoma . . . are there?* he wondered.

"What now?" Jacqueline asked, at the end of her rope.

They looked up to see Ian's monster truck making its way toward them, devouring trees and debris as it went. It stopped a few feet from them. They watched, stunned, as the driver's side door opened and Ian jumped out.

Both Jacqueline and Alexander were too filled with emotion to speak at first.

"I'll help you get him in the truck," Ian said, hurrying over to Joseph.

"Careful, I'm not sure if there's damage to his spine or not," Alexander warned.

"I've got a board in the back of the truck. We can put him on that," Ian said, before running back to the truck.

"We're going to make it," Jacqueline said, with tears in her eyes. "Do you hear that, Grandfather? We're going to make it!" she declared, flashing Alexander a relieved smile.

Once Joseph was safely in the truck, Ian made haste getting them all out of there.

By the time they got back to the main house, the rain had slowed to a drizzle. Pam ran out, with Cookie close behind her. They worked to get Joseph out of the truck with as little jostling as possible. Cookie led them inside to Joseph's room.

"Are you all right?" Pam asked Jacqueline, who stood frozen by Joseph's bed watching with a warned look as Cookie tended to him the best she could.

The phone lines were down so they could not contact Doc Brown.

Jacqueline willed herself to speak, tearing her eyes away from Joseph. "I don't have the time or luxury to be anything else," she answered. "I've got to find a horse and then check the rest of the property. I need to make sure everyone is accounted for."

"Your horse is in the stable. A few men brought her back about half an hour ago," Pam informed her.

Jacqueline hugged Pam, surprising her completely.

Pam smiled, confused. "It's just a horse, Jacqueline."

"No, it's much, much more," Jacqueline told her before casting a longing look at her grandfather and, hurrying toward the stable.

She entered to find Thomas elbow-deep in a bucket of water.

"Where is she?" Jacqueline asked. "I've got to go check on the others and I need her to——" She froze, seeing Pepsi lying on the ground in a nearby open stall.

"She's sustained some pretty serious injuries, Jack. I'm doing the best I can. The phone lines are out so I couldn't call the vet."

"Wh-what happened to her?" Jacqueline asked, kneeling beside the horse.

"Probably hit by the branches when a tree fell, so far as I can tell. She's burned pretty bad on one side and she's got some pretty deep gashes on her hind legs."

Jacqueline wished she could stay with Pepsi but knew she could not. There were people depending on her, and as the woman in charge she couldn't afford to let them down. "Take care of her, Thomas," she said somberly as she stood. "I'll need your horse."

"He's already saddled."

"Thomas?" Jacqueline said, mounting the stallion.

"Yeah?"

"Where's my father's horse?"

Thomas turned regretful eyes on Jacqueline. "I found him lying near Pepsi. A tree fell and . . ." He wiped his forehead before continuing. "He didn't make it, Jack."

Jacqueline felt her heart sink, but there was no time to dwell on misfortune. She mounted the horse and kicked it into motion.

She spent the entire day riding from one end of the ranch to another helping with anything she could. She was relieved to learn that Joseph's were the only serious injuries sustained. She tried not to worry about him too much, knowing he was in good hands with Cookie looking after him.

Jacqueline heard a muffled sound from somewhere behind her. She pulled on the reins of the horse she rode, turning in the direction of the noise. She waited quietly, listening hard. Again she heard it. It seemed to be coming from an area just beyond the next ridge. She recognized the sound as a bull in distress and increased the speed of her approach. She was just about to slow down again when her horse stopped abruptly.

Jacqueline flew over the horse's head like a bullet shot from a gun. She closed her eyes as images of Jasmine took shape in her mind, followed by hot, searing pain that quickly consumed her senses. *God, take care of my baby,* she thought before everything went silent and pain was replaced by total oblivion.

* * *

Alexander, who was also surveying the damage to the grounds, watched, horrified, as Jacqueline was thrown from her horse. It must have sensed the oncoming danger. From his vantage point he could see that the entire hillside opposite their approach had collapsed after a mud slide. He spotted a large Angus bull stuck up to its neck in the muddy earth. The entire area had become a virtual quicksand trap. He floored Thomas's truck, in an attempt to reach Jacqueline before it was too late.

Alexander grabbed a rope from the back of the truck before hurrying to lie prostrate on the ground at the top of the ridge. He threw the rope toward Jacqueline, who by now was just beginning to get hold of her senses again.

"Grab the rope!" Alexander yelled.

Jacqueline moaned in response, opening her eyes in time to see the last of the bull's snout going under the earth. She felt herself slide farther into the mud. Knowing she would be next if she didn't act quickly, she grabbed the rope, pulling herself up as Alexander pulled from his end. She gritted herself against a white-hot pain so fierce she couldn't tell where it came from.

Once on top of the ridge, Alexander checked Jacqueline for injuries. It was evident that her arm was broken when he touched it. She nearly took out his eardrum with a deafening scream.

He gasped when he saw the side of her leg, which was cut nearly from knee to ankle. It was so bad, he could almost see the bone.

"What? What is it?" Jacqueline asked, trying to sit up, but again her efforts were rewarded with pain.

"I think your arm is broken and your leg . . ."

"What is it? What's wrong with my leg?" she asked, panicked as she cradled her injured arm close to her.

"You've got a pretty bad gash in it. We'll have to get you to the ranch A.S.A.P."

"Is it broken? Jacqueline asked, feeling dizzy from the pain.

"It's not broken, but it's bad. You're going to need stitches and probably surgery to close this thing, and you've got quite a bit of mud and grass in it. We've got to move quickly before infection sets in, Jack."

Jacqueline screamed with pain when he tried to lift her. "No! It's broken! There's too much pain for it not to be, Alex. Leave me here and go for help."

"Even with the truck it will take me an hour to get back to the ranch. We have to move you and we have to do it now," Alexander insisted.

"What are you, a doctor or something? How would you know if my leg is broken or not?" she asked angrily.

"I've seen enough injuries like this to last me a lifetime! Now will you quit challenging everything I say and just believe me for once!" he growled in response.

Alexander looked at Jacqueline when she remained silent. It was obvious the day had finally caught up with her. Hot tears rolled down both cheeks and she looked nearly ready to pass out again.

"I'm sorry, Jack," he said softly. "That was stupid of me. You're going to be fine. Everything is going to be fine. I promise."

He took a small jackknife from his back pocket and began tearing long shreds of his shirt.

"I've got to get you into the truck so I can get you back to the ranch. In order to do that, I've got to stop your leg from bleeding and your arm will need a splint as well. I'm going to tie these around your leg to make a tourniquet of sorts, all right?"

Jacqueline nodded, sniffling and wiping at her eyes in the process.

"Here we go," Alexander warned and then busied himself with the task. He was impressed when Jacqueline dug her hands deep into the muddy earth by the handfuls but did not pull away from him.

"There, the worst is over," he said when he finished. He smiled, but it faded quickly with the realization hit him that Jacqueline was slowly losing consciousness. He did not want her going into shock before they could make the hour-long drive back to the main house. "Stay with me, Jack," he urged, shaking her gently. "Stay with me."

Chapter Twelve

Jacqueline woke slowly. She recognized the sweet scent of Jasmine and squinted against the brightness of the noonday sun.

"Ah, you're awake," Cookie said with relief. "I'll let him know."

Him who? Jacqueline wondered. *Dear God, please tell me she didn't call my father and tell him what happened!*

"Hello, beautiful."

Jacqueline smiled. "Alex," she said hoarsely. She forced her eyes to focus. "Are you okay?"

"I'm fine," Alexander answered, kissing her gently. She winced. "Am *I* okay?"

Alexander chuckled. "You will be soon," he answered.

Jacqueline loved the look and scent of him. He smelled like the ranch, a mix of wildflowers, earth, and pure male. She found the combination sexy but tried to hide the fact.

Alexander leaned down to whisper in her ear, "Heal quickly. We've unfinished business to attend to . . . and not in a barn."

Jacqueline moaned at the exciting thought. She tried to sit up, but pain prevented her.

"Whoa, slow down," Alexander said, putting a hand on her shoulder. Your leg has been stitched up and you've fractured your arm. It'll take some time, but you'll heal faster if you lie still for a few days."

Jacqueline took in her surroundings, realizing she was in her bedroom. So Alexander had gotten her there without incident. She spotted Cookie's worried face. She was about to assure the older woman that she would be fine, but a frightening thought flooded her mind.

"Where is Joseph?" Jacqueline asked. When neither answered, she tried to sit up again, but her head swam and she felt a sudden wave of nausea. She fell back in frustration. "Where is my grandfather?" she managed. "Did something happen to him? I—I can't remember and . . . what do you mean I have stitches?"

"He's resting, Jack," Cookie answered, approaching the bedside. "He's going to be okay."

"Wh-what happened to him? I remember . . . something . . . I think . . . what happened to him?" she repeated.

"Take it easy, Jacqueline. Your grandfather is going to be just fine," Alexander said soothingly. "There was a fire. Do you remember?"

Jacqueline searched her clouded memory through her pain. She remembered rain, the smell of burning wood, Pepsi, mud, and then pain. "It's all so jumbled in my head. I can't make sense of it," she said in frustration.

"It's all right. It will come back to you soon enough. Just know that Joseph is here. He'll come up to visit you as soon as he can. I promise." He stroked the side of her neck as he spoke.

Cookie smiled down at Jacqueline. "Just rest for a few more days, Jack, and then you—"

Jacqueline frowned. "A few *more* days?" she asked, confused. She eyed Alexander suspiciously. "How long was I asleep?"

"You were exhausted. You said you hadn't slept or eaten well in nearly a week and then there was the fact that—"

"How long, Alex?" Jacqueline asked insistently recognizing his stall tactic as the same one her parents used.

"A week. You've been in and out a few times, but not very coherent. We weren't sure . . . You've got a pretty big knot on the back of your head and you'd lost a lot of blood by the time I got you back here."

"I understand," Jacqueline said solemnly. She knew Alexander was trying to tell her they weren't certain she would make it at all. Truth was, she wasn't so sure she would either. She remembered small flashes of pain, Jasmine's muffled sobs, Cookie's gentle ministrations, and the sound of Alexander's comforting voice.

"I need to see Jasmine. Could you help me sit up?" she asked.

"I'm not sure that's such a good idea, Jack," Cookie stated. "You're not well and you look far too pale. You'll only worry her more."

"Well enough or not, I won't have my daughter

worried that her mother is in a coma, or worse, that I'll never regain consciousness." She looked at Alexander pleadingly. "I can hold it together if you'll help me, Alex."

Alexander hesitated, but nodded, knowing Jacqueline needed to see her daughter as much as her daughter needed to see her.

He pulled back the covers before helping her to a sitting position. He hated to hear her painful moans but knew she would have tried on her own had he not helped her.

"I'll get a brush and the water basin. We'll clean you up a bit before I send for Jasmine," Cookie offered, leaving the two alone.

"I've got to get better and soon, Alex. The rodeo is only a few weeks away and the damage the storm did . . . There's work to be done and I can't do it if I'm lying here in bed all day," Jacqueline said.

"The rodeo again?" Alexander said in frustration. "Let it go, Jacqueline. It's not worth the—"

"Yes, it is!" Jacqueline took Alexander's hand. "It's worth it to me, and it's worth it to the ranch hands. The rodeo is the only way I know for my dreams to come true. It's a way for all of us to prove something to my father."

"Prove what?"

"That we can do it," Jacqueline answered, squeezing his hand as she spoke. "This rodeo will be the first time we've done anything on our own. We've planned this thing ourselves from beginning to end. My father had no input whatsoever. Thomas and I chose every head of cattle that will be up for auction during the rodeo. We've fed them and we've raised them ourselves."

Through her pain, Jacqueline beamed with excitement. "Alexander, this isn't just a rodeo. It's a celebration of our independence and it will show not only my father that we're ready to run this place, but it will show everyone else as well. I can't cancel the rodeo, Alex. It would be too much like canceling everyone's dreams and I won't do that, no matter what," she stated, releasing his hand.

"I've got everything we need," Cookie said, entering with a large pot of water, towels, and other items. "The girls are downstairs looking for you, Alexander. I told them you'd be right down. I'll let you tell Jasmine her mother is awake. Give us half an hour and then send her up. Now shoo so I can get Jack ready."

Alexander kissed Jacqueline's hand before leaving.

After spending time with Shasta and Jasmine, Alexander made his way down to the barn. He stood in the entrance, then travelled through the crowd of male and female ranch hands who had assembled for a meeting. He came to a halt after reaching the front.

"We've got to get these pens reassembled, and arguing about it isn't getting the job done any quicker! We've all got things to do, so let's just settle this dispute and move on," Thomas said over the disapproving grunts and groans that filled the room.

Ian leaned sideways to whisper in Alexander's ear, "Jack's plan was to assemble the bull pens on the southern side of the ranch and then bring over the steers. Seems like too much work to most of us when we can just assemble them where the bulls are, on the north side of the ranch."

"Where are the plans?" Alexander asked.

Ian pointed. "Up there with Thomas."

Alexander instinctively walked forward to join the two men. He looked down at the plans spread out on a large bale of hay.

"Why can't you see the logic in what we're saying?" someone called out from the back of the room.

"Because your logic doesn't sign our paychecks!" Thomas shot back.

"It's a stupid idea and someone needs to walk right up to the house and tell Jack that it doesn't make sense!"

"Actually . . . none of you are making sense," Alexander said. The room grew quiet in response.

"What did you say?" Thomas asked, with an encouraging smile.

"I said, given these plans and the layout of the ranch, this doesn't make sense," Alexander answered, pointing down at the plans.

"Who is he to say the plans won't work? He's a city slicker who doesn't know anything. What's he doing here?" a ranch hand called from the back of the room.

"Yeah!" numerous shouts from the crowd agreed. "Get him out of here!"

Thomas raised a hand at the angry crowd. Silence ensued. "Let him speak."

Alexander held the plans high as he spoke. "As you have all said, the current plan doubles your work. The other thing is, how wise is it to put the bull pens at the rodeo entrance?"

"See, he don't know nothin'!" another man shouted.

The owner of the voice was a large, burly man of about Alexander's height and age. He stepped out from the crowd. "Jack wants them there so everyone can see our stock. She thinks that people who wouldn't otherwise think about buying bulls will get interested if they see them. If they aren't there, then no one will see them. We need them at the entrance so folks can get a gander and spend some money," he concluded.

Several heads nodded in agreement.

"I see. Well, has anyone thought about the stench that goes along with the stock?" Alexander asked. His question was met by several quizzical glances. "I realize you were all born and raised on a ranch, but let's face it. Not everyone was. Some people will be allergic or just plain offended by the smell. There is also a safety issue that worries me as well."

"Safety?" Thomas asked, concerned.

"Yes. I've seen the bull pens. It wouldn't take much for a curious child to get between the rungs and inside a pen. Once that happens, it's over . . . for the kid and the ranch."

"We hadn't thought about that and I don't think Jack had either," Thomas confessed.

Alexander pointed to an area near the lake. "You need to move the pens back here."

"But the lake area suffered a lot of damage. There's no way we can have it ready by the time—"

"You don't need to get the area ready. All you need to do is set up a huge tented or enclosed area. Make sure it's large enough to have bleachers and a podium. We can set up the pens behind the tent." Alexander was growing increasingly frustrated by the quizzical expressions. "An auction. We can *auction* the bulls. We'll bring them in ten at a time and set up a small corral where they can roam while patrons get a closer look."

"An auction! Yes, an auction!" It wasn't long before everyone echoed his or her agreement.

"How would you organize it?" Thomas asked.

"Me? No, no. I was just giving you an idea to work with. I'm not the rodeo type and—"

Thomas stepped forward, placing a hand on Alexander's shoulder as he spoke. "You can draw up your plans, carefully. Tomorrow you will present them to Jack. I'm sure she'll like them."

It wasn't a request, Alexander realized. He knew any protest would have been ignored. He nodded in response. Thomas turned back to the crowd.

"Ian," he called, wanting the man to step forward. "Assemble a team and meet Alexander down by the lake," he said.

"All right, people. That's it for the moment. You know what to do and I want it done by week's end. Let's get busy!" Thomas shouted as the crowd dispersed.

Alexander pulled Thomas aside. "How am I supposed to do this? I'm a businessman, not a rancher."

Thomas took Alexander by both hands. He turned them palm up and raised them to eye level between the two of them. "The calluses are old, but they say otherwise," he said before releasing him and walking away.

Alexander stood with his hands still extended in front of him. He studied them for the first time in years. The hard lines, scars, and calluses did indeed tell the true story of his past.

"I have the crew ready. Do you need a lift down to the lake?" Ian asked. "Alexander?"

"What? Oh, ah, yes. I'll be right there." Alexander waited until he was alone in the barn. He bent low, grabbing a handful of earth. Bringing it to his nose, he inhaled the scent deeply before opening his fingers and allowing it to scatter. While the scent was slightly different from what he was used to, he smiled in response.

Alexander entered Jacqueline's house exhausted but oddly energetic at the same time. Since her injury, he'd taken to staying over to watch her while Cookie slept and took care of Joseph. Of course, Pam and Shasta had taken to staying there as well. While his body ached from hours spent helping disassemble and move the bull pens to the other end of the ranch, internally he felt refreshed.

He entered the kitchen, surprised to find Pam sitting at the table. A foil-wrapped plate sat in the center of its surface.

"What are you doing up at this hour?" he asked, heading for the refrigerator.

"I . . . well . . . I . . . How did it go? Word is you've stepped in to help with the rodeo organization in Jacqueline's stead," Pam answered uncomfortably.

Alexander chuckled. "Well, I don't know whose words those are, but they aren't correct. I came up with a plan for one small part of the preparations. People like it, so we're going with it," he said, getting the lemonade and pouring himself a glass.

"We?" Pam asked.

"Well, the ranch hands anyway." Alexander downed the beverage before replacing the pitcher in the refrigerator. "How's Shasta?"

"Fine," Pam answered, distracted. "She fell asleep around nine, so Cookie put her to bed in Jasmine's room. She told me to ask if we can stay here for the rest of the week."

"I'm glad she's made a new friend in Jasmine, but we're out of here in the morning, now that Jacqueline's better."

"That reminds me," Pam said, turning to face him, "Ms. Ross called. She faxed your information to you and it's on the bed in the spare room Cookie set up for you."

"What did Beverly want?"

"She told me to have you call her tomorrow. She didn't say why."

"Fine. I'll make sure I——"

Alexander's words were cut off when Ian entered the kitchen. He'd come by the house to check on Joseph. He froze in the doorway, looking directly at Pam. She nearly jumped out of her seat but made a quick recovery as she leaned back. "I thought . . . I saved you some . . . Are you hungry?" she finally managed.

Ian flashed a handsome smile. "Famished," he said, joining her at the table.

Pam slid the plate and utensils toward him. She watched in silence as he unwrapped it.

"This is mighty nice of you, Pamela." He smiled, digging his fork into a huge piece of steak.

"Can I get you some juice? I helped Cookie make a fresh pitcher of lemonade . . . and there's peach cobbler for dessert," she said hopefully.

He nodded briskly. "Mm, sounds delicious."

Alexander watched Pam busy herself with the tasks. She reclaimed her seat at the table.

"Was the work very hard?" she asked.

Ian shook his head. "Not really. We had a lot of help. Even the tenderfoot pitched in," he said with a nod toward Alexander who'd moved to the corner of the kitchen and was watching them with great interest. "Where'd you learn to tie fencing like that? And you did a fine job organizing the bull pen setup," he complimented.

"Just luck, I guess," Alexander answered, leaning back against the counter.

"I see." Ian picked up a whole baked potato slathered in butter and sour cream. He took a huge bite and downed some lemonade.

"You're going to choke if you don't slow down, Ian," Pam said with a laugh.

"Sorry," he apologized. "I tend to devour what I like. Guess I've grown too accustomed to eating out on the range with the men. I'll slow down though so as not to offend your delicate senses," he teased.

"No apology is necessary, Ian, and . . . my senses aren't as delicate as you might think. Please, devour away."

Ian's and Pam's eyes met and held. Though neither said a word, they understood one another perfectly.

"I'm going to bed!" Alexander said loudly, interrupting the two. He walked by the table but stopped before opening the door. "It's getting late, Pam. I'm sure Ian won't mind finishing his dinner alone if you're tired."

"I'm not tired," Pam informed him.

"We're leaving pretty early tomorrow. You might want to get a good night's—"

"I'm fine, Alexander," she said without looking at him. "Don't let me keep you up. You look tired. Get some rest."

How the devil did she know what he looked like? She hadn't so much as glanced in his direction since Ian entered the room, and since when did she start calling him Alexander? Alexander inwardly grumbled, but finally left Ian and Pamela alone.

"See you in the morning," Pam said with a wave, though her focus was still on Ian.

"Good night boss," Ian said with a smile before returning to his food.

Upstairs, Alexander showered and changed into a pair of shorts. He frowned as Ian's words repeated themselves in his head, "Good night, boss." He wasn't sure how being called boss by a ranch hand made him feel, nor was he sure he wanted to stick around to find out.

Alexander turned out the bedroom light before falling across the bed. He grunted, realizing he wasn't sure he wanted to leave before finding out either. He put the thought out of his mind only to find Jacqueline's image invade the space. He could almost inhale the sweet strawberry scent of her. He moaned, recalling the firmness of her powerful but sexy thighs. He put the pillow over his head to block out the sound of her laughter as it echoed somewhere between memory and drowsiness. Rolling onto his side, he recalled the words that had plagued him since she'd spoken them, "I would never and could never give you my heart."

Alexander left the bed to stand outside on the balcony. He inhaled sharply, realizing the course had been set. He would not play this game any longer. He knew who he was and he knew what he wanted. He wanted her, needed her, and he would have her, body, soul, and heart.

Chapter Thirteen

Cookie walked by Alexander as if he weren't there. She wasn't the first person he saw who looked more than a little stressed out and preoccupied. He saw Thomas hurry down the stairs and out the front door, slamming it in his wake. "What the devil is going on around here?"

"She's got a temper like her father's!" Cookie grumbled, walking by him again. Cookie exhaled a long breath before speaking. "I think you should just get Shasta and Pam and go, Alex. There's nothing you can do."

"Do about what?"

Cookie looked over both shoulders and down the hall suspiciously before speaking. "She knows," she whispered conspiratorially.

"She knows?" He watched as Cookie nodded frantically. "She knows what?"

Cookie leaned in close, causing him to bend down. "About you, Alex. She knows how you changed the plans, how Thomas put you in charge, how the men have agreed to listen to you. She knows . . . everything," she said worriedly. "If you have the sense the good Lord gave you, you'd pack your bags, your daughter, your babysitter, and you'd hightail it for parts unknown before that girl gets up and about again," Cookie advised.

"But I didn't ask the men to—"

"Doesn't matter. They had a meeting in the barn at dawn and they decided you were the one to take over for Jack. And to make matters worse, Joseph okayed everything."

Alexander felt as though his heart dropped to the pit of his stomach. He tried to swallow but his mouth went dry.

"She's madder than a wet hen," Cookie whispered.

"Let me guess. She thinks I've planned this whole thing so I could steal the ranch out from under her, right?"

Cookie nodded.

Alexander walked a small circle around Cookie as he rubbed his temples. He stopped, looking her in the eye. "No. That won't be necessary."

Cookie's eyes grew wide with surprise.

"That's right, Cookie. I'll stay here until the rodeo is over or until Jacqueline is on her feet, whichever comes first. If it's permission you need, find Joseph, tell him what I said, and I'm sure he'll green-light my decision. If you need me for anything I'll be upstairs talking to his bullheaded granddaughter," he told her before heading up the stairs.

He didn't see Cookie straighten her back and smile approvingly. "It's about time," she whispered, walking toward the kitchen. "It's about doggone time!" She chuckled.

Alexander felt a migraine coming on as he paced Jacqueline's bedroom floor. He was getting tired of discussing the same issues repeatedly, but Jacqueline tenaciously insisted on not only getting her point across, but making him see things her way, which he had absolutely no intention of doing.

"This is my ranch, Alexander, and those are my plans! You can't just waltz in here, take over, and expect me not to put up a fight!" she said from her perch in a chair near the bed as she rubbed her bad leg, which was elevated on an ottoman.

"For the umpteenth time . . . I—am—not trying to steal the 1850 out from under you, Jacqueline."

"Then why did the men decide you should take my place? And why was changing my plans the very first thing you did with your new power, and why in God's name did Joseph condone any of it?" Jacqueline asked angrily.

"The men liked my plan so they're using it." Alexander said as calmly as possible. "They didn't put me in charge of anything, Jacqueline. They are ranch hands. They do the labor, not the planning. Without you they probably had no direction. I'm just a stand-in, not a replacement. Joseph knows it, I know it, and so do the men."

"I won't let you do this, Alexander. I'd rather cut off my leg than let you take the ranch from me and mine!" Jacqueline said, trying to stand.

Alexander rushed over to prevent her from getting up. Jacqueline struggled until the pain in her leg became too much for her to handle. Alexander sat on the edge of the ottoman opposite her. He watched Jacqueline fight not only her tears, but her fear of losing the 1850 as well.

"Jacqueline, baby, listen to me," he said soothingly. "I know this is hard to believe right now, but I swear to you I have only your best interest at heart."

Jacqueline snorted.

Alexander stood abruptly. "That's it. I'm not going to do this with you, Jacqueline," he said, looking down at her. "You're the one who said the rodeo had to go on. You're in no position to make that happen right now, so Joseph and the men have put me in charge. I don't know why they did it and frankly, at this point, it doesn't even matter anymore.

"The fact is that I'm going to do my best to make certain your rodeo is the best damned rodeo Oklahoma has ever seen. I'll make sure the day is successful financially, and once it's over, I'm outta here!"

He took several breaths to calm his temper. Jacqueline's continued fears that he was still out to take her ranch upset him more than he was willing to admit. He exhaled a final ragged breath. "Think about what I said and I'll check with you later this evening, but under no circumstances are you to risk your health by trying to stand on that leg again. You've got a daughter who needs you, and I mean all of you, Jacqueline. She doesn't need a mother who made herself lame because she was too damned stubborn to listen to reason," he said before exiting.

Alexander walked down the hall where he nearly collapsed into a chair. He took another long, set of deep breaths to calm himself.

"You did fine."

Alexander looked up to find Cookie standing beside him. "I don't know, Cookie. She's scared. She'll do anything to protect the ranch and everyone on it," he said worriedly.

Cookie rubbed his back. "You did a good job, Alexander. I'm proud of you. You made her listen to reason. She'll come around."

"How can you be so sure?"

Cookie smiled knowingly. "Because she'll do anything to protect the ranch and everyone on it, even if that means letting you run the 1850 until she's up to it again." She patted his shoulder reassuringly, before going downstairs.

Alexander took a few more breaths before following suit. Shasta and Jasmine met him halfway.

"Dad, Joseph said he would teach me how to ride if it's okay with you. Oh, can I, Daddy, please!" Shasta begged excitedly.

"No, Shasta. I've told you before that I don't want you anywhere near the horses, understand?"

"But our horses are safe, Mr. Hawkins, honest. They wouldn't hurt a fly, I swear!" Jasmine chimed in.

"I know, sweetie, but I'd prefer that she not." He forced himself to smile.

"But, Dad, I promise to be careful and—"

"I said no, Shasta!" Alexander growled.

Both girls stopped on the last step.

"Yes, sir," Shasta said sadly before walking away with her head down. Jasmine took her by the hand, walking beside her.

"Shasta."

Shasta turned teary eyes on her father. Alexander

approached her, kneeling down. He took her free hand in his. "I heard two more calves were born last night."

Shasta nodded.

"I think they'll be in need of names, don't you?"

"But Ian says all the calves will get sold away at the rodeo. Why name them if we won't get to see them again?" Shasta asked.

"Hm, good question," Alexander said playfully as he rubbed his chin. "Well then, I guess I'll just have to buy two Angus bull calves for my two favorite girls, won't I?"

The girls nearly knocked Alexander over as they showered him with grateful hugs and kisses. He put a hand over his ear to protect his eardrums from their excited screams.

Cookie came running out of the kitchen. "What on earth is going on out here?" she asked, seeing the trio.

Jasmine ran to Cookie. "Mr. Hawkins is going to buy the two new calves for us! We get to name them and everything!"

"Wow," Cookie said, unenthused. "And just who is going to pay for the feed for those two new baby calves when they're big ole two-thousand-pound bulls?" she asked, shooting Alexander an inquisitive look.

Shasta grinned. "My dad will!"

"What's going on out here?" Pam asked as she made her way down the hall. "A girl goes to the ladies' room for a moment and comes out to find screaming little girls jumping about."

Before the girls could answer, Ian entered the house. "We need you down by the lake, Alexander.

We can't figure out how you want the bleachers set up beneath the canopy."

"Tell everyone to take a break. I have business to attend to and then I'll be right down," Alexander answered, taking both girls by the hand.

"What do you mean take a break? There's work to be done. We've got—"

"Daddy is taking us to name the new baby calves!"

"And he's buying them for us so we can keep them!" Jasmine explained.

Ian frowned. "We can't keep them. They're going to bring in a fortune."

Both girls looked sadly at Alexander.

"But you said, Dad," Shasta whispered sadly.

"Can't it keep until after we set up the bleachers? Those calves aren't going anywhere, Alexander," Ian prodded.

"No, it can't keep. I said I'd be down after a while and I will," Alexander said through gritted teeth.

"But we've got ranch business, and ranch business comes first!" Ian insisted.

"Not anymore, it doesn't!" Alexander nearly shouted back.

"Daddy!" Shasta yelled, near tears.

"What?"

"You're hurting my hand."

"Mine too," Jasmine agreed.

Alexander released the girls' hands. "I'm . . . I'm sorry. I didn't mean to squeeze them so tight." He shot Ian an angry glare.

"I could take them . . ." Pam offered.

Both girls shook their heads and the tears in their eyes threatened to fall.

"No. I said I would take them and I will. The men will wait," Alexander said firmly.

Ian glared at Alexander in disbelief. "This isn't exactly the best way to start your leadership, Alexander. The minute I tell the men you begged off to go name some baby calves with the girls, there will be hell to pay."

He shrugged. "I don't care, Ian. My girls come first," he growled. He took a breath and looked at Jasmine and Shasta. "Well, ladies, are you ready to go see your new baby calves?"

Both girls smiled, nodding emphatically.

"Then let's go," he said, taking them by the hands again. "I was thinking you guys could name one of them Ignacious," Alexander teased.

Shasta frowned. "Ignacious?"

"Ew!" Both girls protested as the front door closed behind them.

Cookie wiped a tear from her plump cheek as she watched them walk away. "He called them *his girls,*" she said with a hiccup.

"Yes, he did." Pam nodded, sniffing back a sob of happiness.

"Lord help us," Ian said, rolling his eyes.

"What do you mean?" Pam sniffled, shooting Ian a curious look.

"Things are about to change around here, that's a fact. But I don't know if I can take a bunch of crying women every time a man does something good."

"Yeah, but that kind of good warrants tears, Ian," Pam said, still staring at the closed door.

* * *

Alexander knocked lightly on Jacqueline's door. After he returned from a hard day's work, Cookie suggested he go up to talk to Jacqueline since she'd had time to cool down.

"Enter," Jacqueline said from the other side.

"Is this a bad time? I can come back later if you want to be left alone," Alexander said, hesitating at the doorway.

"I want to talk. Would you mind coming in and sitting down for a few minutes?" Jacqueline asked, tapping the ottoman in front of her chair.

Alexander obliged. He sat down gingerly, making certain not to hit Jacqueline's leg. He looked down at the bandages. "How does it feel?"

"It hurts, but not as bad as it did before." Jacqueline sighed heavily as she searched for the right words. "Alexander, I owe you an apology. My behavior earlier today was immature and unfair. I accused you of trying to steal the ranch, the men's loyalty, and probably a dozen other things I can't remember at the moment. That was wrong of me," she said sincerely.

Alexander nodded. "Jacqueline, you've been through a lot lately, so—"

"Please, Alexander, let me finish. I've been cooped up all day with nothing to do but think about what you said, how I felt, and what I was going to say when I saw you again. Let me say this, okay?"

Alexander nodded.

Jacqueline sat back thoughtfully in her chair. She looked at Alexander wondering where to begin. "I've spent my whole life waiting for the moment I could run this ranch on my own. I've dreamt about many things and shared one of them with you. The problem was that you were never a part of anything I imagined." She smiled slightly. "You see, while I knew I wanted to turn the 1850 into a historical working ranch, I never thought I would need help doing it. But you came along and were able to see my vision and offer me a way to bring it to fruition. While that was sweet of you, at the same time, as you know, I questioned your motives. I was, however, able to get over it enough to do what was best for the ranch. She pulled out a large envelope from a pocket on the side of her chair. She handed it to Alexander and waited nervously for a response.

"I'd still like to be your partner if you're still interested," Jacqueline offered.

Alexander opened the envelope to find the legal documents for their partnership. He checked the last page and was visibly relieved to see Jacqueline's signature there.

"As I said before, there are a few changes my father's lawyers thought I should make, but they are minor and should not cause a problem."

Alexander nodded. "This is great, Jacqueline. I know how hard it must have been for you to give me these, but I promise you I will respect our agreement. I have no ulterior motives here."

"I know, Alexander. I do believe you one hundred percent," she said, fidgeting in her chair as she spoke. "There is something else you must understand though. When I was told the men voted you in to take over the preparations for the rodeo I felt betrayed and I lashed out at you. I shouldn't have done that. I saw it as the men teaming up with another man, to take what was mine.

I reacted without thinking. I just want you to know

that I believe you had no intention of usurping my authority, or of stealing the ranch from me." She paused momentarily.

"It's just that I finally made it to the point where the 1850 was mine and what happens? I get injured and confined to my room and a stranger gets his hooks into my dream. Not just part of it, but the whole enchilada. I was nearly blind with fear and anger."

"I can imagine," Alexander said honestly. "But, again, I would never do anything to hurt you, Jasmine, or the ranch, Jacqueline."

Jacqueline smiled. "I just needed to work through my own fear, that's all. Now comes the toughest admission of all." She straightened up in her chair. "After Bryce . . . my husband . . . died, I put any thoughts of love, romance, passion, and sharing my life with a man completely out of my head. I pushed away anything that wasn't related to my daughter or the ranch. So, when you came along, I pushed you away as well. I never expected to feel the way I do about you, Alexander. I didn't know how to deal with it. I wanted you, but I didn't want you to get too close. At the same time, there were moments when I thought I wouldn't be able to breathe unless I saw you."

Alexander looked surprised at the statement. He smiled. "Well, you did a terrific job of hiding it. I was beginning to think you regretted our being together in the barn. I figured I'd help out around here until you were feeling better and then get back to the city and my own life." He chuckled.

"I know, and I'm sorry. It's just that I'm not accustomed to needing or wanting a man in my life. I guess I thought of it as a weakness I couldn't afford. As you once told me, I have a daughter to raise and a life to live. There is no time for foolishness."

"I don't think those were my exact words, but they're close enough." He chuckled once more and then grew serious. "Jacqueline, I know you must have loved Bryce tremendously and I'm sure he loved you as much. I don't want to replace him, I know I never could, but—"

"You're wrong, Alexander."

"About what?" he asked, puzzled.

"I loved my husband very deeply, but what Bryce loved was the ranch. Not me," she confessed sadly. "Like most of the people here, Bryce was born and raised on the 1850. We grew up together. He was my best friend and . . . God, my father loved him like a son."

Jacqueline wiped a tear from her cheek as she spoke. Alexander didn't think she even realized she was crying. He leaned forward, taking her hands in his. "You don't have to do this, Jacqueline."

"Yes, I do. Please, I want you to know. I need for you to know so you can understand, Alex," she pleaded.

She continued when he gave her hand a gentle squeeze. "Bryce was a born rancher. Everything he touched prospered. There wasn't a task on the 1850 he couldn't perform with his eyes closed. I truly think he was created for this kind of life. He was magnificent.

"I used to spend hours watching him ride, rope steer, catch horses, mend fences . . . I couldn't get enough of him. He was poetry in motion as they say." She smiled reminiscently.

"Now, don't get me wrong. Bryce was good to me. He just didn't love me the way I loved him. To him, I think . . . I was a best friend, a confidante, someone he knew would always look out for him and take care of him when he needed it, which wasn't often, but the times he would soften . . ." Her words trailed off.

"He didn't neglect you, then? I mean, did he give you what *you* needed?" Alexander asked softly.

Jacqueline thought about the question for a moment. "I suppose he did for that point in my life, and even if he didn't, I don't mind because he gave me the best gift I could ever have. He gave me Jasmine." She smiled brightly.

"I only wish that he could have lived to see her. He would have loved her completely, I think, don't you?"

Alexander saw the hurt in Jacqueline's eyes. "Yes, I'm sure he would have," he answered confidently.

"More than the 1850?"

"More than the 1850," Alexander assured her.

Jacqueline nodded and then laughed as she wiped the tears from her eyes. "Look at me, I'm a mess." She chuckled. "I didn't mean to get all sappy. I'm sorry."

Alexander leaned forward slowly. "You have nothing to apologize for," he said, kissing her softly at first.

"I—don't know how I could have been so cruel to you, Alex," she said against his lips. "I'm sorry for—"

Alexander deepened the kiss. Jacqueline moaned in response.

"I'm here for you, Jacqueline," he said, after he ended the passionate kiss. "I'm not after the ranch or the loyalty of your men. I want *you*."

"I'm here, Alex, and whether you like it or not, I'm all yours."

"Like it?" Alexander grinned. "Woman, I'm damned near ecstatic about it! Now we just have to get that leg healed so I can show you just how happy I am."

Alexander kissed her again, long and deep, before standing. "It's late and I've got to get some shut-eye. Let me help you into bed," he offered.

"That's okay. I can manage," Jacqueline said, sitting forward and grabbing the crutches from the floor near her chair.

Alexander ignored her statement. In one easy motion, he carefully swept her into his arms. He laid her gently on the bed. "You really have to work on that whole accepting help thing," he said playfully before kissing her again. "Now get some rest," he instructed before pulling the sheets up. "Hmm, these feel nice," he crooned, rubbing the material between his fingers.

"One hundred percent real Egyptian cotton," she said, raising an eyebrow at him. "Care to join me?"

"You're too much, Jacqueline."

"Ain't I just enough?" Jacqueline purred. "Good night, Alex."

Alexander turned out her light before leaving the room. He made it into his own room only to throw himself into bed, fully clothed. For the first time in weeks, he slept soundly, too tired to dream.

Chapter Fourteen

The next morning, Alexander headed to the stables after checking on Jacqueline. She was still asleep when he'd entered her room and he didn't disturb her, knowing how much her body needed the rest.

He headed toward Zeus, formerly Bryce's horse, which he had taken to riding since Solomon's was killed in the fire. Today he planned to survey the entire 1850 on horseback so he would know the layout of the ranch in time for the rodeo.

Alexander checked Zeus's saddle. He put one leg in the stirrup to mount the horse when he heard someone enter the area. He groaned, put his foot down, and leaned against Zeus's massive torso.

"We need to talk to you, Alex," Thomas said, with Joseph and Ian in tow.

Alexander rubbed his temples briskly for a moment before exiting the stall. He knew the news Thomas was about to deliver would not be good.

"You won't like what we have to say at first, but

we're confident once you calm down, you'll see the logic in our suggestion," Ian offered diplomatically.

Alexander grunted. "So basically you're telling me you're about to say something that will tick me off and you know it will tick me off, but that's okay because given time, I'll come around to your way of thinking. Is that right?" The men nodded. "Well, let's get it over with then. What is it?"

Thomas spoke up. "Jack rides in the rodeo every year, but with her injured, she can't ride. If she doesn't ride, then that means she can't win. If she doesn't win, then she doesn't get the prize money, and if she doesn't get the prize money, then that throws off our financial plans."

Ian stepped forward to explain further. "If she won, we'd planned to use some of her prize money to pay the application fees and for the state and government contracts to turn this place into a historical working ranch. And we were going to start work on renovating some of the buildings before someone comes out here to survey the properties again.

"With Jack not entering, that means we won't even have the chance to win the twenty-five thousand. And before you ask, no, there isn't anyone else here who can win the women's division. The competition is going to be stiff this year. So—"

"We need you to ride in the men's division because the prize money for that category is nearly double the amount for the women's competition so it will make up the difference."

Alexander didn't so much as blink before cutting Thomas off. "No," he said clearly and then walked by them as he spotted Zeus's feed bag in the corner.

"Alexander, we need you to do this for us, for the ranch, and for Jack!" Thomas insisted, losing his patience.

"Get someone else to ride," Alexander called over his shoulder.

"I can't help you. I'm just a dumb city boy, remember?"

"Don't you want to know who the top contender for the men's division is?" Ian asked anxiously.

"No."

"His name is Quincy. Quincy Terrance," Ian told him anyway, knowing the answer would change Alexander's mind.

Alexander stopped what he was doing immediately. That was a name he hadn't heard in a long time. He growled deep in his throat but did not speak. Alexander leaned forward, placing both hands on either side of a barrel of oats and apples. He exhaled long and ragged as if he'd been punched hard in the stomach.

"We know you can do it, Alex. There's no other way. Jack told Joseph about your partnership, but we don't want you to pay for everything. There are other ways you can contribute. You're a part of the 1850 family now, Alex. We have to work together on this," Thomas said evenly.

"You don't know what you're asking," Alexander said, sounding winded.

"Yes, we do," Thomas assured him.

"I . . . There's no way I . . . No . . . I don't have the skills and there's not enough time to . . . What makes you people think I can do this?" Alexander asked, clearly confused.

"This," Thomas said, holding a piece of paper toward Alexander.

Alexander froze, paling considerably. Once able to collect himself, he took the newspaper clipping from Thomas's hand.

He didn't have to read it. He knew what it said. He looked at the image of himself at eighteen years old, standing on the winner's block as the champion in that year's most prestigious rodeo. Next to him stood an angry second-place contestant—Quincy Terrance, or Q.T. as Alexander had called the boy—who had been upset for the first and apparently last time in his life.

Alexander's hands shook as he held the clipping and an old familiar hatred swept over him. The feeling was soon replaced by a sense of loss so deep, Alexander felt he might collapse under the weight of it.

"No," he said firmly before shoving the paper hard against Thomas's chest. He walked past them, back to Zeus's stall where he tethered the bag of oats and apples to the saddle. He mounted Zeus and without a word rode out of the stable.

Ian started after him, but Joseph prevented him by placing a hand on the tall man's shoulder. "First anger, then he will come."

"But we need to talk about the—"

"No talk, Ian. He will do what needs to be done in his own time and in his own way," Joseph assured him.

"But we don't have time to wait for him to come around. And if we don't talk to him, who is going to help him get over whatever happened to make him stop riding?"

Joseph sighed at Ian's impatience. "Jack," he said, taking the newspaper from Thomas and leaving the barn.

Chapter Fifteen

Alexander used a stick to poke angrily at a small cooking fire. He turned the rabbit on the spit, not particularly caring if it burned. While the anger inside him still raged, he found solace in the clear starry sky, the open range, and the sound of a coyote's howling somewhere in the distance.

"Is there enough for two?"

Alexander turned quickly, surprised by the voice. He softened and then stood. "Jacqueline? What are you doing here? How did you get here?" he asked, hurrying to help her make her way toward him.

She smiled, walking to the campfire. "I can manage, Alex. I borrowed Thomas's truck. It's parked at the base of the ridge."

He marveled at how well she managed with just a cane. He noticed the cast and sling on her arm and felt guilty that she was there. He waited for her to sit down.

"You aren't supposed to be up and about, Jack."

Jacqueline laughed.

"What's so funny?" Alexander asked, putting his saddlebag under her leg to elevate it.

"You called me Jack. I guess that's what you do when you're mad at me. It caught me off guard."

Alexander thought about it. He had indeed called her Jack, and he was upset with her for coming outside when she was still healing from her injuries. "I guess that's right. Why would you risk your leg healing properly to come out here?" he asked.

"I knew something was wrong. Pam told me you were in a bad mood when you got in. Why didn't you stop by to see me?"

Alexander looked into the fire. "I should have, and I'm sorry. I guess I couldn't face you. I was angry and . . . I just needed . . ."

"Privacy?" she asked.

"Yes," he answered.

"Well I heard you've had a whole day to yourself, so I hope that's been enough. I promised Pam, Shasta, and the men I'd bring you back."

"How is Shasta?" Alexander asked, ignoring her statement about the men.

Jacqueline turned the rabbit before speaking. "She's fine." She smiled vaguely. "She told me to tell you she was having fun with Jazzy so take your time. She confided to me that she thinks you're out here thinking about whether or not to move back to Manhattan. She seems to think the longer you stay out here, the more positive the answer will be."

Alexander chuckled. "That's my girl, thinking positive as always."

"Alex—"

"Are you hungry?" Alexander asked, not wanting to discuss why he was there.

"Yes, a little, I suppose."

"Good, because there's plenty," he assured her, taking two plates from another saddlebag.

"Alexander—"

"So, how's your leg holding up?" He took the rabbit from the spit and pulled a small hunting knife from his pocket.

"Fine. Doc Brown took my stitches out yesterday. I just have to keep it wrapped when I'm in motion. I've got a pretty angry-looking scar, but overall it healed well. And before you ask, my cast comes off at the end of next month. Just after the rodeo," she added somberly.

Jacqueline's pain at having to miss riding in the rodeo wasn't wasted on him, yet he was not going to let her use it as a sympathy card to coerce him into doing something he didn't want to do.

"If you came all the way out here to convince me to ride in the rodeo, I'm afraid you've wasted your time. I already told your grandfather, Ian, and Thomas that I won't do it, and I meant it. I won't," Alexander said defiantly.

"Okay."

Jacqueline had a difficult time hiding the smile that threatened to break out on her face in response to Alexander's shocked expression.

"So why did you come up here?" Alexander asked, unable to decipher Jacqueline's expression.

"To listen."

"Listen?" Alexander frowned. "Listen to what?"

"To you."

Alexander rubbed his temples, but Jacqueline

leaned forward, taking his hand in hers. "That's a very telling sign of distress, Alex." She smiled. "Calm down. I didn't come up here to convince you to do something you didn't want to. I came up here so you would know that you aren't alone. Whatever this is that you're going through, I'm here. Not to lecture, or make suggestions, I'm here to just . . . listen," she said reassuringly.

Jacqueline released his hands. She wrapped a blanket Alexander had brought with him around her shoulders as she sat near the fire. "So this is me . . . listening," she said with sincerity.

"I don't know what you want me to say," Alexander mumbled as he stoked the fire. He glanced up at Jacqueline, but her expression was still unreadable. "They read the newspaper clipping, which I'd love to know exactly who and where they got it from, but they don't know diddly-squat about me. They think they do, but they don't."

Alexander groaned and sat back. He looked up at the stars, closing his eyes tight, and Jacqueline thought he looked as though he was praying. Opening them, he looked at her.

"Whatever I say, however I say it, just know something, Jacqueline. I love you. I'm not the person I used to be. I've changed and you are the reason for that change. I need you to think of the person I am now, not the person I was then, when I was lost and angry. Can you do that?" Alexander asked desperately.

"I see you, Alex." Jacqueline smiled peacefully. "I will always see you," she promised.

Alexander believed her. If he didn't, he knew he would not be able to talk about the things on his mind or in his heart. He focused on the red and orange flames and allowed himself to be drawn in by the heat from the fire. He spoke softly, keeping his voice at an even cadence as if entranced.

"I used to have a twin sister. Her name was Alexandria. I called her Drey for short. She was a tomboy through and through, so much so that I really didn't realize she was a girl until I was five or six." He smiled sadly. "We did everything together. We had friends we grew up with and the four of us became known around town as the Inseparables, me, Drey, Lana, and Q.T. The four of us were rodeo fanatics. We roped, trick-rode, raced, and competed our way through our school years. We all dreamt of starting a ranch somewhere in Texas and opening a riding school on the grounds."

Alexander inhaled sharply. "Just before graduation my sister came down with a high fever. My folks took her to the doctor in town and he gave her an antibiotic. She took it and at first it appeared that she got over it, but I couldn't shake the feeling that something was still wrong.

"It was May fifteenth, the day of the year's largest rodeo competition, we were all abuzz, or at least most of us were. . . ."

Alexander shivered slightly. Jacqueline put a spare blanket around his shoulders, but she didn't think he noticed.

"I walked into Drey's dressing tent to find her doubled over in pain. She refused to let me call for help and begged me not to tell anyone. I didn't agree . . . I couldn't. Drey said she would see a doctor as soon as the trick-riding competition was over. You see, the four of us had this plan. We had each entered a different competition and if we all won we would put the money in a savings account and let the interest grow until we graduated from college. Then we would use the money to start our ranch."

Alexander looked at Jacqueline, who was sitting as still as a tomb. The flickers of light from the campfire revealed the trails of tears streaming down her face, yet she did not make a sound. Alexander looked back at the flames, rocking slightly as he spoke.

"I told her she had to see a doctor before she rode and I made her promise to wait in the tent until I returned with help. She promised me she would," he said, almost angrily.

"I found a doctor and I ran toward Drey's tent. But it was too late. They announced the women's trick-riding competition and she was the first rider. I froze when I saw her face as she rode out to the circle. Her skin was ashen and her eyes met mine, but I couldn't move."

Alexander's words came quickly as he continued. "The buzzer sounded and she kicked her horse into a dead run. The first half of her routine was flawless. She was amazing and the crowd was with her the whole way. She ran into trouble when she had to bend to throw her hat on the ground. That's when I knew she wasn't going to make it. She kept riding and when she came around again to pick up the hat, she bent low . . . and kept falling. She was trampled beneath Jezebel's hooves."

Alexander's breath came in long gasps. Jacqueline wanted to hold him and promise him everything would be all right, but she knew it was time he faced his demons and he had to do it alone.

"When the EMS workers ran out to help Drey,

Jezebel reared and kicked wildly. Each time she came down, she landed on my sister. No one could calm her, not even my father. I finally got my feet to move and ran out there, past the workers, past the crowd of officials, the police, and the firemen."

He suppressed a deep sob. "I knew she was dead before my father picked up her lifeless body. Her eyes were open and she seemed to be staring at me. I fell down on the earth and cried like a baby.

"Do you know what hurt almost as much as losing my sister?" Alexander asked. He didn't wait for Jacqueline to answer. "Two weeks later Q.T. and I were drinking, something we both did far too frequently after losing Drey, and he got pretty drunk. We both did. He started bawling like a preschooler and told me that he'd gone to see her and convinced Drey to ride while I was off looking for help."

"In my mind, I saw him as the man who murdered my sister. I wanted to kill him. I—" Alexander was flooded with the same level of rage he'd felt back then. He released several deep breaths to calm his nerves before he spoke again.

"The truth is, I wanted Q.T. dead. I needed him to be dead, but I knew that wouldn't bring my sister back. The next day, I called Lana, and told her what happened. We emptied our bank accounts, headed for New York City, and never looked back.

"Actually, that wasn't the brightest thing I've ever done, bringing Lana with me, I mean. I would have left her behind if I'd have known she would develop a penchant for the finer things in life and leave me for a rich movie producer after six months of marriage." He chuckled softly, remembering the naievety of his youth.

Jacqueline's heart skipped a beat. It was the first sign of hope she had seen in him since his arriving. She felt Alexander's pain, but knew he was working through it, and the fact only made her respect, admire, and *love* him even more. She gasped at the realization that she did love him. She could not imagine a life without his strength and passion, nor would she want to. Now she had only to figure out how to tell him so.

"Alex, I can't take away the pain of your past any more than you can mine," she said, standing. "But if you'll allow me, I promise to spend the rest of my life giving and sharing moments with you that can replace the hurt with love and the very best of me."

Alexander was speechless. Was she saying what he hoped she was?

Looking her deeply in the eyes, he said, "I love you too, Jacqueline. I can't explain why, but I fell in love with you the moment I first saw you at the grill. Somewhere deep in my soul I knew you were meant for me and that feeling hasn't quieted or stopped my longing for you from that moment until this." He moved toward her and kissed her passionately, moving his tongue inside her mouth with wild abandon.

Alex, please," Jacqueline said, struggling. "I need you," she begged.

Alexander watched, mesmerized, as she pulled her poncho and tank top over her head, revealing full, pert breasts. She pulled Alexander toward her and he kissed her again as he began unfastening her jeans.

When her jeans, panties, and boots were removed, she busied herself with undressing him until he stood naked before her.

"I want to say this now, before we make love, so you won't think it's nothing more than passion's throes that made me say it." She waited for him to nod before telling him what was in her heart.

"I love you, Alexander Hawkins. I fell in love with you the moment you tried to jump the fence when you thought my daughter's life was in danger. If that wasn't enough, I knew I couldn't live without you when I saw you holding my grandfather in the midst of that fiery inferno during the storm. I fell in love with you the moment you told me you had already given me your heart that night in the barn.

"Most of all, I love you deeply and passionately not because of the way you feel about my family, but because of your amazing heart. You aren't the man of my dreams, Alexander," she said, smiling at the insulted look on his face. "You are the man I was afraid to dream of because I didn't dare think I could ever be so blessed. You are far better than anything I could ever have dreamt."

Alexander laid Jacqueline down gently on the bedroll he had spread out earlier. He kissed her with all the unspoken love he had harbored for far too long.

He broke their kiss to take preventive measures. Then he moved toward her.

"I don't want to hurt your leg," he said, hesitating to get on top of her.

"No problem, cowboy." Jacqueline smiled as she climbed on top of him. She didn't speak as she lowered herself slowly and determinedly down onto his shaft, enjoying the tremendous thickness and length of him. "I believe this is where we left off anyway," she panted.

"Jacqueline, God help me, you're going to be the life and death of me!" Alexander grunted, placing both hands on her hips and pulling her down deeper.

"Time will tell, my love," Jacqueline said between pants, "time will tell."

They made love passionately throughout the night beneath the starry sky with the distant calls of the coyotes and wolves as their chorus. They fell asleep, naked and perfectly satisfied, shortly before dawn.

Chapter Sixteen

Alexander heard approaching footsteps. He quickly covered a still-sleeping Jacqueline and rose to slip on his pants. He zipped his jeans and looked up just in time to see Thomas and Ian come over the ridge.

"Damn it! What are you two doing here?" Alexander whispered loudly so as not to wake Jacqueline as he walked in their direction.

"We thought Jack might need a little help convincing you to come back to the ranch," Ian said, "but it looks like—"

"Watch it, Ian," Alexander warned.

"Sorry, Alex. I was just kidding."

"I think they've moved beyond the kidding territory and into serious ground," Thomas said, gesturing to Jacqueline.

"Over here," Alexander said, moving away from the camp.

"Now tell me why you're really here, because I

know you didn't drive two hours to see if I was coming back. My daughter is still at the ranch, so the question was an obvious excuse. Now what's going on?" Alexander inquired.

"Fifty head of cattle are missing and so are nearly seventy horses, all mares so far as we can tell," Thomas blurted out.

"What?" Alexander roared, surprising both men. "What do you mean they're missing?"

"Calm down, Alex. This sort of thing happens all the time. This is cattle rustling territory, so—"

Alexander stood up abruptly. He paced back and forth in contemplation. They needed every one of the horses and steers back and they needed them before the rodeo. Jacqueline had sunk nearly every penny into purchasing the Angus bulls, and the sale of the yearlings and cows and bulls was the only way they were going to stay afloat regardless of who won the riding competitions. He knew it and so did they.

"Get back to the ranch. Take Zeus with you. Ride around a few of the other ranches with him in a horse trailer and—"

"Why do we have to take Zeus? We can go a lot faster if we leave him in the stable," Ian said.

"You said only mares were taken, right?"

Ian nodded. "Yeah."

Alexander rolled his eyes with irritation. "The horses we are auctioning are all part of Zeus's herd. Trust me, if anyone is going to find those mares, it's going to be their stud. If we can get him close enough, he'll smell them and probably raise all hell trying to get to them."

Understanding dawned on both Thomas's and Ian's faces.

"Damn, he's good!" Ian admitted.

"How did you think of that?" Thomas asked, amazed at the logic.

"Get going. Jacqueline and I will leave shortly. Don't forget Zeus. I'll drive Jacqueline back in Thomas's truck."

Alexander waited for them to leave before returning to Jacqueline. He laid beside her and she woke slowly.

"Mm, good morning, handsome," she said with a smile, turning to face him.

"Good morning, beautiful," Alexander said. "I have something to tell you."

"Mm, will it keep until you give me a proper good morning greeting?" She asked, sliding her hand down the front of him.

Alexander wanted nothing more than to make love to her, especially in her seductively disheveled state, but he wasn't sure how she would react to hearing Thomas's and Ian's news.

"That's just it, love," he said, putting his hand on hers and holding it still. "I don't know how you are going to react to what I have to say, so I thought I would at least tell you now and let you decide how . . . and when you wanted to move going forward."

"Forward, backward, up, down, I can move any way you want to, Alex," Jacqueline teased, kissing his neck. She felt him tense and looked up at him. Realizing he was serious, she released him. "I'm listening," she said with concern.

Alexander explained the situation in detail. Once

she got over the initial shock of it, she responded, "Your decisions were excellent, Alex. I honestly don't think I could have done better. You're right, we need to get back to the ranch and figure this all out."

"I'll get everything ready to go," Alexander said, getting up.

"Whoa, slow down there, cowboy," Jacqueline said, pulling Alexander back down. "I said we needed to get back to the ranch, but only a crazy woman would walk away from a naked man with your physique to rush off for a dusty drive and a long day at the ranch. You're not going anywhere yet, mister," she informed him.

Alexander smiled with relief. "Thank God, because I was wondering how I was going make that drive without having kissed, tasted, or filled you up this morning, woman."

Jacqueline laughed, but the noise was soon replaced with sexy moans of pleasure as they made love beneath the midmorning sky.

"Daddy!" Shasta screeched, running at Alexander full-force.

He managed to get both feet on the ground and close the door to the truck just in time to scoop his exuberant daughter up in his large arms.

"I missed you, Dad! Did you miss me?" Shasta asked, showering her father with wet kisses all over his face.

Alexander laughed. "Of course I did, pumpkin! A day without you is like a lifetime without air and sunshine," he said with a growl.

Shasta giggled excitedly.

"Goodness, girl, I think all this Oklahoma fresh air and food has made you grow!" Alexander said, putting her down.

"Daddy, you're not supposed to talk about a lady's weight or her size. It's rude!" Shasta said, putting one hand on her hip.

"Oh, I'm sorry, pumpkin, I just mean that I think you're getting taller," Alexander said quickly.

Shasta's eyes lit up. "Really? Do you mean I might not be short like Mother, but maybe I'll be tall like you?" she asked hopefully.

"It's quite possible," Alexander said thoughtfully.

"Did you have fun out on the range, Daddy? Did you catch any wild horses?" Shasta pulled on Alexander's shirt, causing him to lean down toward her. "Someone stole our horses while you were gone, Daddy. I told Pam they only did it because you weren't here. If you were here, you would have prevented them from stealing," she whispered.

"That's why I'm here now, pumpkin. The men and I will find them."

"And, Dad, someone stole Peaches and Cream, too," Shasta said sadly as tears welled in her eyes.

"Peaches and Cream?" Alexander asked, perplexed.

"My and Jasmine's new baby Angus bull calves. Did you forget about them already?"

"Oh yes, Peaches and Cream. No, I didn't forget about them." Alexander knelt down in front of his daughter. "Don't cry, pumpkin. I'll find your calves and have them back here by the end of the week. I promise." He hugged her tightly. "Now go inside with Jasmine. There's going to be a lot going on out here and I don't want the two of you getting hurt."

Shasta kissed Alexander's cheeks. She hugged him and whispered in his ear, "I trust you, Daddy, and I'm glad you and Ms. Jacqueline are together now. She makes you look very happy," before running off hand in hand with Jasmine, who had given her mother just as exuberant a welcome.

Thomas approached Alexander.

"Did Zeus find the horses?" Alexander asked.

Thomas shook his head. "Not yet."

"Get everyone here and . . ." He paused as his cell phone went off.

"Hello? Beverly, can I call you back? I'm right in the middle of something and I . . . What! Are you certain? No, I'll handle it myself!" Alexander hung up. "Damn it!" he said angrily.

"Alex, what is it?" Jacqueline asked.

Too angry to speak, Alexander walked to the truck, got in, and started the engine.

"Where are you going?" Jacqueline asked, standing near the driver's-side door.

"To town," Alexander said through gritted teeth.

"I'm coming with you," Jacqueline said, preparing to go around to the other side.

"No!" Alexander growled. "Not this time, Jack." He drove off and left a cloud of dust in his wake.

"Thomas, Ian!" Jacqueline called. The men came running. "Follow him in Joseph's truck, and don't let him out of your sight," she instructed.

"He's probably just going to town to pick up an important fax or something," Ian offered, though he didn't quite believe his own words.

"Whatever he's going to do, there's going to be trouble," Jacqueline said stiffly.

"What makes you say that?" Thomas asked.

"He called me Jack."

The two men looked at one another. They nodded in understanding before getting in Joseph's truck.

Alexander had spent the drive into town talking to Beverly on his cell phone. He skidded to a halt and turned off the engine. He got out, slamming the door behind him.

"Call information and get the number for the bank here. It's First National Bank and Trust of Verona, Oklahoma. Call the bank, get the fax number, and send me the information."

"Alexander, are you going to be okay? You sound upset," Beverly said worriedly.

"I'm fine, Bev, now get me that info A.S.A.P. And thanks, you did an excellent job," he said, hanging up and entering the bank.

Alexander walked to the doors leading to the back offices. A tall, gangly security officer guarded them.

"I need to speak to the manager," Alexander said, trying to get by the guard.

"Is he expecting you?"

If he expected me, he'd have run for the hills by now, Alexander thought angrily. "No," he answered impatiently.

"You can call to make an appointment or leave a message with one of the ladies at the desk up front," the guard suggested. Folding his arms across his chest, he spread his legs, planting them firmly.

"I need to speak to him now," Alexander insisted.

The security guard pulled a walkie-talkie from his side. "Is Mr. Davis busy, Pearl?" he asked, speaking loudly into it.

"Benjamin is always busy, Bill, you know that," came the answer.

The guard replaced the walkie-talkie. "Sorry, he can't see you right now. Just leave your information at the front desk and I'll see to it that he gets it."

"I don't think you're understanding me," Alexander said through gritted teeth. "I need to see Benjamin right now, and one way or another I'm getting through that door."

Alexander saw the man nod to someone behind him. He didn't have to turn around to know two more guards approached.

"Is there a problem here?" one of the guards asked from behind Alexander.

"Not unless you don't let our friend here pass," Ian said in a deep and intimidating voice from behind the two guards.

Alexander felt relief wash over him. *Thank God for stubborn country boys,* he thought. While he didn't doubt he could take on the three guards, he wasn't certain he wouldn't have gotten arrested by the time he was through with them and able to see Benjamin.

He turned around to see Thomas and Ian standing just as firmly behind the two guards. Thomas stepped through the small group to stand before the original guard at the door.

"Let him pass," he said.

The guard hesitated but eventually moved aside. "He's got five minutes," he said as if the threat mattered to anyone but himself.

Once inside, Alexander entered Benjamin's office, closing and locking the door behind him.

"What the devil?" Benjamin protested, standing up.

"Sit down, Ben," Alexander said firmly.

"How dare you barge into my office! I'm calling security!"

"There are twenty-seven bones in the human hand, Benjamin. Touch that phone and I'll break every one of them," Alexander threatened. Benjamin released the phone. "Now sit down." Alexander waited for him to take the seat behind his desk.

"My name is Alexander Hawkins. I—"

"I know who you are, Mr. Hawkins. I know everything there is to know about you," Benjamin assured him. "Truth is, I was expecting you. Actually, I'm surprised it took you this long to figure things out. You disappoint me, Alex."

Alexander ground his teeth sharply. "What the hell's going on around here, Ben?" he asked suspiciously. "Who started the fire down by the lake at the 1850? Who stole the horses and the Angus bulls? How can a man who is at the top of the beef supply industry be in debt to a town full of people? And while you're at it . . ." Alexander leaned forward, coming face-to-face with Benjamin. "Perhaps you can explain how a ranch that produces millions of dollars in revenue each year suddenly stands knocking at bankruptcy's door."

Benjamin sat back, unintimidated. He withdrew a cigar from an expensive box on his desk and picked up a gold lighter. He brought the cigar to his lips to light it, but Alexander reached forward, snatching it from him so quickly Benjamin froze in surprise. He watched as Alexander crushed it, allowing the tobacco and paper to fall to the desk.

"Are you sure you want to play this game with me, Ben?" Alexander asked menacingly. "Because, trust me, I can guarantee that I'm a hell of a lot better at it than you are."

"Be careful, Alex," Benjamin warned, "I only have to push this little button and the room will fill with security guards."

"You mean the ones that are out there shaking in their boots and huddled in a corner? Or perhaps you mean the Moe, Larry, and Curly who cowered the moment Ian and Thomas walked in?"

"I—I have more than just three or four guards," Benjamin said unconvincingly. "They're in the back guarding the vault."

"Then they should enjoy seeing the rest of the men I sent for, who should be here—" Alexander checked his watch—"right about . . . now."

Benjamin's beady eyes widened almost hysterically. "I'll call the police," he threatened.

Alexander was growing tired of Benjamin's lies. He was wasting time. He needed information, and he needed it now. He had made his daughter a promise and he was determined to keep it even if it meant beating Benjamin to a bloody pulp.

"I don't have time for this!" Alexander said, rounding the desk and pulling Benjamin up by his collar. "Start talking before you haven't any teeth left to—"

"All right, all right!" Benjamin yelled, throwing his hands in the air in surrender. "I'll tell you what I know!"

Alexander was grateful the little weasel didn't call his bluff. He released Benjamin the moment he heard the fax machine on the edge of his desk begin producing papers.

"Don't even think about lying, because I've already got most of the information I need right here in black and white," he threatened, retrieving the pages.

"Are you sure you want answers to your questions, Alex?" Benjamin asked, narrowing his eyes at him.

"You know what they say, Ben. Knowledge is power."

"Yes, but knowledge can also be a burden."

"Just tell me what I want to know so I can be on my way."

Benjamin sighed. "I told him it would come to this, but did he listen? No." He withdrew several folders from a locked drawer in his desk. "He told me everything would run smoothly and said I shouldn't worry. He said you'd be too busy chasing your tail to ever get wise to the plan." Benjamin threw the folders on the desk and sat back in his chair. "It's all there."

Alexander took the folders to a chair near the door. He sat down and began reading.

Half an hour later, Alexander looked up, stunned. "This can't be right," he said with disbelief.

"Check the signatures. Here's a bank draft from three months ago."

Alexander got up to take the slip of paper from Benjamin. He checked the signature against those in the folder.

"It doesn't make sense," he said, sitting down again.

"It's what he wanted." Benjamin felt sorry for Alexander. "Look, you don't have to worry about it. Jack's going to be okay. She'll have a hard time at first, but—"

"But, why would her father want her to think the ranch was on the brink of bankruptcy, and how could he have gotten so many people to play along with the farce? Solomon would have had to pay off an entire community to pull this off."

"Folks around here don't need a reason to help him when he asks for a favor no matter how strange the request, and that includes me," Benjamin answered.

"I don't get it." Alexander mumbled. "The old man leaves his daughter in charge of the ranch while he travels abroad for a year. He lets her believe everything is fine, then sneaks around town talking store owners and bankers into lying to his own daughter thereby making her think she's in debt up to her ears? He even goes as far as to let her spend nearly every dime of her savings to save the place? Why?"

"Maybe his plan is to sweep down at the last moment to save the day. He'll look like the hero and Jack will think herself a failure to the point that she'll finally stop badgering the old man for more responsibilities around his ranch."

Alexander considered Benjamin's words. Finally, he shook his head in disagreement. "No, I'm not buying that. I spent months working with Mr. Carr, and that doesn't sound like him. I'd be willing to bet that this was a test to see just how badly Jacqueline wanted to keep the ranch running and how hard she was willing to work at making it a success. She had to either use her own money, or let the place sink."

Alexander stood, handing the fax papers to Benjamin as he did so. "What better way to see how resourceful, intelligent, and determined someone is than to strip them of everything they thought they had, and leave them with nothing but their own devices?" he wondered aloud.

"Maybe the old man's just lost it."

Alexander wasn't certain why, but Benjamin's comment angered him.

"Where are the horses and livestock?" Alexander asked, forcing himself to remain in control of his senses.

"I'm afraid I can't tell you that."

"If you don't, I'll be liable to break your neck!"

Benjamin's eyes widened. He brought a hand up to rub his neck. He wrote something on a piece of paper. "Memorize the directions and then burn the paper. I wouldn't want anyone to find it and recognize the handwriting," he said, passing the paper to Alexander.

Alexander read it and left the office.

As he walked down the corridor, he tried to process the new information. It still made no sense to him. Jacqueline stood to lose everything she held dear because one man had the ability to take it all away. Why would Solomon do something so callous? he asked himself, but then remembered his original intent had been worse.

Alexander strode past Ian and Thomas. He stopped when Ian called his name before he could get in the car.

"What happened? What's going on?" Ian asked.

Alexander handed him the piece of paper Benjamin had given him. "We'll find the bulls and the horses there. We'll go as soon as we get everything we need," Alexander said, getting in the truck.

Ian passed Thomas the paper. "What the devil are they doing all the way out there?" Thomas asked.

"The question is, how did Benjamin know they were there?" Ian commented.

The two stood, looking at Alexander for answers.

"Let's get back to the ranch. We've got horses and cattle to rustle and a rodeo to put on next weekend," Alexander said before closing his door.

He started the engine and drove over to them as they walked to Joseph's truck. He rolled down his window and they stopped.

"Thanks for backing me up, fellas. It was—I appreciate it," he said before driving off.

"What do you suppose happened in there?" Ian asked no one in particular.

"Don't know and don't care. He's riding for us and that's what matters," Thomas answered.

Alexander sat on the edge of Shasta's bed. He held her small, delicate hand in his as she slept. It had been an emotionally draining day and he was grateful for the few stolen moments he was able to muster to read to her until she fell asleep.

He put the book down on the nightstand before kissing her soft cheek, turning out the light, and exiting the room making certain he closed the door quietly. He checked his watch, knowing Pam would return momentarily.

He was startled to find Jacqueline sitting in the chair outside the room.

"I didn't want to intrude on your time with Shasta," Jacqueline said, standing.

"Were you waiting long?" Alexander asked, walking with her down the hall.

"Not long at all. I got Jasmine bathed and in bed and we talked for a bit. She wanted to sleep up here with Pam and Shasta, but I told her she needed to get some rest, which is something poor Pam needed as well. I know the two of them have been running her ragged." Jacqueline smiled. "She fell asleep shortly after that. She's growing so fast, Alex."

"I know what you mean. I swear they've both grown two inches in the few months we've been here," he agreed. "So is everything all right?" he asked as they descended the stairs.

"I was going to ask you the same thing," Jacqueline said, raising an eyebrow at him. "You left so suddenly and then didn't tell me what happened once you returned. Thomas said you located the cattle and horses, and are going after them in the morning, but he wouldn't say anything beyond that."

"Nothing else to say."

Jacqueline put a hand on his arm to stop him. "Alex, I know something is wrong. What is it?"

Alexander wanted nothing more than to tell her what he'd discovered, but he wasn't quite certain what it all meant. He thought it best not to discuss it until he had time to sort it all out in his head.

"Are you hungry?" he asked, trying to change the subject. "I'm hungry. Why don't we go see if Cookie has anything we can scrounge up?" He hurried ahead of her before she could answer.

"Alex," Jacqueline said, stopping him in his tracks. "I thought we'd already established that you could tell me anything and I'll listen. While you and I have ventured into romantic territory, I'll remind you that the 1850 is still my ranch and what goes on here is my business. I'm sure you think you're protecting me, but I don't need protection, I need answers. These are my bulls, cows, and horses out there and I want to know where they are and how the devil they got there."

"Jacqueline, please. I have to work this out in my head. I know I can talk to you, but now is not the time."

"But—"

Alexander's cell phone rang. He held up a finger to stay her words when he answered.

"Hello . . . Lana . . . what do you . . . yes, I've got a minute." He walked away from Jacqueline and into the library, closing the door behind him.

Jacqueline stood as if frozen. So that's how it was? He could keep secrets from her and not share information? His ex-wife could call and get his undivided attention even if he was in the room with her? Jacqueline stifled a jealous surge. *Fine,* she thought, *talk to your ex, but don't come running to me when you have problems.*

Chapter Seventeen

The next morning, Jacqueline was nearly trampled in her yard by a group of excited children as they ran past her.

She chuckled. "Hey, where's the fire?"

"Sorry!" a chubby little boy called over his shoulder.

"Ollie, where is everyone going?" Jacqueline asked, watching as several other groups dashed by.

"To see the hawk!" Ollie said impatiently.

"What hawk?" Jacqueline tried to recall anyone telling her about a new baby hawk or an injured one, but drew a blank.

"He's practicing his trick routine and he's funny to watch. His horse throws him off and then he curses, remounts, and then tries again. He's very, very funny!" Ollie said, wobbling off in the direction of the corral.

What kind of hawk rides a horse? Jacqueline wondered. Suddenly, she gasped in horror. "No!" she said, filled with fear before using her cane to do some waddling herself.

Jacqueline watched as the horse stopped abruptly, causing Alexander to go flying. He landed with a loud thud and the crowd groaned in unison. She spotted Thomas, Ian, and Joseph and began making her way through the crowd.

"You're riding too high, Alex. He doesn't like it. Sit back in the saddle until it's time to make the catch, then lean down and forward!" Thomas instructed.

Alexander tried again, and again the horse threw him.

"You're still too high! Try it again!" Ian shouted.

"It's not me, it's this damned stubborn horse!" Alexander said, getting up and brushing at his jeans. "Do that again and I'll punch you so hard you'll see stars. Now hold still!" Alexander threatened the horse.

Ian cracked up. "It's like a scene from Blazing Saddles."

"Get him down from there," Jacqueline said, nearly out of breath.

"Jack, hey, good to see you out and about," Thomas called down to her from his seated position atop the wood fencing.

"I said, get him down, now!" she insisted.

"What's gotten into you, Jack? He's a little raw, but—"

"Thomas, I'm not kidding! I want Alexander down and off that horse."

"Give it a minute, Jack. The horse is bound to throw him again," Ian said, laughing.

Jacqueline was about to let loose her temper when Joseph approached her. "What is it, Granddaughter?" he asked, concerned.

Jacqueline turned tear-filled eyes on him. "We can't ask him to do this, Grandfather. You have no idea what he's been through. You can't ask him to ride against that horrible man. Not for our sake or for the ranch. We'll find the money some other way! Please, Grandfather, make him get down," Jacqueline pleaded.

Joseph looked up at a stunned Thomas, who had never seen Jacqueline cry before. Ian also looked perplexed. Joseph nodded and Thomas called a halt to the practice. Disgruntled ranch hands slowly began to disperse.

Alexander rode over. "What's the deal? We've got at least another half hour before—" He too was stunned by the expression on Jacqueline's face. He immediately dismounted, squeezing between the rungs in the fence to get to her quickly. He stood worriedly looking at her. "Jacqueline, baby, what's wrong? What's happened? Are the girls all right? Is it your leg?" He paused. "Oh God, is it your parents, are they—"

"Come," Joseph said, gesturing to Ian and Thomas, who were mesmerized by the scene. When neither man moved, Joseph hit Thomas so hard on the shoulder that he nearly fell off his perch atop the fence. "Come!" Joseph reiterated before walking away.

Jacqueline watched them walk away. She kept her head turned away from Alexander, not wanting him to see her tears.

"Jacqueline, talk to me," he said softly.

She looked at him then. "Please don't do this, Alex. Please don't ride in the rodeo. I know they talked you into it, but don't do this. Not for me, Alexander, please," she begged.

Alexander kissed Jacqueline's tear-streaked cheek. "Baby, I'm doing this for you, for the ranch—"

"But you don't have to! I'll find another way."

Alexander held a finger over her lips. "But I'm also doing this for myself . . . and for Alexandria. I've been running away for ten long years, Jack. I ran away from Texas, a home I loved, and my parents. I ran away from my sister's memory and friends I used to have. I've been running from myself for so long, Jack, that I don't even know if I'm the person I used to be anymore," he explained.

"You're the person I need you to be, Alex. You're the man I love and the man I want . . . forever. You are doing this for all the wrong reasons. You can't retrain your body in a week!"

Alexander blanched at her words. "Thanks for the vote of confidence," he said coldly.

Jacqueline dried her eyes. "Alexander, think about it. You know your mind has to be clear and in-the-moment when you ride. Concentration is key to doing something so dangerous."

"I don't want to argue with you, Jacqueline. We'll talk about this later. Right now I've got to get the men ready to ride. We've got cattle and horses to get. It's taken longer than I expected to find enough cattle trucks to collect the steer and—"

"There's nothing to talk about later. You cannot ride in the trick-riding competition and you know it. You're just being pigheaded. This is about taking revenge on Quincy. You're going to get yourself killed out there if you don't—"

Alexander turned to walk away. He stopped and then turned back to face her. "I'm riding, Jack. Deal with it," he said before walking away.

Jacqueline was tempted to hog-tie Alexander until the rodeo was over. Why did men have to be so bullheaded? she wondered.

"Mama! Mama! They're here!" Jasmine said, barging into the kitchen and skidding uncontrollably across the newly waxed linoleum floor. She managed to grab the side of the kitchen table, stopping herself.

"Whoa, slow down, Jazzy. What are you talking about, who's here?" Jacqueline asked, snapping peas and throwing them into a bowl on the table.

"One of these days that child is going to give us a heart attack," Cookie said, winded from just watching Jasmine.

Pam chuckled.

"Nana and Pop-Pop! They're back. They're here!" Jasmine screeched.

Jacqueline felt the blood drain from her face. "What do you mean . . . here?" she asked, hoping her daughter meant they were on the phone.

Jasmine rolled her eyes. "They're here, Mama, outside! They're getting their stuff out of the car! Come on, Mama! Come see them!" she said, before making a mad dash for the door.

Jacqueline's and Cookie's eyes met.

"Dear God," Jacqueline breathed. "I've been expecting the men for the last half hour, not my parents!" She stood, and nearly knocking the bowl of beans to the floor in the process.

"Calm down, Jack," Cookie said, rounding the table to take hold of Jacqueline's hands. She held them firmly in her own. "The 1850 is yours, remember? You rule the roost here, not Solomon or Leila. When you walk out there, you walk with confidence, you hear me?"

Jacqueline smiled nervously. "Oh yeah, sure, Cookie. I'll just stroll right up to them and say, Hi, Mom and Dad, welcome home. Don't worry about the black earth down by the lake that was burned to a crisp during your absence, and, Dad, Alexander rode your horse into a fire and got it killed. What's that, you ask? Who is Alexander? Well, he's a man I've slept with. He also saved my life when Pepsi threw me into a sinking pile of mud, which is how I got this horrendous scar on my leg.

"Alex is also the guy who originally wanted to kick us all off the ranch, but he kinda likes me so he changed his mind . . . Oh, and he pretty much runs things around here.

"I'd introduce you to him but, gosh, I can't 'cause he and the men are out trying to find the cattle and horses that were stolen from here yesterday, and by the way, we're nearly *bankrupt* because you left us all in debt and I had to use my savings to pay off half the damned town!" she said in a tumble of hysterical words. "Sure, Cookie, I'll be cool as a cucumber . . . when my father sends me packing!"

Pam chuckled. "I see now where Jasmine gets her exuberance."

"You listen to me," Cookie said gravely. "You are Jacqueline Renee Carr and *you* run the 1850. I don't care if the house burned down to the ground and your parents drove up to a pile of smoking ashes, this is your ranch, Jack. Do you hear me?" she asked, shaking Jacqueline soundly.

"Now you just march yourself out there and greet your parents like everything is right as rain. Whatever questions they have, you can either answer or put off until later, but you do not, under any circumstances, cower, cry, or get hysterical," she said with a firm shake between each word. "You are a grown woman, not a child! Remember that. Do you understand me?"

"Yes, but—"

"But what?" Cookie asked with a frown.

"But you're going to rattle my brain if you don't stop shaking me like that," Jacqueline informed her. She made her eyes cross dramatically for emphasis.

Pam burst into peels of laughter. Jacqueline chuckled and Cookie thought they were both crazy.

"I love you, Cookie," Jacqueline said on a serious note. She bent down to kiss the short woman on the cheek. "Let's go face the music," she said, turning around.

Cookie pulled her hand away. "Uh-uh," she mumbled. "That's *your* music, not mine. You go out there and handle your business and Pam and I will stay here in the kitchen handling ours."

"So you're just going to abandon me and throw me to the wolves?" Jacqueline asked, surprised.

"Um . . . yep!" Cookie confirmed.

Jacqueline smiled. "All right. Wish me luck!" She winked before leaving.

* * *

"Jack, dear!" Leila chirped, holding out her arms in greeting. "My sweet Lord, what on earth happened to you?" she said upon seeing her daughter limp down the porch steps with a cane.

Jacqueline made her way through the crowd of women. "I'm fine, Mother, just a minor mishap," she said, hugging her mother and then wincing.

Leila released her when she felt Jacqueline cringe. "What's wrong?" she asked.

"My arm is just a little sore, that's all," Jacqueline answered, trying to sound as casual as possible.

"My sweet Jesus! Sol, did you hear that? Our baby broke her arm while we were away. And just look at her leg. My poor, sweet Jack, what happened to you?" she asked, bending slightly to look at Jacqueline's leg.

Jacqueline inwardly cursed herself for choosing today of all days to wear shorts. She couldn't stand the feel of anything against the raised tender skin of her scar. Pam had finally talked her into wearing shorts as a way to relieve the discomfort of her pants rubbing irritatingly against it.

"I'm fine, my leg is fine, and my arm is fine. Everything is fine . . . really." Jacqueline smiled, hugging her mother with her uninjured arm.

Solomon walked over to them. "She probably got injured at a party she threw after we left. Too much celebratory spirits and not enough gumption to handle it, eh?"

He smiled, but Jacqueline could see the concern in his eyes.

She hugged him as best she could and relished in

the momentary comfort of his arms. "Welcome home, Dad," she said, refusing to give in to an unexpected flow of tears. She straightened, forcing herself to be jovial. "Let's get the two of you in the house and—"

"He's here! He's here! He's here!" Shasta screeched, running to Jacqueline and hugging her around the waist. "My dad is back! He's coming with the other men and they found them, Ms. Jacqueline, they found them all! I knew he would do it! Didn't you?" She beamed up at Jacqueline.

Jacqueline smiled as she pushed stray strands of sandy-brown hair out of Shasta's face. "Yes, Shasta, I knew he could do it and I'm glad he's back, too." She bent low, kissing her on the forehead.

"Did he find our babies?" Jasmine asked hopefully.

"I couldn't tell, but my dad always keeps his promises," Shasta assured her.

"And who is this adorable little lady?" Leila asked, smiling brightly at Shasta.

Jasmine turned to face her grandparents. "Nana, Pop-Pop, this is my very best friend in the universe!" she said proudly.

Shasta curtsied. "My name is Shasta Dinay Hawkins. I am very pleased to meet you, Nana, and Pop-Pop."

"My goodness, that's a lovely name for a lovely little girl with such lovely manners." Leila smiled, liking the child instantly.

Solomon laughed. "We'll keep her."

Jasmine beamed. "That would make them your grandparents too, Shay."

"Only if your mom agrees to marry my dad, which it seems to be taking forever for him to ask," Shasta said, obviously frustrated with her father.

"Yeah, what's taking him so long?" Jasmine whined.

"I don't know," Shasta said, throwing her hands in the air as she spoke. "I thought he would ask her after we caught them in the barn together that night and—"

Leila gasped, Jacqueline covered Shasta's mouth, and Solomon roared with laughter. "Okay, girls, enough chatter for now. Grab a bag and take them into the house," Jacqueline said, releasing Shasta. The girls obeyed.

"She's adorable. Whose child is she exactly?" Leila asked, raising an eyebrow at her daughter.

Jacqueline opened her mouth to speak but stopped when herds of black Angus bulls passed by only a few yards away.

"What in blazes . . ." Solomon started.

Leila noticed her daughter's face practically light up. She followed Jacqueline's line of vision to see a handsome, well-built man approaching on a massive black stallion.

Alexander, Joseph, Ian, and Thomas dismounted in unison. Several of the ladies standing nearby began whispering excitedly. Jacqueline realized they were quietly arguing over which was the most handsome. She was pleased when they unanimously agreed on Alexander.

Alexander strode up to Jacqueline, kissing her soundly on the lips. "Still mad at me?" he asked with a playful wink. He put a hand around her waist, pulling her close.

"Alexander, I'd like you to meet *my parents*," Jacqueline said, nudging him.

Alexander did not release her. Leila smiled, believing he had actually pulled her slightly closer to him.

"Solomon Jacob Carr," Solomon said, extending a hand to Alexander.

"So we finally meet," Alexander said, shaking his hand firmly. "My pleasure, sir."

Solomon got the distinct feeling that Alexander thought it anything but a pleasure.

"Mrs. Carr." Alexander shook her hand as well.

"Please, call me Leila."

Alexander smiled handsomely.

"Dad!" Shasta called as she exited the house and ran towards him.

Alexander let go of Jacqueline and knelt on one knee. He hugged Shasta tightly. "How's my girl?" he asked.

"Better now," Shasta said, resting her head tiredly on her father's shoulder. Alexander looked up to see Jasmine holding Leila's hand.

"Oh, I see. Your grandparents are back so you don't need an old city boy like me anymore, huh?" he teased.

Jasmine released Leila's hand immediately and ran to Alexander. She hugged him tightly and he relished the moment with his two special girls.

Leila raised an eyebrow at Jacqueline who looked away quickly.

"We found your calves," Alexander informed them. Both girls cheered loudly. "It's too dangerous for either of you to be outside right now with all the bulls and horses moving about, so I want you both to go inside. I'll send Ian around later to bring you down to the barn. For now, go inside and play, okay?"

The girls nodded and did as they were told.

Alexander watched Joseph, Leila, and Solomon greet one another. He looked at Jacqueline to see her reaction.

"It's going to be all right, Jacqueline," he whispered, leaning toward her.

Jacqueline offered him a nervous smile, but quickly replaced it with a cocky stare. "No problem," she said.

Alexander chuckled.

"Is that . . . Thor?" Solomon asked, shocked.

"Alex caught him," Ian boasted.

"Good job there, son. How did you tame him?" Solomon asked, amazed.

"I didn't," Alexander answered honestly. "We sort of have an understanding. I give him quality oats and fresh ripe apples and he lets me ride him . . . for a while anyway," he added, rubbing his hip.

Ian and Thomas laughed.

"Thor threw him off twice during the ride back," Jake told them, smiling at the huge animal.

"Amazing. Well, you've got yourself one fine piece of horseflesh there, Alexander, my boy. He's a bit younger and larger than my horse, but he'll do well enough. Perhaps we can go riding together sometime after the rodeo," Solomon suggested.

"Ah, actually, sir, Thor isn't my horse. He's yours and . . . well, sir, about your horse, he's . . . he's dead," Alexander felt Jacqueline squeeze his hand in support. Alexander confessed somberly.

"What?"

Alexander moved everyone inside and explained about the fire and Zeus's death.

Solomon sat quietly for a moment. "That's bad

news," he said, clearly upset. "I raised that horse from the time he was a colt. He was a good horse indeed."

"Again, I know it isn't much, sir, but I'm sorry," Alexander reiterated.

Solomon straightened. "Nothing to be sorry about. Things happened as they should have. You saved my wife's father. Seems to me losing a horse in the process is minor by comparison, and as for me taking Thor, no, thank you. That horse has too much youth in his eyes. Me, I'll just be needing a tame old horse with a calm temper. You keep Thor for yourself," he suggested.

Alexander looked at Jacqueline. She winked approvingly.

"What was that?" Leila asked, smiling.

"What was what?" Solomon asked.

"Jack knows what I was talking about, don't you, dear?"

"No," Jacqueline lied.

"What are you talking about, woman?" Solomon asked irritably.

Alexander stood. "Well, it was nice meeting you both, but I'd better get back to work before Thomas and Ian come in to carry me out."

"Oh, do you have to leave so soon?" Leila asked, hoping to grill him about the wink she saw.

"I'm afraid so. You folks enjoy the rest of your day. I'll see you later tonight with a report, Jacqueline," Alexander said.

Jacqueline nodded. She watched him exit and then turned back to her parents, who were staring at her as if she'd grown horns before their very eyes.

"What?" she asked, shifting in her chair uncomfortably.

Solomon frowned. "I take it you hired him. Why? Seems to me we've got all the help we need with Joseph, Thomas, Ian and the rest of the men."

"Seems to me, you left me in charge of the 1850, Father, which means I can hire whomever I want," Jacqueline cut in.

Solomon's surprise at his daughter's stern response was evident in his expression, though he successfully hid his approval.

"You see, Leila, I told you the girl would find her voice," he whispered proudly to his wife.

"Sit down for a moment and I'll bring you up to speed on the goings on around here since the two of you have been away," Jacqueline said, gesturing towards the sofa.

Solomon sighed, tiredly. "I've managed to keep in touch with a few discreet ranch hands so I know about the fire and most everything else. There's no need to—"

"Sit down, Father," Jacqueline insisted. Once her parents were seated she began explaining everthing that had happened since their absence. She stumbled only once as she explained how Alexander, Shasta, and Pam came to reside at the 1850. She saw her father's disapproval but ignored it, choosing instead to focus on her mother's loving expression.

The three agreed there was far too much information to process in one night. Her parents opted to save any questions until morning. It had been a long day for all of them.

Chapter Eighteen

"There you are," Leila said, sitting down on the living room sofa next to Jacqueline.

"I'm glad you're back, Mother," Jacqueline said, though she was surprised she really meant it.

Leila chuckled. "You could have fooled me. I thought you were trying to avoid me all afternoon and evening."

"I was busy checking last-minute arrangements for the rodeo. I also went down to the barn with the girls, to see their baby calves. From there I checked pre-ordered ticket sales and got the girls into bed, which was a feat in and of itself," Jacqueline said tiredly.

"It's hard to believe the rodeo is only a few days away," Leila said thoughtfully. It seems like it was just yesterday we were saying 'next year's rodeo'." Jacqueline nodded in agreement. "So what's going on between you and Mr. Hawkins?"

Jacqueline was caught off guard by the change of subjects. "What do you mean?"

Leila tilted her head and raised an eyebrow at her.

Jacqueline was too tired to pretend there was nothing going on. She exhaled sharply.

"He's the most stubborn man I've ever met," she confessed. She went on to tell her mother everything about her and Alexander's complex relationship.

Leila sat back contemplatively. "I see," she said with a frown.

"He's wrong, isn't he, Mother? I'm right, aren't I?" Jacqueline asked, frustrated. "He'll get himself killed out there if he rides in the rodeo. He just won't listen to reason!"

"Whose reason, Jacqueline?"

"What do you mean, whose? Only one of us is being reasonable, Mother, and it's me!" Jacqueline insisted.

Leila smiled lovingly. "Yes, your points are all valid and therefore reasonable, but I can understand Alexander's point of view as well."

"But his point of view is totally distorted by pain and some insane belief that winning the rodeo will give him some sort of retribution against Quincy for losing his sister."

"Yes, I know, but you're forgetting something, dear."

"What?"

"You're forgetting that men aren't made like women. You lost Bryce and you learned to deal with it. You focused on raising your daughter and working on the ranch. Alexander is a man, sweetheart, and men don't like feeling as though they have no control.

"He needs to ride in the rodeo to beat Quincy on an emotional level because he thinks that will make the pain he's lived with for so long go away."

"He's wrong. It won't!"

"He doesn't need you to tell him he'll lose. He needs you to tell him that even if he loses, you'll be there for him, and then if he loses, you need to stand by him and be there for him just like you said you would."

"But—"

"There are no buts, Jack. You either love him enough to stand by him or you don't." Leila said. "I'm glad to see you smiling again." Leila added, changing the subject abruptly again.

"What do you mean? I smiled before I met Alexander," Jacqueline said, taking offense to the statement.

Leila placed her hands on either side of Jacqueline's cheeks. "But love makes you radiant," she said before kissing her on the forehead. "Get some rest. I've a feeling you are going to be very busy for the next few days."

"What do you mean?" Jacqueline asked, watching her mother stand. "Mother?"

Leila was about to speak when Solomon entered the living room. "And how are my two favorite ladies doing this fine evening?"

Jacqueline couldn't help but smile at her father's appearance. The time away from the ranch had obviously done him good.

"We're fine Father. Care to join us?"

"Thank you, Jack, but I was actually just about to go check on—"

"Of course he'll join us," Leila smiled demurely,

which immediately clued Jacqueline that something was going on. "Your father has had something to tell you for some time now, dear. Haven't you, Sol?"

Solomon frowned, confused. "I have?"

Leila raised an eyebrow at him.

"Oh! Yes, yes of course I do," he stuttered. "Ah-well-yes . . ."

"Why don't you sit down, Father?" Jacqueline suggested.

"What's that? Oh, no, no, I'm fine, here. Close to the door." He added the last part in a low, incoherent whisper.

"Relax, Sol. I'm sure your daughter will understand everything once it's said. Now, wipe the sweat from your forehead, straighten your back, and let's get on with it, shall we?" Leila coaxed.

Solomon stood before his daughter. "Well, Jack, I-well, you see," he paused momentarily to collect his thoughts. "The 1850 isn't really having financial difficulties. We don't owe anyone in town a dime and never did. I asked all our friends to stretch the truth a bit so it would appear as though we were in debt and I had Benjamin, down at the bank, present a few *slightly* bogus financial records should you insist upon checking things out for yourself," he concluded.

"And . . ." Leila prodded.

"Oh, yes, and I like your ideas about turning this place into a working historical ranch . . . always have, actually."

Solomon stood nervously awaiting his daughter's response. The silence that fell over the room and the utter look of disbelief and horror in his daughter's eyes were nearly more than he could stand. He tried to soften things by adding, "but I did it all for you, Jack. I needed to prove to you that you could make this place work under the worst of circumstances. Staging all this was a bit difficult and perhaps a tad bit extreme but I did it for your own good."

"What!" Jacqueline yelled so loud, that even the ranch hands working down by the lake froze in response.

Alexander threw the pliers on the ground with a curse.

"Need a hand?" Solomon asked.

Alexander looked up from his kneeling position by the fence.

"I take it you just told your daughter about your insane plan and you're looking for a safe haven," Alexander said dryly.

"Indeed. I'd much rather brave the wolves and the weather than stay in there with Jack madder than a wet hen," he confessed. "You know," Solomon said, conspiratorially, "While I knew Jack would be too busy running the ranch and preparing for the rodeo to discover the ruse, I knew you'd figure it all out. Glad you didn't let me down, my boy." He smiled knowingly.

"Don't look so pleased with yourself. I was tempted on more than one occasion to tell Jacqueline what you were up to."

"So, why didn't you?"

Alexander looked at Solomon. "I guess the father

in me realized, I'd do whatever it took to help my daughter believe in herself after suffering tragedy the way Jacqueline did."

Solomon looked pleased. "Thank you for understanding."

"Don't thank me. I only said, I understood your reasoning. I didn't say I agreed with your methodology. Now if you'll excuse me, I have work to do," Alexander mumbled before picking up the pliers.

"It's awfully late for this kind of work. You can't see what you're doing, can you?"

"It's a full moon. I've got enough light," Alexander assured him.

Solomon put a hand on Alexander's shoulder. "Is it really that fence you're working on, or something else?"

For a moment, Alexander didn't move or breathe. Finally, he put the pliers down and stood. He looked at Solomon, trying to judge what to do or say next.

"It might go easier if you just start talking," Solomon suggested.

"I love her. I love everything about her. I'm crazy about Jasmine and so is Shasta. I want them in my life every day . . . for the rest of my life." Alexander paused, giving Solomon a chance to react. When he said nothing, Alexander continued.

"I can't ask her to marry me when I have no stable environment in which to raise the girls or take care of a wife, yet . . ." Alexander leaned forward, resting both arms on the fence. "I can't live without them. My original plan was to purchase the 1850 for Shasta and myself. I'm in a custody battle with my daughter's mother . . . sort of. She never has enough time to spend with Shasta, so she sends her away to a year-round boarding school. I don't want that kind of life for my daughter. She should be home—with me.

"I've gone to court five times over the last seven years, but no judge will give her to me. I travel a lot with my job, so I spend most of my time at one hotel or another. For the couple of months I'm actually in Manhattan I rent the penthouse at a fine hotel. That's no life for a child, I know, but she's mine and I want her. I thought the 1850 would make the perfect environment for her. I didn't plan to fall in love with Jacqueline. I wasn't looking for a relationship. Damn it, why did I have to fall in love now?" Alexander growled.

Solomon laughed. "Well, my boy, it seems you're no different from the rest of us after all. The papers and magazines have hailed you as America's most eligible bachelor and an impossible catch. It seems those city girls were just using the wrong bait!" he said, slapping Alexander on the shoulder.

Alexander looked at Solomon. The man looked far too pleased with himself.

"You—you had something to do with all this, didn't you?" he asked, already knowing the answer.

"Well, as you know, my daughter is a stubborn woman. She thought the ranch hands and I were all the father figures my granddaughter would ever need. And as far as love goes, she didn't think she had it in her. Not for anyone but Jasmine anyway.

"And you, I've been keeping up with your career for years. I knew about your struggle to get your daughter and I knew about your residency issues. I was told you were too pigheaded to accept any proposal I could make, so I put you in a position to make your own."

Alexander shook his head. "And the information I mysteriously received about the 1850 as well as the photos of the ranch and its estimated worth. Those were your doing as well?" he asked.

Solomon smiled proudly.

"But—how did you know so much about me and what I was going through? There isn't a newspaper or magazine who knew, so you couldn't have read about it."

A serious look crossed Solomon's face and a long silence followed. "I was at your sister's funeral, you know?" he asked rhetorically. "You were the angriest teenager I'd ever seen. Your parents thought they'd lost you when you left. We felt for all of you."

"Y-you knew my parents?" Alexander asked in shock.

"Knew them? Hell, boy, your father and I were like brothers. You were probably too young to remember, but your folks used to come up here from Texas all the time. We had a falling-out one year and we grew apart. Your mother called me when your sister . . . well, after the accident. Your father fell into such a deep depression she was afraid for him.

"Leila and I drove down and we stayed for nearly three weeks until I was finally able to talk some sense into him. He was determined to find you," Solomon said, looking sadly at Alexander, "but I told him you had to come around in your own time and in your own way. Finally, he listened to reason. But he'd come around only to realize he'd lost both his children in so short a period of time."

Alexander pushed himself away from the fence. "I didn't mean to hurt him. I was just so . . . angry and confused that I . . ." He rubbed his temples slowly and then looked at Solomon again. "I love my parents. I didn't leave because I was angry with them. I left because I thought I had let them down. I should have made Alexandria see a doctor if I had to carry her there kicking and screaming. She died because of me," Alexander said angrily.

Solomon put both hands on Alexander's shoulders. "No, boy. Your sister died because she was as stubborn as your father . . . and you. Still, she did what she felt she had to do, for whatever reason."

"I know," Alexander admitted, smiling faintly. "It took me a long time to see that, but I know it now," he said with confidence. "But that still doesn't tell me how you knew I needed a place for Shasta and me, nor does it explain—"

"Your father called and explained everything. He's been following your every move. Don't ask me how, but he has. He knew my Jacqueline had lost her husband and was raising a daughter by herself as well. We put our heads together and came up with a plan. I would give Jack the ranch and you the chance to win them both. Once you were interested, Leila and I just had to hit the road long enough for the two of you to figure the rest out on your own."

Alexander bent forward, placing both hands on his knees.

"I know it's a lot to take in, my boy, but—"

Alexander shot upright. "Damned right it's a lot! You're basically telling me that you and my father secretly planned everything that's happened this summer!" he said furiously.

Solomon remained calm. "No, son, not everything. We didn't plan for you and Jacqueline to fall in love. We're two old men who could only hope you would."

Alexander grew silent. He rubbed the back of his neck as he paced. He stopped only inches from Jacqueline.

"I know the two of you meant well, but that doesn't change the fact that I can't ask your daughter to marry me without having a place of my own. She'll never leave the 1850 and she'll never leave you and Leila."

"Never is a long time, son," Solomon said with a smile. "Now let's go up to the house. You need to get some rest. There's nothing else you can do out here tonight and nothing else you can solve at this hour."

Alexander nodded and the two headed for home.

"I have two more questions, Mr. Carr," Alexander said without slowing their pace. "Do you really expect Jacqueline to forgive you for setting her up the way you did?"

"We'll talk," he said thoughtfully. "I'm sure we can smooth things over." He was quiet for a moment, allowing Alexander to ask his next question.

"Other than finding a house and settling down, how do I get Jacqueline to trust me enough to marry me? I know she loves me, but—"

Solomon nodded in understanding and cut him off. "How did you break Zeus so quickly and get him to trust you?"

"I didn't break Zeus. He's still wild. I told you before, I give him what he needs and he does the same for me. He bucks and even throws me every now and again, but I think that's mostly show. He's reminding me that he's allowing me to ride him, but—" Alexander stopped short as understanding dawned. "I get it," he said, smiling.

Solomon chuckled. "I knew you would, son."

Alexander had just drifted off to sleep when he heard Jacqueline's whispered voice.

"Alex? Are you awake?"

He sat up groggily. "Jacqueline? What is it? What's wrong?"

"Nothing. May I come in?"

Alexander turned on the lamp above his bed. "Sure."

Jacqueline tiptoed into the room, closing the door behind her.

Alexander groaned at the silhouette of her naked form beneath her silk nightgown. He tried to focus on something else as she sat on the edge of the bed.

"Look, I don't know how else to do this, so I'm just going to come right out and say it. I'm sorry. I didn't mean it when I said you couldn't possibly beat Quincy at the rodeo. You can if you try hard enough. I figure you were roping and riding from the time you could walk and you didn't stop for eighteen years. You haven't ridden for ten, but that's okay.

"You just need a good teacher and you'll do fine. Thor, however, is another story. I talked to Joseph and he's going to work with him. That animal is more stubborn mule than horse, but if anyone can train him, my grandfather can. Joseph is going to enlist my father's help in the morning as well. So to-morrow you'll have the best roping and trick-riding teacher the 1850 has to offer."

"Thomas or Ian?" Alexander asked sleepily.

Jacqueline grinned. "Me."

"But you can't. Your leg . . . your arm," Alexander said, fully awake with concern.

"I said I would teach you, Alex. I didn't say I would ride. Actually, Pepsi could use the exercise. She has healed up nicely and aside from a few leftover burn scars, she's her old self again. I just won't put a saddle on her."

"Jacqueline," Alexander frowned. "I don't know if this is such a good idea. I was thinking earlier that maybe you were right. Maybe I can't win."

"Alexander Hawkins, you are going to win the men's roping and trick-riding competition. You are going to be so good that Mr. Quincy Terrance will regret ever having entered our rodeo. Now, I won't listen to anymore foolishness from you. Get some sleep and meet me at the north pasture tomorrow at sunup," Jacqueline said firmly.

Alexander grabbed her by the arm to prevent her from leaving. He pulled her down on the bed with him. "Fine, no more negative talk from me, if . . ."

"If what?" Jacqueline asked sexily as she lay on the mattress looking up at him.

"If you help me get back to sleep. It is your fault I'm awake at this ungodly hour after all," he said, kissing her neck softly.

"Alexander! I—we can't! My parents . . . the girls . . . there's no way we—"

Alexander slid his hand beneath the top of Jacqueline's nightgown. Freeing her breasts, he suckled one hungrily while teasing the other between his fingers. Jacqueline drew in a breath, exhaling on an excited moan. "I'm sorry, were you saying something?" he asked before moving to the other breast.

"Alex. Wh-what if someone h-hears?" Jacqueline said, only slightly worried.

"Everyone's asleep, Jack. Who is going to hear?" he asked, sliding a hand beneath her nightgown and finding the already wet nub he so enjoyed loving with his hands. "Mm, there's a part of you that doesn't give a damn about who hears," he said in a deep low tone.

"Alex . . . Alex . . ."

"What is it, baby? What do you need?" Alexander asked, sliding a finger deep within her.

"You, Alex," Jacqueline cried out, not caring who heard her. "I need you."

"Then let me in, Jack," he said, opening her legs and getting between them. She stopped him abruptly.

"Protection. Alex, we need protection."

Alexander hated these moments, but knew they were necessary. He leaned across her to reach into his wallet on the dresser. He pulled out the prophylactic, opened the package, and put it on. "Now, where were we?" he asked.

"Let you in," Jacqueline said breathlessly. "I was about to let you in."

"That's right, Jacqueline, let me in," Alexander said, sliding into the warm tightness of her. "Let me into your love," he said, pulling out so that nothing but the tip of him remained, "let me into your mind and thoughts." He entered her again. "Let me into your body and soul," he groaned, barely able to hold on as he withdrew most of himself from her again. "but most of all, Jacqueline Renee Carr, let me into your heart," he said, thrusting deeply into her and causing her to cry out passionately.

"You have my heart, Alex," she promised on a moan. "You've always had my heart."

Chapter Nineteen

Jacqueline stopped in the entryway. Her heart skipped a beat at the sight before her. Alexander wore a white shirt Leila had made for him that accentuated his barrel chest, large biceps, and deliciously muscled triceps. It boasted turquoise and onyx beads with silver collar clips at the tip of each wing.

Her eyes traveled down to a pair of jeans worn beneath his chaps, and a new pair of boots. His black Stetson that was made specifically for him topped off the look. She had to force herself to breathe as he slid his large hands into leather roping gloves.

"I swear you had better not get hurt today, Alex, because when this is over, I'm not letting you out of my bed for a week," Jacqueline said sexily.

Alexander turned toward her. He groaned deep in his throat at the sight of her. She wore a well-fitted black shirt with silver beads that hung down from fringes at her wrists. He eyed her carefully, realizing that until that moment, he had never seen her in a skirt before. The one she now wore was made of black suede. It was a straight skirt that came to a V at the bottom.

She wore black suede and leather boots, which he found particularly sexy. It was also the first time he had ever seen her with her hair brushed back from her face and in a ponytail. Atop her head was a black suede Stetson that only enhanced her sexy gray eyes.

"Forget the rodeo, woman, I vote we hit the bed right now," he said, walking toward her like a predator seeking its prey. He swept her up in his arms, kissing her soundly.

"Excuse me."

Alexander didn't bother looking up as he set Jacqueline down on her feet. "What?" he growled, not taking his eyes off Jacqueline.

"Alexander? Alexander Hawkins?"

Alexander froze and Jacqueline felt him stiffen.

He looked up and a low vicious growl that momentarily frightened Jacqueline emanated from deep within him. Jacqueline didn't have to wonder who was in the doorway. Every sensory organ in her body told her it was Quincy Terrance. She turned, surprised at what she saw.

The picture in her mind was nothing compared to the reality of him. He was nearly as tall as Alexander, and while built, he was leaner than Alex in certain areas. His rich, dark chocolate complexion was offset by eyes so light Jacqueline could think of no way to describe them other than ice blue. He was a handsome man to be sure and even the thin scar that ran down the side of his face from the edge of his eyebrow to his jawline was somehow almost sexy. He was a hard-looking man with a certain stillness that put one instantly at ease.

"Q.T.," Alexander said coldly.

"I just wanted to stop by to wish you luck," Q.T. said, offering what appeared to Jacqueline to be a sincere smile. He held out a hand toward Alexander.

"Get out," Alexander said in a harsh tone. "And when the rodeo is over, I want you out of town. Better yet, I want you out of Oklahoma entirely."

Q.T. frowned. "When this thing is over, you and I are going to have a talk, Alex. It's been ten years and we need to clear the—"

"Get out!" Alexander roared, trying to step around Jacqueline, but she held on to his arm.

Q.T. looked at Jacqueline, tipped his white hat, and left the room.

"Damn him!" Alexander said angrily.

"Focus, Alexander. Don't you dare forget anything I've taught you. Your competition starts in fifteen minutes. Forget him, do you hear me? As a matter of fact, go down to the stable and spend a few minutes with Thor," she insisted, nudging him toward the door.

Alexander opened the door but turned back to face Jacqueline. "I'll win this competition, Jack, but when it's over . . ." He pushed his hat down lower on his head. "Q.T. and I are going to go a few rounds and you will not stand in my way." He left her staring worriedly after him.

Jacqueline couldn't have been more pleased with the crowds of people who showed up for the rodeo.

She had attended the livestock auction earlier in the day and was speechless at the exorbitant amount of money made. It far exceeded her expectations.

She had watched with pride as Jasmine did her trick-riding routine perfectly, including the back flip that she insisted upon learning. She won the gold medal for her age division.

Cookie won the barbecue cook-off as well as the dessert contest and was still, hours later, proudly sporting her two first-prize medallions. A young man from the 1850 won the trick-riding competition for his age division, a young woman swept the teenage girls' roster walking away with five gold medals, while Ian took the gold for the men's races and Thomas took the silver. Joseph was still pouting over not being able to compete because of his still-aching back.

"Mama! Nana and Pop-Pop said to slow down. They've been trying to find you for the last hour," Jasmine said, out of breath.

"My dad is riding next, Ms. Jacqueline!" Shasta said excitedly.

"I know!" Jacqueline said, wondering how her life would ever be the same when Shasta and Alexander left at the end of the summer. She couldn't imagine being able to breathe let alone focus on anything without the two of them. She pushed the thought out of her mind, as she watched her parents approach.

"My goodness, you get around," Leila said, winded.

Jacqueline smiled. "Sorry, I've been keeping tabs on everything from finances to food."

"Well, it's getting ready to start. We'd better find good seats, dear."

"Jake and Jade saved us some right up front," Jacqueline informed her mother. She looked at her father. "How are you holding up?" she asked, concerned.

Solomon laughed. "Excellent! You won't find a shindig like this in the Highlands."

Jacqueline escorted everyone to their seats. She said a silent prayer for Alexander.

"My dad is going to win, won't he, Ms. Jacqueline?" Shasta asked nervously.

Jacqueline smiled down at her. "Win or lose on the field, he's a winner to us, isn't that right, pumpkin?" she asked, tweaking Shasta's nose.

Shasta smiled. "Yep! He's the best!"

Jacqueline grinned. "I agree. Now hush and sit still until it's over."

"You were amazing!" Jacqueline said, entering Alexander's dressing room. She threw herself into his arms, kissing him wildly.

She released him, smiling broadly. "The way you sat your horse was amazing and the way you performed was beyond anything either of us could have hoped for. I'm so proud of you, Alex! You were perfect! The way you threw down your hat and then kicked Zeus into a wild run and then bent to pick it up . . . and you did it three times!

"I thought I would die, the way you threw yourself over one side of Thor and landed on your feet while he was still galloping, only to do the same thing after throwing yourself over the other side, was just . . . amazing, Alexander!" Jacqueline raved.

"It did look amazing, didn't it?" Alexander asked

with a smile of his own. Jacqueline nodded exuberantly. Alexander chuckled. "Yeah, right up to the point when Thor threw me off him," he said angrily. He threw his hat down like a spoiled child.

"Alexander, I don't care about that. I'm just glad you're in one piece," Jacqueline confessed. "You were going pretty fast."

"I lost, Jack. I lost to that egocentric piece of—"

"Dad! You were great!" Shasta said, barging into the room and into her father's arms.

"Yeah, we're all really proud of you, Mr. Hawkins," Jasmine said, beaming.

"You did a fine job out there, son," Solomon said, with Leila nodding emphatically behind him.

"Thanks, guys," Alexander said, putting Shasta down as he spoke.

"Dad, you aren't going to be sad, are you?" Shasta asked.

"Maybe just a little," Alexander answered honestly.

"But you're a winner in our book already, Dad. Winners aren't always the ones who cross the finish line first. Winners are the ones who keep trying even when they know they won't cross the finish line first. That's what you did today, Dad. When Thor threw you off him, you calmed him down, got right back up there, and finished your routine. That's what makes you a winner to all of us. You never stopped trying. You didn't give up, Dad," Shasta informed her father.

Alexander hugged her close. "Thank you, pumpkin," he said, wondering if anyone could love her more than he did.

Shasta winked at Solomon in thanks for giving her the speech. He winked back in return.

"Excuse me," Q.T. said from the doorway.

Alexander released Shasta. "Jack, take the girls and your parents out of here . . . now."

"Dad, what's wrong?" Shasta asked, frightened as she looked from her father to the stranger and back again.

"Jacqueline!"

"Mom, Dad, take the girls for a waffle-cone ice cream, please." She waited for them to leave.

"Q.T., your ride was amazing. Congratulations," Jacqueline said as she walked between the two men.

"Thank you," he said, tipping his hat to her.

"Leave, Jack," Alexander said, though he was staring at Quincy.

"I don't think so, Alex," Jacqueline stated firmly, but she did walk over to sit in a chair off to the side.

"I'm not here to start any trouble, Alex," Quincy said evenly.

"What do you want, Quincy?" Alexander asked, folding his arms across his broad chest.

"I want you to understand something, Alex. I want you to take the time to listen to what I have to say, whether you agree or disagree. I want you to hear the whole story."

"I know the whole story," Alexander said crossly.

"Really? Then you know the physician called a week before the competition to tell Alexandria she had leukemia?"

Alexander's shock was obvious.

"Here," Quincy said, handing Alexander an old wrinkled paper. "Alexander, I didn't let your sister wait for the rodeo doctor because I knew there was nothing he could do to help her. Your sister made me promise not to tell anyone about her illness. I made her promise that the moment she was done riding that day, she would let me drive her to the hospital there in Texas and that she would tell all of you what she knew."

Alex twisted his face in confusion. "I—I don't understand. Why did she ride if she was that sick?"

"We're talking about your stubborn sister here, Alex. She wanted us to have that ranch and she wasn't about to risk not getting it by failing to ride in her portion of the rodeo."

Alexander thought about Quincy's words. "All right, you've told me. Now get out."

"Not until I give you something else, too," Quincy said, handing Alexander a small piece of paper.

Alexander took it. He looked down, frowned, and then looked back at Quincy. "What is this?" he asked, staring hard at the three-hundred-thousand-dollar check.

"I've saved all my winnings for the past ten years. I was never sure what you and Lana were doing, but we had a deal and I stuck to my end," he said, turning to leave.

"Wait," Alex said, "let's talk."

An hour later found Jacqueline and Alexander sitting alone in the small room.

"You did good, Alex. I know how hard that must have been for you," Jacqueline said, offering him a beatific smile.

"I just can't believe it all. This morning I was ready to kill that man, and now here I sit, about to start a ranch of my own in Texas with him as my ranch manager and partner. Drey would be so proud of us. She always wanted a school to teach kids how to rope and ride and help them understand the importance of taking care of animals and such. A ranch that is also a school . . . Ten years ago I would never have thought Q.T. and I would eventually start one," he said, filled with amazement.

"Well, Lord knows that between the two of you, you've got more than enough money to do it." Jacqueline laughed, but it faded quickly.

"What's wrong?"

"I just don't know how I'll . . . I'm going to miss you and Shasta terribly, Alex." Jacqueline sniffled, teary-eyed.

Alexander smiled nervously. "You don't have to miss us, Jacqueline."

"Wh-what do you mean?"

Alexander got down on one knee before Jacqueline. "Marry me, Jacqueline. Marry me and I promise to spend the rest of my life making you and Jasmine happy," he blurted out.

"Oh, Alex, I wish I could," Jacqueline said, the tears coming quickly now. "Don't you think I've thought of this? The truth is, I know you would never move to the 1850 with Jasmine and me permanently. You're too proud for that. But I can't leave my home or my history. Manhattan isn't the kind of place I can bring up my daughter. God, I love you, but I just don't see how it could work. Besides I've got to figure out how to raise the money to turn the 1850 into a historical ranch."

"Then let me help you," Alexander said, taking both of her hands in his. "While Quincy and I are looking for a place to build our ranch, and while it's being prepared, Shasta and I can stay with you and Jasmine on the 1850.

"Once our place is ready, we can all split our time between there and the 1850. As far as Manhattan is concerned, I can sell my half of the business to my partner, Beverly, who has been dying to run things on her own for quite some time now. We can use that money to start work on this place . . ."

"No, Alex. That's your money for you and your daughter. I could never—"

"Now who's being too proud?"

"I think it's time for me to go home, Jacqueline. My parents, my family, everything I am in love with—except for you and Jasmine are in Texas. We'll build the ranch there. It's only a few hours' drive from Texas to Oklahoma. We can divide our time between the two ranches. What do you think?" Alexander asked, hopefully.

Jacqueline didn't hesitate. "I think I'm marrying the most wonderful man on the planet." She grinned. "You are amazing, Alex, and I love you."

"So, does that mean . . . will you marry me Jacqueline Renee Carr?" he asked again.

"Yes, Alexander Hawkins, I will marry you," Jacqueline said, kissing him deeply.

Two very shrill and recognizable, ear-shattering screeches sounded from the open doorway. Jacqueline and Alexander looked in that direction with surprise. The girls jumped up and down excitedly, hugging one another while babbling something about being sisters. Solomon put an arm around Leila, who was so filled with joy she was crying.

Ian and Pam stood behind them grinning at one another like two lovesick teenagers, while Joseph danced about in the background singing something in his native tongue. Thomas remained his usual calm self.

Alexander leaned forward to whisper in Jacqueline's ear, "Do you think we'll ever get enough peace and quiet to enjoy that week in bed you promised me?"

Jacqueline kissed him and then smiled. "Only time will tell, Mr. Hawkins," she answered. "Only time will tell."

Epilogue

Hundreds of cars dotted the designated parking areas on the 1850. Throngs of people, some with bags containing keepsakes and presents purchased from one of the gift shops on the property, walked about the grounds, entering and exiting newly erected structures. Children took full advantage of free pony rides and adults enjoyed several slide shows and videos of vintage footage taken of what life was like years ago on the beautiful ranch lands.

"How does it feel to see your dream come to fruition?" Alexander asked, pulling back on Thor's reins.

Jacqueline smiled as she observed the busy ranch from her vantage point atop the highest hilltop overlooking the 1850. She stroked Pepsi's long neck calmly as the horse whinnied and moved closer to Thor.

"This is beyond anything I ever dreamed," she confessed. "I knew turning the 1850 into a historical working ranch would be a good idea, but I never thought it would be so successful and I hadn't realized how much revenue tourists would bring the town once we opened the ranch. I'm just as amazed a whole year later as I was the first day we opened our doors to the public." Jacqueline smiled.

"And you? Did you think we would be so successful that we'd be interviewed by every magazine and news show in the country?"

"I can't say that I did," Alexander confessed. "You've done an amazing job, Mrs. Hawkins," he added proudly.

"I couldn't have done it without you, Mr. Hawkins," Jacqueline beamed. "If it hadn't been for you, I wouldn't have been able to get the government grants pushed through so quickly. Let's not forget that it was your brilliant idea to provide sections for the 4-H and equestrian competitions in addition to the Future Ranchers of America summer camp for kids."

"Well, I had a little help on the last idea," Alexander confessed. Both adults turned their attention towards Jasmine and Shasta who sat astride their ponies on either side of their parents. The girls chatted excitedly with one another.

"And just what are the two of you up to?" Alexander asked his mischievous daughters.

Jasmine smiled up at her handsome new father. "Shasta and I were wondering if we get to go to the Future Ranchers of America School for free since you and Mamma own it and our adopted uncles run it."

"Adopted uncles?" Alexander looked to Jacqueline for an explanation.

"They are referring to Ian, Thomas, and they've added Q.T to the list since he opted to teach at our school rather than start a ranch of his own in Texas," Jacqueline provided.

"I see," he said, turning back to the girls. "Even so, you won't be attending for free. You'll have to apply and your mother and I will have to pay for your classes each summer just like everyone else," he answered.

The girls whispered amongst themselves momentarily.

"We understand, Daddy," Shasta said diplomatically.

"Well, we'd better head back down there. We close the gates in two hours and as usual there will be plenty of work to do once the tourists are gone."

"When will Grandpa Joseph and Cookie be back from their honeymoon, Mamma? I don't like eating at the cafeteria. The food is good, but it's not as good as Grandma Cookie's." Shasta whined. Jasmine nodded emphatically in agreement.

"They'll be back Thursday," Jacqueline answered. "Cookie promised to do all the cooking for Uncle Ian and Aunt Pam's wedding on Saturday."

"Will Nana and Pop-Pop be back then too?" Jasmine asked hopefully.

"Yes. Their year away ends tomorrow actually, but their flight doesn't get in until Wednesday. They were gone an extra month because they flew home to check on us last summer after the big storm, remember?"

The girls nodded before heading down the hill.

"Have you and your father resolved the matter of him having the town think you were broke, or should

I expect a little tension when he arrives?" Alexander asked with concern.

"I never could stay mad at him for long," Jacqueline confessed. "We talked a lot after the wedding and while I don't agree with his methods, I understood his need to make certain I would be all right running things on my own. We're fine now."

Jacqueline was about to kick Pepsi into a trot when Alexander leaned forward to hold Pepsi's reigns.

Jacqueline looked puzzled, "What's the matter?"

"Nothing. I was just wondering if I'd told you how proud I am to be your husband."

Jacqueline thought her heart would burst from pride. "You've told me every night when you lay beside me and wrap me in your arms and again every morning when you kiss me awake. You tell me every time you hug Jasmine and you tell me every day that we wake up on 1850 soil rather than having to split our time between here and Texas.

"I love you too, Alexander Hawkins and nothing's going to change that. I promise."

"I just hope you feel the same way in six months after our third child is born and he's crying his head off while you're trying to focus on the girls or the ranch, or—"

Jacqueline leaned across Pepsi to pull her husband close. She kissed him passionately. "I'll always feel this way, Alex. Never doubt that," she promised. "And as far as our son is concerned, he is going to grow up to be as loving and as gorgeous as his father, of that, I am certain." She kissed him again and he surprised her by lifting her effortlessly and sitting her sidesaddle atop Thor.

"So, how fast do you think we can ride with you in

your condition and me in mine?" Alexander asked, hungrily.

Jacqueline didn't have to ask what he meant by 'his condition' as his hunger for her was evident as she sat in his lap.

She smiled seductively before taking the reigns from Alexander and prodding Thor into a trot knowing the girls and Pepsi would follow. "Time will tell, Mr. Hawkins. Time will tell."

Dear Reader:

The Bible is the best book ever written. As a child I enjoyed reading its stories of kings and queens and their faraway kingdoms. As a young adult I engrossed myself in its recounting of lost loves, battles fought, and wars won. As a woman I have found solace in its promises of peace, whispers of hope, and seeds of rebirth.

As a writer I have found this special book to hold within its pages some of the most lovable, detestable, fascinating, unbelievable, and colorful characters ever written. As a reader I have laughed, cried, and been both confused and enlightened by its stories.

I acknowledge the Bible as the foundation from which my passion for reading and storytelling was birthed. I thank my parents, Althea Cooley and Frank Lawson, for ushering me to church every Sunday morning to mix the cement of my future. Thanks, Mom and Dad, you're the best!

To my fans, I thank you as well for your wonderful e-mails and letters. Your encouragement means so much to me.

Blessings Always,

Francine E. Matthews
ladyhawk3940@aol.com

ABOUT THE AUTHOR

Francine E. Matthews lives in Oklahoma with her husband of twenty-one years and her three teenaged children, Crystalyne, Jonathan, and Christopher.

She enjoys an eclectic selection of reading material, such as Christian, motivational, romance, nonfiction, mystery, science fiction, time travel, historical, and multicultural, to name a few.

She loves animals, especially horses. She is determined to learn to ride the moment she can stop gawking at them with wide-eyed amazement long enough to jump on!

Francine is an incurable romantic who has fallen head over heels for the black cowboys of Oklahoma, their families, and their history.